Praise for
Silent Night Violent Night:
a Cory Goodwin Mystery

"Captures you from the first sentence and keeps you 'hooked' until the last period. Terrific romp from start to finish! All the 'clues' are there, but it still keeps you guessing!"
-- *KF, Amazon.com*

...and don't miss CJ Verburg's
Croaked:
an Edgar Rowdey Cape Cod Mystery

"*Croaked* has everything I want in a mystery: Wonderful kooky characters, a plot that keeps you turning pages, terrific dialog, humor, great local color, ...oh yes, and murders, too. I enjoyed every minute of it. Highly recommended!"
-- *SW, Amazon.com*

"A thoroughly enjoyable murder mystery . . . Plot, characters, and setting combine for enough twists and turns to keep readers guessing, and reading. Highly recommended."
-- *CW, Goodreads*

"A real page-turner . . . Great Cape Cod color, terrific fun, and a must for anyone who loves to curl up with a good mystery." --*CC, Amazon.com*

"A wonderful mystery where every step is interesting (and important), and every character is authentic and credible."
-- *"CG," Amazon.com*

NOTE: This is a work of fiction. None of the people, places, or situations in this book are intended to represent actual people, places, or situations.

SILENT NIGHT VIOLENT NIGHT: a Cory Goodwin Mystery.
Copyright (c) 2011 by CJ Verburg. All rights reserved. Printed in the United States of America. No part of this book may be used or reproduced in any manner whatsoever without written permission except for brief quotations embodied in critical articles and reviews. For information please address the publisher at: info@Boom-Books.com.

Third printing

ISBN 978-0-9834355-3-2

Christmas-light garlands by Richard Arnold
www.ceccobravo.com

Cover design, with thanks, from a photo by www.tOrange.biz

SILENT NIGHT VIOLENT NIGHT

A CORY GOODWIN MYSTERY

BY
CJ VERBURG

A publisher's Christmas party. A blizzard.
Rival scientists. Secret romances.
Murder.

Boom-Books.com

For Howard

CHAPTER ONE

As I swung out of Copley Square onto the Mass Pike, the band on my radio swung into "Hernando's Hideaway." Desultory snowflakes were drifting through the orange sky like petals. Half an inch, the weatherman predicted. I'd picked this station because Oxbridge, Connecticut, is a three-hour drive from Boston and the rest were all playing Christmas songs.

My dad taught me "Hernando's Hideaway" longer ago than I care to remember. He'd stand me on his shoes and we'd sing it together as we tangoed across the parquet floor of our Manhattan living room. Dad's a ballroom virtuoso. As my mom says, he'll always have that to fall back on when he irks the State of New York into revoking his detective license.

What I hadn't noticed until now is that Robert Frost wrote "Stopping By Woods on a Snowy Evening" to the same tune:

My lit, -tle horse, must think it queer
To stop, without, a farmhouse near . . .

Try getting that out of your head when your alternatives are "The Little Drummer Boy" and "Jingle Bell Rock."

At Route 128 the projected snowfall rose to an inch. OK, I thought. No problem. Being a media person myself, I'd thrown my heavy boots in the car just in case. I've spent enough nights stranded in airports and motels to take weather forecasts with a bag of salt.

Dinner around seven-thirty, Lilah Darnell—or, rather, Lilah Easton—had told me on the phone. Cocktails whenever you get here. Come early, Cory, OK?—so we can catch up before the horde arrives.

Right. I was still too astonished to grapple with details. Lilah in suburbia? Hostessing a semiformal dinner party? Never mind that this was a fate we'd been groomed for since birth. The core of Lilah's and my friendship was our vow, copied from Jackie Bouvier (later Kennedy, later Onassis): *Never to be a housewife.* And now the notorious Delilah, legend of the Ivy League, was happily married to a textbook publisher? Unthinkable! You might as well imagine Jerry Garcia designing neckties, or Bobby Seale writing a cookbook.

It must be fifteen years since I'd seen her. Not often after we left college, in the wake of the Vietnam war. Lilah was my senior sister when I was a freshman: back then, a vast age gap. Over the years we'd become contemporaries. Sisters again, too, evidently, or why would she ferret through the Old Girl Network to find me?

The other question—why was I driving halfway across New England to see her?—had more than one answer. Curiosity, certainly. I'd picked Lilah Darnell for my role model before that term existed. She was bold, brilliant, and beautiful—just the kind of uncommon woman I planned to become at Mount Holyoke College. My second week on campus she electrified the grapevine by dumping Harvard's class president for a local woodworker. In January she flew to Japan to spend semester break studying calligraphy and the tea ceremony. In March she won a summer apprenticeship at a foundry in Perugia. Her plan after graduation was to become a famous sculptor, start an artists' commune, and launch a series of international affairs.

With this Amazon for my mentor I flourished. When Lilah sold a terra-cotta demon to a New York collector, I caught a bus to Boston and pitched my first story idea to *Phases*. While she skied the Alps, I covered the D.C. demonstration against President Nixon's bombing of Cambodia. She chiseled, I wrote; she exhibited, I published. Shortly after *Phases* hired me as a stringer, I received a handmade invitation to her wedding in the East Village. There we sat up half the night promising each other that our love lives would never overshadow our work. Several years later she turned up on my Back Bay doorstep, divorced; praised my series on urban gentrification, bought me a dinner worth a month's rent, and left me a baggie of ganja from her Jamaican lover. That was the last I'd heard from Lilah until her surprise reappearance in Connecticut.

By Worcester I was glad I'd brought those boots. The petals had escalated to confetti. Crossing the state line I spotted the yellow lights of a snowplow. Possible four to six inches, announced the radio. I called Lilah to warn her I might be late, and scratched my plan of stopping in Hartford for gas and coffee.

But I, have pro, -mises to keep,
And miles, to go, before I sleep!

Past Hartford the traction got tricky. My little horse—an old VW beetle, restored over the years like the Tin Woodman—progressed down Route 84 in a series of glides. As the snow thickened, Friday night's rush-hour traffic had thinned. The forecasters now were issuing stern travelers' advisories.

I peered through the troop of tiny kamikazes hurling themselves at my windshield; picked out a truck with bright lights and lots of tires, and pulled in behind it.

Lilah's directions depended on spotting landmarks: bank, mall, Burger King. Maybe I'd better call her again at Oxbridge . . .

But I didn't make it to Oxbridge.

The balance tipped a few miles before my exit. I'd been too busy keeping my wheels in the truck's tracks to notice how much the weather had worsened. Now I glanced at my gas gauge and saw I should have filled up in Hartford after all. While I was taking that in, the truck pulled left to pass a van—the only other vehicle in sight. I started to follow and felt the VW skitter like a water drop on a griddle.

My stomach crowded my esophagus as I tucked in tight behind the van. You get used to navigating strange roads in rented cars, losing your way and finding it again, and you get cocky. You forget that travel holds greater dangers than arriving after check-in.

At the Oxbridge exit I bid the van a reluctant good-by and inched onto the snow-lined ramp. The next thirty seconds were predictable: The VW took off downhill like a kid on a playground slide. We skidded past a guardrail, twirled across the road, and landed nose first in a snowbank.

The radio was playing "Blue Christmas." Otherwise the world had gone silent. Snow fell past my headlights, beautiful and implacable.

I surveyed the area. No bank, no mall, no Burger King. All I could see beyond my car was a distant glow where the highway must be.

I called Lilah's home number, twice, and got nothing. I tried her cell phone and got voice mail. My emergency road service regretted that due to unusually heavy call volume, all representatives were currently helping other customers.

I switched off the radio and pulled on my boots.

My husband, Larry, laughed when he found the bag of kitty litter I keep in my trunk. (He could afford to; he drives a Jaguar.) Later I would take a moment to savor his chagrin when he found out how right I was. Not now. For now I didn't dare think about Larry or vindication or the painful thinness of my driving gloves or why I keep refusing to buy a new car or anything else but getting out of here.

There was already half an inch of snow on my roof. Another round of phone calls produced the same results. Now what? Stay iglooed in the VW all night, or risk a potentially futile (or fatal) search through the storm for help?

I found a window scraper under my seat. I dug snow away from my wheels. If my flashlight batteries would only hold out till I finished . . . I'd dimmed the headlights and lit a flare but left the engine running. With the gas gauge on E, I couldn't take the chance that, once stopped, it wouldn't start again.

Not that any of these decisions were conscious. My brain had downshifted some time ago. All my energy was in my fingers.

I chopped. I scraped. I scooped. I cursed. I felt like an archeologist trying to extricate a mammoth from a glacier. Fresh snow refilled the holes I dug and blew into my eyes and mouth. Though my feet ached with cold, inside my coat I was sweating. How many eons had I been here? How many seconds till the motor died?

Then lights, and the rumble of an approaching car.

Don't even think it, Cory. He'd be a fool to pull over. His only hope on this sloped, slippery road is to keep going.

He didn't pull over but up. "Hey!" A laconic baritone. "You need some help?"

"Yeah," I croaked.

It took me half a minute to reconnect my brain. Meanwhile my knight-errant had emerged from his car (a vintage white Lincoln Continental) and inspected the damage.

Given that he wore a dark sheepskin coat, fur hat, and fur-lined leather gloves, I couldn't tell much about him but that he was a few inches taller than me—five-ten, maybe—

and not apparently short of funds. His manner was friendly, comradely even, without the smarminess one comes to expect from roadside rescuers.

"Got any rope?" he asked, as matter-of-factly as if this were a ranch and we had calves to brand.

I nodded. The key was still in the trunk. I opened it and fished out the heavyweight line I keep coiled beside the kitty litter in case of emergency.

He twirled the end approvingly. "Yippie-i-o-ki-ay! Now, if we tie this to both bumpers—"

"Not enough traction. You'll slide right off the road."

"Take a closer look."

I peered at his face—about my age, clean-shaven, distinctly handsome under the hat—before I realized he meant the Lincoln.

"I made them put on chains when I rented this sucker." He looped the rope through his bumper. "And is that cat litter? Oh, hell, podner, we're all set!"

He was right. Two false starts, a hearty heave, and the VW was back on the road.

We untied the rope. Now that my brain was revving up again, I noticed that my hands were numb and trembling. The right one had blood on it. Where were my gloves? There, on the snowbank next to my flashlight. Oh, lord, how could I possibly find the Eastons' house in this zombie state? Was I even fit to drive?

A moot question. Rule Number Three of the freelance journalist: What is necessary can be managed. If it can't be managed, it's not necessary.

"Where are you going?"

"Oxbridge," I answered; and added with unreasoning hope, "Bruce and Lilah Easton's. It's off Old Mill Road, wherever that is."

"You haven't been there before?"

"No." Glancing around for something to wipe my hands

on, I found a tissue in my coat pocket; and only then registered his change in tone. "Do you know them?"

For a moment he seemed undecided. "I did," he said at last. "In another lifetime."

Cocooned as we were between two pairs of headlights, my fists thawing in my pockets, snow sparkling all around us like glitter, this struck me as a reasonable statement. "That's when I knew Lilah. We went to college together. I haven't seen her in—oh, eons."

He nodded as if reassured. "You can follow me. It's on my way. What's your name?"

"Cordelia Thorne." I held out my hand.

"OK, Ms. Thorne." He rubbed my chilled fingers between his palms. "Now it's your turn to play good fairy. Don't mention me at Eastons'. Not to them, their guests, nobody. OK?"

"Sure . . . but who is it I'm not mentioning?"

He grinned back at me—sardonically, I thought, though all I could see was the tip of his nose, a medium-thin mouth, and a square chin. Without a word he climbed into his car.

"Hey, wait! At least let me say thanks!"

As he gunned the Lincoln into a skidding takeoff he powered down his window. "Hi-yo Silver!" he hollered through the snow. "Awaaay!"

Between the snowstorm and the darkness, there wasn't a chance I'd have found the Eastons' mailbox on my own. They'd plowed their driveway (or had it plowed) up to the road. I idled there in the mouth of safety and waved to my nameless rescuer as he patched out in another cloud of snow.

This is going to be a hard story not to tell, I thought. How will I explain . . . ? But when I looked at my watch I discovered that, thanks to the missed coffee break in Hartford, I wasn't even late enough to apologize.

The Eastons' driveway wound through woods and across a field. Along the verge stood wrought-iron street lamps, each hung with a holly wreath. On any other night I'd have paused to admire the view: snow draping hedges and trees like cheesecloth, the lawn an unstained sweep of white sloping down toward twinkling house lights. Maybe that's why I accepted this invitation, I reflected; because Lilah as a pillar of the country-club set must be seen to be believed.

On the phone her conspiratorial tone had assured me we were still allies. Only the world had changed. Protest marches were out, pragmatism was in. The Cold War had followed the Age of Aquarius into history, with the dot-com boom on its heels. Walt Disney, that kindly gentleman, had morphed into a mega-corporation. No one cared if China stayed red as long as it went green. OK, a revolution is not a dinner party, no Mudd Club or CBGB; but everybody has to eat, and with America's supermarkets stocking fresh bean sprouts and soy sauce, basmati rice, salsa, and couscous, at least our quest to imagine all the people sharing all the world had made headway.

Her husband, Bruce, said Lilah, was president and publisher of Communicore's Higher Education Group. I wouldn't have envisioned college textbooks as a plush line of work; but Bruce Easton, I learned when I nosed around, was pushing the envelope.

Bruce's most inspired coup was reviving the Caxton Press imprint. (This from *Phases*' business editor.) During the post-World War II science boom, Caxton was *the* cutting-edge publisher of science books. Over the next half-century, as a succession of larger companies gobbled up it and then each other, its star faded to barely a twinkle. Bruce Easton revived it just long enough to rebrand it. He signed prestigious (though expensive) textbook contracts with a dozen Nobel science laureates and hopefuls. Then he folded Caxton Press back into Communicore except for its logo, which survived as a highly coveted decoration on the spines of selected titles.

Well, you figure, big deal. Textbooks: what could be duller? Not so. Suppose that the eminent Professor X wants to write a book about physics. If he aims it at a general audience, his publisher has to convince thousands of bookstore managers and Amazon browsers that fractals and string theory are a better way to spend $34.95 than pizza and a movie. On the other hand, if Professor X aims his book at college freshmen, his publisher can sell a hundred, five hundred, even a thousand copies at a crack, for a sum that once would have covered a year's tuition, just by persuading fellow professors to require it for their classes. And that market rolls over every semester.

My *Phases* informant put it another way. "It's big bucks, Cory, which means power, which means politics. Big fish eat little fish, and when the little fish are gone, the big fish start chomping each other's tails."

"What sort of fish is Bruce Easton?"

"Bruce Easton," he replied unhesitatingly, "is a piranha."

As the wife of a corporate honcho myself, I understood he meant it as a compliment. Nor was I surprised. Lilah had indicated on the phone how drastically her taste in husbands had changed since the previous one. Numero Uno, as she called him, was a fellow sculptor living in a drafty SoHo loft whose kitchen comprised a tiny porcelain sink, a hot plate, and an avocado tree growing out of a toilet. OK when you're young and dedicated, said Lilah with crisp finality, but I'm not anymore. Can you believe?—suddenly there I was at gallery openings, lusting after pin-striped suits and calfskin attaché cases!

Believe, yes. Empathize . . . well, not so much. On the surface my story sounded like an echo: a summer romance in Paris with a fellow writer who turned out to be Larry Thorne of Thorne Cosmetics. Au revoir to pastis and cahiers on the

Boul' Mich'; hello to lattes and laptops on Charles Street! But when Larry set aside his novel two years ago to accept a vice-presidency, and I agreed to quit journalism and teach prep school, our marriage imploded. Only after a rollercoaster series of breakups and reconciliations had we vowed to find common ground. I would share my husband with the family firm, and he would share his wife with *Phases*. Some public functions he'd have to attend alone; but when I wasn't on the road I'd go with him, and I'd wear cosmetics.

Lilah's reappearance in my life couldn't have been timelier. If she could thrive in a mixed marriage, so could I. Even comparing notes on the phone made our schoolgirl sisterhood feel like a prophecy. Bruce's Mercedes, Larry's Jaguar. Their house in Connecticut, ours on Beacon Hill. Lilah's work with Planned Parenthood and the Parks Commission, mine with Oxfam and the Opera Company.

I was about to ask how she and Bruce dealt with the dual-identity issue (Larry calls my office the Bat Cave) when Lilah said practically: "But let me tell you why I called."

Among the Eastons' noblesse oblige gestures on behalf of Communicore was their annual Christmas party. A-list authors and staff were invited out to the Connecticut house for a sumptuous dinner, after which they helped Bruce and Lilah decorate their tree. This year's guest of honor was Professor Henry Howrigan of Harvard, whose forthcoming biology textbook promised to keep the company in paper clips for the next decade.

"*Not* my best subject, biology, as you may recall! You know how these corporate parties are, anyway. So I'm thinking, Oh, *gawd*, another night of bone-crushing tedium, and suddenly I flashed on that interview you did with Henry a few years ago. Remember—when Harvard threw their snit-fit about commercializing academic research? I *loved* what you wrote, Cory. I mean, it was so *him*, I could literally hear his voice. So I thought, Perfect! Cory knows Henry, she knows science, and publishing—she can come keep me company!"

Friday the twentieth. Larry would be at Thorne Cosmetics' northwest regional sales meeting in Seattle. His mother had already proposed that I donate my empty Saturday to the sachets-and-potholders booth at her church's Christmas fair.

As for Harvard and Henry Howrigan, I'd heard a new snit-fit was brewing which threatened to defoliate the groves of academe. Over what? That was the six-figure question. No one in the local media could find out—not even Rik Green's hand-picked cadre of campus spies. When it comes to stonewalling, Harvard is four hundred years ahead of the rest of us.

"So I tracked you down through the alumnae office, and I'm phoning instead of writing so you can't say no. The guests all leave after dinner, then we're on our own. There's a marvelous little museum here, and a new bistro I've been dying to try—"

"Lilah," I interrupted.

"—or actually it's more of a tearoom; and the annual Christmas walk—"

"Yo! Lilah!"

"What?"

"You know I'd love to see you. But what's this about? I mean . . . why *now?* After so long? Ten days before Christmas?"

Three seconds while she chose a tack. Three more to pick the words for it. When she finally answered, I thought she was changing the subject.

"Cory! How are your parents these days?"

"Fine. We're spending New Year's with them."

"Your mother, the fearless traveler! And is your dad still a—what's it called?—private investigator?"

"Right." Was there a method to this meandering?

"We all had such a crush on him. Fathers' Weekend, lining up to dance with Cory's dad!" She managed a chuckle.

"It's so perfect you went into journalism. Don't you think? Even back then, how you'd jump into any kind of a problem—algebra, or who stole whose lab report—that nobody else could solve, and bingo!"

"Lilah, what are you getting at?"

There was a tiny pause. "Oh, gawd. Who knows? Nothing."

"Is there a problem you want me to—?"

"No, no. I just meant— Oh, you know. Old times! 'We shall overcome' and all that. Our glorious carefree youth!"

No, I reflected; of course there was no problem. When you've got money, status, education, charm, and every other imaginable asset, the one thing you're not entitled to is problems.

"So you *will* come, Cory, won't you? Since you know my heart will be utterly broken . . ."

She was always like that. She'd play a card at bridge and wheedle her opponents into letting her take it back. She'd hand in papers three days late and still get better grades than those of us who'd sat up all night typing.

"Lilah," I had to ask, "have you cut your hair?"

"Cory! *No!* Never. Have you?"

"No way. I wear it up a lot, but all I ever cut is the tips."

"Me too. Bruce would kill me." She giggled. "Men are so *primitive* about women's hair! Oh, and Cory, I have to ask: Is it true what I heard? You ran off with a rock star? I mean, not to pry, but— Are you and Larry still—?"

In clearing that up—yes, we were, and whatever she'd heard was much exaggerated—we established without further discussion that I would come to her Christmas party.

Not for a minute did I believe all Lilah wanted from me was company for a nostalgia trip. However, I knew better than to think I could find out more by asking her. Back when people used to mix us up because of our long auburn hair, I was known as the straight one and Lilah as the kinky one.

The steps leading up to the house were flagstones, swept recently but refilling fast. I'd followed the driveway past the drift-deep front walk and around to this side door. Servants' entrance? Not unless the servants drove a BMW. I liked what I could see of the house, slung between woods at this end and a hill at the other as if it belonged here.

No one answered my knock. I wasn't in the mood to stand in any more falling snow, especially holding my suitcase, so I opened the door and stepped inside.

I was at the sports end of a long hall neatly stacked with skis, tennis racquets, volleyball nets, and a washer and dryer. At the laundry end stood a woman with her hand on the door frame, speaking to someone behind her. She wore a sweater patterned on a medieval tapestry: one whippet rampant and another couchant on a field of sienna edged with forest green. Her loose-cut pants were the same moleskin color as the dogs and looked virginal, as if they'd never touched human flesh till she lifted them from tissue paper.

But it was her hair I recognized: a reckless coppery cascade that tumbled down her shoulders and took me back instantly to art history class. Jo, James Whistler's wild Irish mistress.

"Lilah!"

"Cory!" Her arms flung open. "Oh, *gawd*, am I glad to see you!"

CHAPTER TWO

Sitting in front of the fireplace half an hour later, my feet in dry slippers and my bandaged hand cupped around a hot toddy, I wondered again why Lilah Easton had asked me here.

She'd kept up a flow of chatter since I arrived that blocked questions. After we'd hugged and exclaimed over each other, she whisked me off on the grand tour. About her house I now knew many new and interesting facts; about Lilah, none.

For example: Bruce had bought this property sixteen years ago while still married to his first wife. He heard about it at a MOMA retrospective honoring its late owner, a painter who'd built it as a weekend cottage in the 1930s. The painter's ex-lover remarked over champagne that the place hadn't sold because it was too small and rustic for a mansion-oriented neighborhood. Bruce left MOMA on the spot and drove to Connecticut; walked around shining his flashlight in the windows; dragged the realtor out of bed and made her draw up a purchase-and-sale.

I could see why. The painter's concept of a cottage was a spectacular two-tiered fantasy in wood and glass. Its main living area, where Lilah and I now sat, was a vast space floating above the rim of a lily pond, walled entirely with windows except for the stone chimney straight ahead of me, the bar to my left, and floor-to-ceiling bookcases to my right. Behind me were a swinging door leading to the kitchen, more bookcases, and a wide archway into the front foyer. All the floors I'd seen were dark red quarry tile.

"Rustic," Lilah repeated humorously. "As in, local stone, local tile, and no hearth—the tile goes right into the fireplace."

Rustic, I didn't add, as in Marie Antoinette's peasant village at Versailles.

The windows reflected a more Bergmanesque aesthetic. Reflected literally: in the room's left corner they made a black mirror, angled sheets of onyx in which shimmered a fruitwood table and chairs. The opposite corner was white: big glass squares in painted frames, like a stamp collection, reflecting patches of a thick white rug and a cubical section from the nubbly white sofa I was sitting on.

By daylight, I guessed, this trompe-l'oeil would reverse. The white grid would dissolve in light, while the black one emerged, framing selected views of the pond and woods.

More a curator's dream house than an artist's, I'd have thought. And more a photographer's vision than a painter's. Night and day, dark and light . . .

"Those white french doors open onto a deck." Lilah pointed right. "I call that corner my sunporch. The black ones behind the dining table fold up like an accordion, believe it or not. In summer it's like eating on the prow of a ship: air all around you and the pond at your feet."

Her head bowed: end of tour. She was half-sitting, half-kneeling, with her back to the fireplace. She'd twisted her hair into an improvised knot to keep it out of her way. The fire behind her lit the tiny wisps around her head into a halo.

Did you know about this, Lone Ranger? I demanded silently. Dammit, why didn't you warn me?

Lilah bent over a coffee table whose ends curled under like a giant scroll. Not marble as it looked, she'd confided, but pressed goatskin. Her right hand turned the crank of a shallow plastic cylinder which her left hand held above a mirror.

"Bruce will be here any second. Can you believe, he's e-mailing the phone company! I said, Like they'd come out in this? I just hope Melinda and Henry get through. Melinda Doerr is Henry Howrigan's editor, did I say? She flew to Boston this morning to tie up loose ends and then drive down with him for the party. They're pushing this book of his as if the future of humanity depends on it. Bruce actually thinks the *Times* might review it . . ."

I gazed past her into the fire. I didn't want to watch her hands, nor her intense dilated eyes, nor hear her babble about Henry Howrigan's biology textbook.

Cocaine is a drug I've always disliked. I don't care to use it nor be around it, for both its short-term impact and the long-term havoc it can wreak. Lilah's expertise disturbed me. The mini-Cuisinart she'd taken from the stereo cabinet. The small round mirror she'd lifted off a nearby wall. The faint note of defiance when she explained she really wasn't that into it, but with a business crowd about to descend on us . . .

A log cracked, shooting sparks against the firescreen. Lilah set down her grinder and picked up a razor blade.

"Shall we wait?" She glanced up at me. "Or let him catch up?"

Oh, hell, I thought. Look at your face in that mirror, Lilah! You're too thin, edgy, you've got circles under your eyes that not even TC's Unshadow can hide. You've lived a rich life by any definition, and you're still the most beautiful woman I know. What do you need with cocaine?

"Your call." I hoisted my toddy. "I'm sticking with rum."

Her eyebrows arched. "You don't—?"

"No thanks."

Her gaze dropped to the coffee table. Out of touch, out of reach.

"Lilah, why did you invite me here?"

That brought her head back up from the silver straw in her fingers. "Well, I thought," she began brightly. Then, with a tiny frown, "I mean, I wanted— I hoped—"

"Good evening," came a cool clear male voice.

Lilah jerked upright. I swiveled.

"You must be Cory."

And you must be psychic, I thought. Unless you eavesdrop.

His smile etched lines that softened the planes of his face. He wore office clothes: an impeccable gray suit, pale blue shirt, soft gray leather shoes like the ones Larry's cobbler sends over from Italy. His tie—silk—was silver, mauve, and cobalt, an assertive pattern which stopped short of aggressiveness. The silver at his temples conferred distinction without compromising his youthful physique. Bruce Easton, I suspected, was used to attracting attention, and skilled at either holding it or thwarting it.

He approached us with the lithe grace of a dancer. As Lilah made unnecessary introductions, he extended his hand over the back of the sofa. "So glad you could join us."

"Thank you."

His grip was firm, his hand thin, clean, long-fingered. Not an artist's hand (I thought of Numero Uno) but a collector's. And cold.

"I waited for you," said Lilah, accurately if not truthfully.

Bruce Easton walked around the sofa. "Melinda couldn't get through about the phones, but she'll keep trying. They should appreciate the urgency, in a no-cell zone. She and Henry stopped in Waterbury to put on chains. ETA half an hour." He sat beside me, leaving an unoccupied square between us. "Lilah, you'll want to tell Mary Helen."

"Yes." She offered him the straw.

He set it down. "I'm sure she'd like to know sooner rather than later."

With a mute nod Lilah rose and headed for the kitchen.

I expected him to apologize. Instead he slipped on the role of host like a smoking jacket. "Such weather! Ghastly for you, driving all this way alone. But then it wouldn't be a real Christmas party without snow." He smiled and indicated the mirror. "Will you—?"

"No thanks."

One of my many objections to social snorting is its guilt potential. Say yes and you're taking on an obligation to repay; say no and you're a spoilsport. I've seen couples who were best friends for years— But that's another story. My impression of Bruce Easton was that he grasped every nuance in this game, and no had qualms about turning the screws when it suited him.

It didn't suit him now. On the contrary. For me he was all graciousness.

"I was so pleased when Lilah told me one of her oldest friends would be here for our little fête." He settled back against the cushions. "She mentioned the famous resemblance. Your wonderful pre-Raphaelite hair. Did you cut yours, or have you—oh, I see. That chopstick holds it up? Marvelous." Another brief smile. "What do you think of Lilah's portrait?"

We both looked at the painting over the fireplace: Lilah in a long white gown, her head bare, a sheaf of lilies in her arms.

I considered. *Derivative?* No, Cory.

"Lovely."

"I commissioned it from Halsey as a wedding present. Long before he was well known." Bruce Easton crossed his legs; laced his fingers around his knee. "Lilah reminded me of Whistler's 'White Girl' the first day I met her. I daresay that contributed to the attraction." He chuckled. "For Halsey as well. He was as eager as I was to make certain her beauty would be preserved."

"Lilah's done a good job of that herself," I couldn't help remarking.

"Yes," he agreed with a collector's dispassion. "She has, hasn't she?"

Cory the journalist was growing more than a little curious about this marriage, or acquisition. Tact prevailed, however, and our conversation drifted among the current hot banalities: Beaujolais Nouveau, the Dow, the euro, ski conditions in Vermont. The tax-policy debate I dodged, since that's an issue Larry and I always clashed about. My view is that nobody with as much money as we've got is entitled to complain.

When Lilah came back she and Bruce inhaled their lines. Instead of speeding her up further, as I'd feared, the coke seemed to relax her.

"This is my favorite part of the day," she sighed. "When it's just us."

She stretched out her legs under the white goatskin-marble coffee table.

Bruce nudged her knee with his toe. "You'll make Cory feel unwelcome."

"Oh, no." A warm grin at me. "She counts as us. My old buddy. Gawd, Cory, can you believe? Who would've ever thought *we* would get *old*?"

That drawled *gawd* I'd heard so many times brought it home as sharply as Westminster chimes from a clock tower or the smell of mystery meat and powdered potatoes. "Like those alumnae we used to laugh at, who'd come on pilgrimages to their old rooms, wallowing in nostalgia for their lost youth."

"But we're not wallowing in nostalgia," Lilah said stoutly. "We're reveling in the present." She scrambled to her knees. "Darling, Cory needs another toddy and so do I."

"Let's all drink to revelry," agreed Bruce, and carried our glass mugs to the bar.

This was a mirrored alcove between the dining area and the swinging door to the kitchen. Over it was a skylight; shelves of begonias and African violets lined each side.

Bruce took bottles and a pitcher from a cabinet underneath. Why not leave them sitting out? I wondered idly. And realized that, except for the blown-glass bowl-within-a-bowl on the coffee table, I hadn't seen one extraneous object in this house. Books in the bookcases, yes—that's hard to avoid—but TV and music equipment, if any, were stowed out of sight. Nowhere was there anything so mundane and personal as a knicknack.

A twinge of uneasiness shivered up my neck. Lilah's dorm room had been a regular rotating exhibit of half-finished terra cotta figurines, wire mobiles, and gifts from her current crew of admirers.

"Darling," commanded the object of my concern, "tell Cory about the rest of our party."

She settled again on the rug in front of the fireplace, an anticipatory glint in her eye, nothing more profound on her mind than keeping her toddy from dripping on her pants.

Bruce alighted rather than sat on the sofa. Though his face was bemused, his body seemed twitchy. I got the idea parties bored him. Were we in for one of those volcanic evenings, then, when FBI lookalikes drink, drug, and goad each other into Saturday Night Live?

Not yet, apparently. Bruce rested his elbows on his knees. His fingertips met as if in meditation.

"As Lilah may have told you, this gathering tonight has a twofold purpose. One, of course, is to celebrate the holiday season. The other is to express Communicore's great appreciation to Professor Henry Howrigan for completing a manuscript which we believe will revolutionize the teaching of introductory biology."

Part of me suppressed a snort; but another part was moved in spite of myself. Bruce's voice, his eyes, even the angle of his head conveyed a depth of conviction that would have done credit to a monk. Though I knew nothing about the teaching of introductory biology and cared less, something in me yearned to join his revolution—to march behind his banner, to link arms with him and storm the barricades of academe. I began to comprehend how Bruce Easton had won himself a divisional presidency.

"We'll start the festivities with a toast to our guest of honor. Then later, after dinner, Lilah and I will invite all our guests to help us decorate our Christmas tree."

"I'm doing the eggnog, darling, don't forget. Organizing the tree is up to you."

Bruce didn't seem to hear. He was moving across the floor to the white sunporch corner, where he dragged the sofa cube out of the way of an imaginary tree. Watching his hands I saw its height, its placement in the window angle, the fullness of its branches, the glitter of its lights . . .

"Reflecting from here over to there," he finished with a sweep, "so that one might be gazing into a starry sky." His hands fluttered downward. "Messy with the needles and such; but the effect will be breathtaking, I assure you."

Evidently I was the one he was assuring, because Bruce addressed me as he strolled toward the fireplace. "You're a writer, yes? Perhaps you can suggest some," he searched for the right word, "auxiliary activities." He lifted a brass poker from its rack. "I had thought of reading the Christmas story; but there's the danger someone might overlook the melodious language of King James's Bible and take its religious content amiss."

"If you want melodious, we can sing carols," Lilah proposed. "That's nonsectarian. We did it every year at school. Cory, do you still know all the words? She has an incredible memory!"

"I think we want something less participatory, darling, or your wonderful eggnog will be wasted." Bruce stirred the logs behind her. "Cory, what's your recommendation? Seasonal poetry?" He swung the poker to the floor and leaned on it like a walking stick. "'A Child's Christmas in Wales' is too long, I'm afraid. Or 'Snowbound.' Robert Frost, perhaps?"

I choked on my toddy. "Oh, yes," I managed. "Robert Frost. Absolutely."

Bruce's voice took on a dreamy melancholia. "Two roads diverged in a wood, and I—I took the one less traveled by."

He dropped his poker back into the rack for punctuation.

"Home is where, when you have to go there, they have to take you in," said Lilah.

"Darling," Bruce touched her hair reproachfully, "that's hardly the mood we're after."

"Birch trees," said Lilah to me. "Woodpiles. That's what he wants. Do you remember those? American poetry 101?"

I was feeling giddy. "Give me a couple more toddies and I'll sing you one."

"Excellent!" Lilah clapped her hands in delight. "Cory will sing a seasonal poem! Now, how about the tree, darling?"

"I expect Melinda will take care of it." Bruce ran a fingernail around the inside of one nostril. "Melinda Doerr is a vice president at Communicore—"

"Bruce promoted her last Spring as compensation when her husband flipped out."

"She was promoted," Bruce corrected, "because she was and is an outstanding editor. She's been my right hand since we moved the Press to New York."

"The steel-trap hand in the velour glove." Lilah slid

around the coffee table out of Bruce's reach. "She's got a whole wardrobe of designer sweatsuits, Cory, all different colors—"

"More significantly, Melinda is skilled at organizing anything in need of organizing."

"As well as disorganizing anything that can stand disorganizing," Lilah said irrepressibly. "She likes throwing her weight around. She's got so much of it."

Bruce swiveled; but instead of the quelling retort I expected, he picked up a paper packet from the coffee table. "We'll put her in charge of handing out ornaments, shall we, darling?" He unfolded a flap and ticked white chunks into Lilah's grinder. "And you can be in charge of keeping everyone happy."

"That's my strong suit," she assured me. "Shall we start with a toast to Henry's book?"

She slid the mirror toward Bruce, who crouched beside her and divided the powder with a razor blade. "Poor old Henry!" he murmured. "Drinks like a fish, sweats like a horse, and won't take off his jacket for fear of committing a faux pas."

"Now now," said Lilah.

"Which it is, given his penchant for polyester turtlenecks." Bruce sniffed a line and handed the straw to Lilah. "Here are some gilt balls for you, Henry, old boy. See if you can figure out where to hang them."

Lilah giggled and cringed. "Really, darling, you're awful to him! You and Melinda both."

"Keep him honest. Henry's nose belongs to the grindstone, so to speak, until he's met his obligations."

I recognized that tone from social-business occasions with Larry. Bruce Easton was not joking.

"I must make sure Gloria has his galleys ready." He rose. "Excuse me, ladies."

He exited through the swinging door to the kitchen.

Lilah wiped the mirror with her finger and dabbed her gums. I was about to ask her about dinner when I noticed her hand was shaking.

"Lilah, are you OK?"

"Oh, Cory!" She forced a smile. "I just can't *tell* you how glad I am you're here!"

"Why? Is something wrong?"

"Not— No. I mean— Oh, pfh! You're still my sister, you know that? Like at school? I've been so *proud* of you! Not just the story about Henry. I subscribed to *Phases* for years to see your name in print. Of course, being a sculptor I've got to keep up . . . But I always looked for you first."

I didn't know what to say. Lilah seemed to mean this scattered speech as some kind of tribute. Why? What was she getting at?

"I would read one of your stories and it was like being back in college. Really! The way you'd walk into some weird scene—that racial violence thing in Southie, remember? and child abuse at day-care centers, and those women who patrolled the subway tunnels shooting rats?— and you never sounded scared. Cool, capable Cory! Just like when Suzanne and I used to bring you our problems. You'd sit there looking deep, listening, the same as you are right now, and then you'd come out with the one perfect comment that cut straight to the heart of it."

God help us, I thought, she's confused me with somebody else. Deep? Cool and capable? Do I look like the Delphic Oracle?

"Lilah," I said helplessly, "every story I've ever gone after I was scared. I never felt so much relief as when I married Larry and I could stop walking out on limbs for a living. And college—what problems did you ever have? You were Delilah, the femme fatale! Heart throb of every man from Princeton to Bowdoin! Not to mention your sculptures, those wonderful gargoyles—"

I stopped because tears were running down her face. She made no move to catch them, though in a moment her mascara would muddy the flow and spoil the youthful complexion she must have spent half an hour recreating.

"Come on, Lilah." I shoved a tissue into her hand. "Don't cry. Tell me what's the matter."

I put another log on the fire while she pulled herself together, blowing her nose in flagrant disregard for the fifty bucks she'd just stuffed up it.

"I don't *know* what's the matter!" Too close to a wail. She took a couple of deep breaths and began again. "I didn't want to say anything because I was afraid you wouldn't come. It's— Oh, *gawd*. I think I'm losing my mind, that's what's the matter. Or else we're under a curse. Maybe both," she added with a damp wry grimace. "That would be perfect, if he cursed all Bruce's projects to fall apart the same as he did, and me along with them."

"Who, Lilah?"

"*Who?* Tony Cyr." She sniffled. "Bruce's ex right hand. Melinda's ex-husband. The ex-head of Caxton Press. My ex-friend Tony," she concluded bitterly.

I thought: I don't want to hear this story. Did I drive four hours through a snowstorm to untangle Lilah Easton's drug-twisted mind? No. Consult me on Robert Frost, draft me for the Christmas tree brigade, but don't turn me into Oprah-wan Kenobie.

"Well," I said, wishing I hadn't given up cigarettes, "I guess you'd better tell me about it."

CHAPTER THREE

Every business is an island to its inhabitants. I'd seen Thorne Cosmetics' sales force hiss when the FDA investigated a moisturizer, and cheer when American women discovered that MsCara truly does thicken lashes. I once spent a three-hour lunch consoling Rik Green after *Rolling Stone* scooped *Phases* on a Springsteen tour. As a journalist, I'd landed on dozens of strange worlds and learned the language of a few.

But—textbook publishing? If I'd ever thought about it at all I'd have dismissed it as a minor satellite of academia, like the food service or campus cops.

So little we know.

"What it was, basically," said Lilah, refilling our mugs, "was *Paradise Lost*."

Milton. God and Lucifer. Terrific.

"Tony used to be Bruce's second in command until he got hooked on power. Then he fell. Flipped out. Told everybody Bruce was the Great Satan. Bruce tried to rescue him—offered him a face-saving job in Boston with reference books. Tony said he'd rather go to Hell than Siberia. So that's what he did."

"Meaning, literally, what?"

Lilah arranged her legs in a half-lotus and commenced her story.

In the beginning was the Word, and guarding the Word was Caxton Press. Back in those prelapsarian days, college publishers functioned as conduits, transferring information from professors into print. As time passed they expanded their role to seeking out projects, and even shaping them to fit curricula. Tony Cyr, the Press's science editor, goosed it into the modern era. His first radical move was to match geniuses with market niches. While his colleagues sat at their roll-top desks sifting through proposals, Tony traveled to campuses and research labs and tapped Nobel Prize winners to write textbooks. His second radical move was to edit their manuscripts.

Melinda Doerr joined Caxton Press as an editorial assistant—that is, a secretary. She'd picked publishing for the usual reasons: "Security and status without guilt. You know? *Books. Education.* Almost as noble as social work, right?—plus it pays better and you get a nice clean desk in a nice clean office."

Melinda owed her foothold on the career ladder less to her B.A. in English than her fast typing and blowsy good looks. Once aboard, she unveiled her other side: a relentless worker, tough, smart, and ambitious. She cut her long dark hair—or, rather, paid a stylist to transform shapeless into businesslike. Aerobics did the same for her figure. Thus lightened, she rose, from editorial assistant to assistant editor.

"And that's when she and Tony got together." Lilah moistened her throat with toddy. "He taught her how to do books—he had to. He was desperate! I mean, he was *the* science editor! Whatever field Caxton wanted to publish in—chemistry, geology, physics, oceanography, you name it—Tony was the man."

So Melinda made her debut as right hand. I didn't need any explanation why she and Tony fell in love. For Larry and me it had been the thrill of exploring Paris together, two American writers chasing feature stories from the Beaubourg to Versailles. For Tony and Melinda it was tracking talent down the Infinite Corridor at MIT and up the slate-roofed turrets at Harvard; sharing notes and sandwiches by the Charles; penciling changes onto manuscripts in Tony's office until the janitors turned out the lights.

Then Communicore, browsing among the treetops like a brontosaurus, stretched its neck from New York to Boston and gobbled up Caxton Press.

As with most takeovers, the initial changes were minor: New computers, updated software. Oak-paneled offices converted to sheetrock-walled cubicles. Three copyeditors urged to take early retirement. The managing editor was heard to mutter that all this modernization boded ill for the future.

And he was right, although not for the reasons he supposed. The upsurge in college enrollments had turned textbook publishing into a casino. CD-ROMs were popping up on the horizon like Cherokees in a cowboy movie. Caxton Press's hallowed policy of releasing no book before its time —its time being defined by a sort of chess game between author and editor in which issues like the serial comma might be nudged around for months—fell under the wheels of Product Development.

Bruce Easton's role in this transformation was angel with a flaming sword. Sent from Communicore's New York headquarters to light a fire under their laggard stepchild, he torched musty piles of manuscript. He flung outmoded contracts, procedures, even furniture onto the pyre. He hacked away dead wood till little was left but stumps. And rallying to his side came a few brave souls like Tony Cyr and Melinda Doerr.

"They adored him! I mean, they'd been the only signs of life in the whole place till Bruce came along. He promoted Melinda to full editor and Tony to senior editor. You should have seen Tony with Bruce behind him—like Butch and Sundance, plotting which market to knock off next. Biochem—*blam!* Calc-based physics—*blam!*"

"Wait a minute," I said. "Did Tony and Melinda know Bruce planned to close down Caxton Press in Boston and move their operations to New York?"

"Of course not," said Lilah. "The last thing Communicore wanted was to scare the Press's authors—that would have wrecked the whole plan. So they couldn't tell the staff, in case of leaks."

"Aha."

"That's why Bruce and I got relocated to Boston. It had to look permanent. Oh, *gawd*, did I miss this house! Luckily, once the phase-out started, he moved the logo here. As a transition." Lilah lifted her mug. "As a wedding present to Tony and Melinda."

I smelled a rodent. "Bruce moved Caxton Press *here?* To Oxbridge, Connecticut?"

"M-hm. The house was empty, since we were in Boston. We obviously weren't going to sell it, so why not rent it to Communicore?"

A big rodent. Yet Lilah lounged with one elbow on the coffee table as though she saw nothing odd in this sequence of events.

I reviewed the chronology.

One: Communicore transfers Bruce from New York to Boston to modernize its new acquisition, Caxton Press.

Two: While signing up books for the Press with one hand—his right hand, Tony Cyr—Bruce starts covertly shutting it down with the other.

Three: Having reduced Caxton Press to a logo, two editors, and a list of high-profile works-in-progress, Bruce moves it from Boston into—

Four: —his own empty house in Connecticut, leased by Communicore as the Press's headquarters until the shutdown is finished.

To me it looked like a high-stakes shell game. Nor did further details change my mind. The rent Communicore paid to the Eastons kept them in a plush Back Bay brownstone while Bruce bolstered and then closed the Boston office. Meanwhile, the company hired a decorator (chosen by Bruce) to convert half of the Oxbridge house into luxury office space, with every convenience from sofas and brass lamps to skylights and landscaping. Tony and Melinda, newly wed, moved into the refurbished studio, where they lived, breathed, ate, and slept Caxton Press. Any author who objected to the new order was wooed back into line with an all-expenses-paid working vacation in the Press's waterfront quarters.

"Plus Bruce and I could still come home on weekends." Lilah sighed. "It was heaven!"

That I didn't doubt. "But was it profitable?"

"Sure. Just as Bruce predicted. Everybody who was anybody in science or publishing wanted a piece of it."

What evil demon terminated this bliss? Who let the serpent into paradise? On that point Lilah was unexpectedly vague. Corporate politics, she said with a dismissive gesture. The economics of publishing. You know.

"But that doesn't make sense. If it was such a success, they should have cloned it, not closed it."

"Well, that's what Tony said." She wrapped her arms around her knees. "You'd think he would have realized by then that Bruce knew what he was doing. But when Tony found out they were pulling the plug, he flipped. Totally went wild. He wrote nasty letters to the directors attacking Bruce—*Bruce*, who'd let him head Caxton Press in the first place!" She hugged her knees tighter. "He also told some of his authors, and *they* raised a stink. Two of them actually sued. The whole thing got so out of hand that he finally had to be fired."

Behind her the flames had died to embers. Her long hair

in the dim light looked black and corrugated, like charred wood. I wished I could see her face instead of a mass of shadows.

"Leaving Melinda to pack up the remains of the Press and move it to New York?"

Lilah nodded.

"But why?" I persisted. "Whose idea was this folding and moving?"

"Everybody's." She shrugged. "The board. Bill Ballantine, the president of Communicore. Bruce told them way back in the beginning they should consolidate everything. I guess it took them that long to see he was right."

"And Melinda didn't object? She went along with losing her imprint and having her husband fired?"

Lilah looked even vaguer. "She filed for divorce. That part was messy. A week before Tony and Melinda were supposed to move out of here, he drank a fifth of Glenlivet, got a gun and shot out every window in those folding panels." She pointed at the black-rimmed panes behind the dining table. "It cost the company a fortune to replace the glass."

I fought down a shudder. "And what happened to Tony?"

"According to Melinda he bought a one-way ticket to Corfu and finished falling apart on a Mediterranean beach."

She said it with a studied nonchalance that covered her feelings like the snow draping the bushes outside her house. Her house once again, now that Tony Cyr was half a world away and Melinda Doerr had accepted a vice presidency with Communicore in New York.

Who was this woman? What had she to do with me, or I with her, that I should be dragged into her mare's-nest of a life? Never mind the face, the hair, the voice. This wasn't Delilah, my old comrade-in-arts. This was Bruce Easton's wife.

I reached for my mug and found my body had gotten

stiff. Oh, hell! Why was she looking at me as though she expected me to say something penetrating? Whatever it was she wanted, all I'd agreed to was a Christmas party. I had no part in this unpleasant tale. Why couldn't we close the book on it and gather everybody for dinner?

Everybody. Bruce. Melinda. Henry Howrigan. Ex-boss, ex-wife, and ex-author of Tony Cyr.

But no; Tony was the ex, not they. I'd heard the term—if you could call it that—whispered at Thorne Cosmetics parties. A harsh monosyllable that made me think of rows of white crosses.

I set down my mug. "And you're afraid Tony Cyr has put a curse on you? Why?"

"Why do I have such a crazy idea? Because ever since we moved back here it's been a string of nightmares. Oh, *gawd!*—you can't imagine!" Lilah gave a laugh that twisted into a sob. "Or d'you mean, Why am I afraid? Because if one more thing happens, I don't think I can take it."

Half of me wondered if a hug wouldn't help her more than this discussion. The other half was arrested by the sleek white coffee table between us, the smudged mirror, razor blade, and straw, and by Lilah herself, poised tensely on the hearth rug like the whippet on her sweater.

"Or did you mean, Why would Tony do this to me? To us?" She was talking as much to herself as to me. "Because here in this house is where he was happiest. People say *he flipped out* or *he lost his mind*, but what does that mean? Where does a mind go when it's lost? Those books downstairs won't tell you. It curls up in fetal position and waits like Sleeping Beauty for a shrink with a magic kiss? What do they know? Textbooks! Maybe you don't have to die to be a ghost."

A log hissed and shifted in the fireplace, sending a feather of smoke up the stone chimney.

"Lilah," I said carefully, "do you have a therapist?"

"Well, sure. The best in Connecticut."

"Have you talked to her about this?"

She shook her head. "I can't."

"Why not?"

"Bruce wants her to coauthor an abnormal psych text. He wouldn't— Oh, crap." Her voice went flat. "There's the door. Henry and Melinda."

She stood in one swift graceful motion. "Come with me, Cory. You should see the studio before Melinda settles into it."

With a faint grin that was more like her old self she added, "I figure, if you want to lay a ghost, stick his ex-wife in his ex-bed."

Meeting someone socially whom you once interviewed for a magazine can be awkward. Had Lilah warned Henry Howrigan that her old friend Cordelia Thorne was also Cory Goodwin of *Phases*? Would he remember the piece I wrote on him? If so, would he greet me as friend or foe?

But Professor Howrigan was a small hurdle next to Melinda Doerr, whose personal life I'd just heard described in unflattering detail by her hosts.

Lilah and I watched from the doorway as two bulky booted and hatted figures emerged from a jade-green Cadillac. I couldn't tell which was who until the driver rushed around to assist his passenger and she shooed him away.

As scarves were unwound, boots stomped, and gloves shed, it became clear that Melinda's thin phase hadn't outlived Caxton Press. I recalled a colleague of Larry's in the skin-care group who starved herself for years till she won a corner office and then gained ten pounds in a month. Melinda carried her weight with the same authority—gusto, even. She embraced Lilah in a bear hug that would have been lethal if she'd meant it.

Yet she impressed me more than I'd expected. Her energy was formidable, crisscrossing the Northeast in a snowstorm. Instead of grumbling about weather, traffic, et cetera, she enthused over Lilah's outfit. Surely that showed character. Hefty and hawk-faced, Melinda in her silver-and-green down coat resembled those cars they used to paint to advertise menthol cigarettes.

Henry Howrigan stayed well back as Lilah and Melinda air-kissed. One hand clutched his briefcase, the other edgily patted the lid of a Maytag. Yes, he remembered me. Yes, he'd liked the *Phases* piece. Period. He'd been just as taciturn at our interview. I suspected one would need to wax passionate about protein structure or membrane permeability to draw out the raconteur in Professor Howrigan.

I was touched, though, by his awe of Lilah. His sagging cheeks reddened when she squeezed his arm. He addressed her with the shy gallantry of a retired colonel in an English novel.

Henry (so he insisted I must call him) fell in close behind Lilah as she led us up the hall. She seemed jauntier, more on top of things, as if talking about her fears had diminished them. Or maybe receiving guests sent her automatically into hostess mode. Or maybe it was the coke. Whatever the cause, I was relieved.

I was also hungry. An intoxicating potpourri wafted from the kitchen: pastry shells, tarragon, roasting meat, garlic, olive oil, mushrooms. Surely there would be hors d'oeuvres . . .

Melinda halted at a half-open door on the left. "My old home!" She flourished her fur hat dramatically. "Oh, Lilah, I do envy you this house!"

Following the hat, I looked in. Just past Melinda's elbow was a steep wooden ladder, presumably to a loft. Wide carpeted stairs led down to a large space enclosed mostly by windows, uncurtained in spite of the darkness outside. On the right stood a grand piano; on the left, an off-white sofa and chairs. A low glass-topped table held a huge bowl of lilies in all the hues of TC's Spring lipstick line—the room's only color.

"It's yours again if you want it," said Lilah.

"Yes." A decisive nod. "I'd love it. Only I'd feel so . . . piggish!"

"Oh, Bruce will make sure you don't have it all to yourself for long." Lilah started again toward the kitchen. "I hope you're still an early riser. He's liable to come barging in to start a meeting or practice his new piano piece."

"If he catches me in my jammies I'll just stay holed up in the loft." Melinda tossed her hat at the sofa and added, "What nicer way to wake up than Bruce playing the piano?"

I glanced at Lilah, but she'd gone on through the swinging door to the kitchen.

Henry stepped aside for me to precede him. If he shared my surprise at Melinda's warmth toward another woman's husband, he didn't show it. "Lead on, Macduff!" he said stoutly. As always when people toss that one at me, I resisted the impulse to tell him it's *lay on* and refers to hacking up your opponent with a sword.

Then we entered the Eastons' kitchen, and the scene changed from *Macbeth* to *Moby-Dick*.

Except for the quarry-tile floor and a minimalist display of copper cookware, the kitchen was white. Starkly, blindingly white. Walls and cupboards, dishwasher, sink, microwave, refrigerator— The stove was a white counter top with discreet marks for the burners. Even the uniformed woman stabbing toothpicks into water chestnuts was white. As we paraded past her into the breakfast room on the right, our reflections shimmered off the shiny white enamel ceiling.

"Henry," I said, "what are you working on these days?"

As an attempt to inject humanity into our blanched

surroundings it was a failure. Henry's answer—insofar as I could decipher it—involved chromosome structure and other phenomena too minute to offset the Eastons' decor. I wanted something juicier. Like a filet mignon.

The controversy at Harvard that had inspired my *Phases* piece centered on Henry's discovery of a mechanism in bacterial RNA replication which was thought to have great potential for agriculture. Chester Chute of Chute Laboratories had offered him an obscene amount of money for his patents. Harvard protested, citing (a) its commitment to protecting pure science from exploitation by philistines, and (b) its dibs on the patents. Chester Chute—a sharp entrepreneur; I'd interviewed him, too—counterattacked. He invited Henry to finish his research in his very own laboratory, staffed with assistants of his choice, plus a salary hike and shares in Chute Labs.

When I spoke with him, Henry was vacillating. I heard later that the scale was tipped by a group of fellow biologists who wrote him a letter (copies to the *Harvard Crimson* and *New York Times*) urging him to uphold the noble goals and traditions of science by spurning Mr. Chute. So he must have done; for he now occupied a chair at Harvard which had conveniently come open a week after our meeting.

If indeed new friction was developing between that chair and its resident butt, I wondered if the cause was Henry's textbook. Chairs don't always entail a lot of work—I gather that's part of their attraction—but Communicore clearly was keeping its author on a short leash.

And then there was Chester Chute's fatal heart attack. The unexpected loss of its CEO had thrown Chute Labs into disarray. His hand-picked successor barely lasted a year. Maybe the current regime, hoping to recoup, had revived its offer to Professor Howrigan.

Lilah led us through the white breakfast room down a short white hall to the foyer. Here the walls were of warm wood, burnished by a brass lamp on a rosewood table. Like stepping out of Rauschenberg into Renoir. Even the eggshell-and-pearl Tibetan rug underfoot looked thick, soft, and cozy.

"Henry, I've put you in your usual room," said Lilah over her shoulder. "Would you like to freshen up before cocktails?"

But as we passed the front door he halted. "Goodness, look at that!"

Lilah and I went to the tall narrow windows on either side of the door. Snow. No longer just falling, but tumbling past the lights like sheets in a clothes dryer.

"You got here just in time," said Lilah.

I envisioned myself staring into that white darkness from my disabled Volkswagen, and I shuddered.

"Oh, dear." She turned abruptly. "I hope Wayne Glynn's had the sense to come in."

"We met him on our way up the drive," said Henry. "I urged him to ride with us, but he refused."

Behind us Melinda said, "Bruce is calling Edgar to haul him in. And Olive and Jeff are up from their naps or baths or wherever they've been."

Without her down coat she looked less like a cigarette ad and more like a corporate right hand. Contrary to Lilah's prediction about sweatsuits, Melinda had on a tweed business suit and leather boots—presumably the clothes she'd worn from New York to Boston this morning and back tonight to Connecticut. No wonder she and Henry were fraying each other's nerves. Her crisp voice, short brushed-back hair, minimal make-up, and folded arms suggested that patience was not Melinda Doerr's forte.

Lilah moved up the hall. Henry followed as close behind her as possible.

"Cory." Melinda stepped into my path. "Bruce asked me to introduce you to our other guests."

On the one hand, I've never cared for being fetched like

a pair of slippers. On the other, where there were guests there would be food. Why not go tackle an easy problem for a change?—like finding out what delicacies the Eastons' chef had speared onto toothpicks?

CHAPTER FOUR

"From here forward is the original structure." Melinda pointed left and right like a flight attendant. "Bruce added this guest wing, and also the hall from the kitchen to the old artist's studio, where I'm staying."

Added on whose tab, Melinda?—his or Caxton Press's? And how do you feel about returning to the studio you shared with your husband? How did you feel about leaving him and your home when Bruce Easton flexed his *droit du seigneur*?

I didn't get to inquire. As we passed through the archway, a swarthy, stocky man flung out his arms.

"Melinda! My angel! My editor!"

He stepped toward us from the fireplace with a glint in his deep-set eyes. Under his sport jacket a Hawaiian shirt hung open halfway to his belt. A beaded rawhide thong peeped through the hair on his chest like a snake in marsh grass. His jeans were faded but his brown-and-green cowboy boots looked new. Not Bruce Easton's idea of evening dress. Whose?

"Professor Jeffrey Abels of Harvard." Melinda stayed well away from his embrace. "Cory Thorne, a college friend of Lilah's. Jeff is writing a landmark majors biology text for us."

I'd heard of him: one of Cambridge's current Young Turks, brilliant and intense. Quite a coup for Communicore to harness him for a textbook.

"And this is Olive Chute, director of Chute Laboratories."

Well, well!

"Cory, did you say?" A pair of green-lidded eyes inspected me over the sofa back.

That was news: Chester's widow running the Labs. And attending the same Christmas party as Henry Howrigan.

"Pleased to meet you, dear."

My evening was looking up. Whatever triangle or trapezoid was forming around Professor Howrigan back in Boston, every vertex of it was represented here tonight.

The clawlike hand Mrs. Chute offered me was so heavy with jeweled rings that I was afraid of crushing her fingers. She asked what I did. I told her, and mentioned the story I'd written for *Phases* some years ago about her husband and Dr. Howrigan. That drew a smile. Aha! Cory Goodwin! Yes indeed. She and Chester had read it aloud to each other. She'd found it a tiny bit, well, *hard*, but Chester was greatly entertained. I said I might call her sometime about a sequel. Certainly, dear. The smile this time was noncommittal. With her hooded eyes, crinkly, weathered skin, and bronzed hair, Olive Chute reminded me of a lizard.

OK, you can't go by appearances. One would get you five, though, that Mrs. Chute didn't feel any more at home among cytosine and mitochondria than I did. Could one become director of a laboratory without having worked in the field? Silly question: Wasn't my husband the writer next in line (following his father and grandfather) to head Thorne Cosmetics? Had Olive inherited Chester's job, then? or a controlling interest in his company?

But Melinda was still heading like a heat-seeking missile toward the bar, where Bruce Easton stood mixing toddies.

He'd changed into gray slacks and a blue cashmere sweater. From honcho to host. Hearing us behind him, he glanced up. Melinda smiled at him in the mirror.

Olive Chute dropped my hand and whipped out to grab Melinda's. "*So* glad you've arrived safely, dear! We were terrified Henry had piled that dreadful great car of his into a snow-bank, and you wouldn't reappear till the crocuses bloomed."

Melinda halted reluctantly. "Olive. You're so tan. Sanibel already?"

"Just a quickie. Thanksgiving with Chet and Priscilla and Tres." Olive preened, touching a lacquered fingernail to an equally lacquered curl.

Melinda mouthed a message to Bruce's reflection.

"I do so agree with dear Ari, don't you?" Olive pitched her voice to the room at large. "One *must* be tan! It's my sine qua non." Her eyes went up and down Melinda's pale plump figure. "Thin, tan, rich, and in love."

There was a silence, broken by Lilah's voice from the kitchen. "Olive, did you bring pictures of Tres?"

She was maneuvering a tray of hors d'oeuvres through the swinging door. I would have hurried over to help her except that Jeff Abels got there first. The chops-licking look he flashed at her was straight out of Little Red Riding Hood.

"Yes, dear, I did. In my purse, wherever I've put it."

"You've got a number of sine qua nons, Olive," said Bruce.

"I'm too old to be indiscriminate," Olive answered tartly. "Someone in this day and age has got to stick up for values."

"Hear hear!" cried Jeff Abels.

Olive lifted her eyebrow at him. "Hardly your line, Jeff, I'd have thought."

He made her a courtly bow and let the door flap shut behind Lilah. "Don't underestimate me, dear lady."

A young woman was staring at him from the rug in front

of the fireplace. Frizzy home-bleached hair, a snug aqua sweater yoked with rhinestones . . . Who was this? Certainly not one of Bruce's art treasures.

I glanced curiously at our host, but he and Melinda were lip-synching in the mirror.

"I'm filthy with values!" Jeff went on. "What's your pleasure? Thrift? Industry? Patience? Fidelity? And speaking of fidelity, who's this Trace? Have you been stepping out behind my back, Olive, you heartbreaker?"

"Oh, for heaven's sake." Mrs. Chute pretended irritation. "Tres is my grandson. Chester Chute the third."

The girl on the rug said, "I don't get it."

She twisted herself up from a lounging to a sitting position and looked from Jeff to Olive. So Byzantine was her eye makeup that I marveled she could lift her lashes.

"Tres is Spanish for three, Gloria." A new party heard from: Henry Howrigan, standing in the archway. His thin fair hair was plastered wetly to his head. He looked shy and sleepy, like a child roused from a nap. "He was born—"

"Henry! At last!" Olive was too delighted to let him finish. "Dear boy, how *are* you? Frozen? Exhausted? Starving? Come sit here by me," she patted the sofa, "and Bruce will bring you a nice hot toddy."

She shifted a suede-booted leg. I liked her jacket, a hand-made patchwork of multicolored tufts.

But Henry crossed behind her, as Melinda had done, to the bar.

"Bruce." He stuck out his hand. "Good to see you."

They shook hands: Henry hearty and awkward, Bruce languidly graceful. Outwardly it was an ordinary moment. Yet Bruce's manner somehow conveyed power asserting itself, so forcefully that I quailed for Henry.

"Do you want a toddy, or shall I open the champagne?"

Henry licked his lips. "Whichever you prefer."

"You're the guest of honor."

He dropped it like a gauntlet. Henry hesitated as if afraid to pick it up.

"Go for the champagne," said Jeff. "We're toddied out."

He strolled over to the dining table, where Lilah was lifting plates of hors d'oeuvres off her tray, and grabbed a fistful of bacon-wrapped water chestnuts by gripping their toothpick handles between his knuckles. This bristling haul he offered to me. "Cory, right? You look hungry."

"Thanks. I am."

"So you and Lilah went to school together." Jeff sidled close enough for the musky scent of his aftershave to mingle with the aroma of bacon wafting from his mouth. "I'll bet a lot of people mistook you for sisters."

Bruce eased a champagne cork out of its bottle with a discreet pop.

"Did she warn you I've got a thing for redheads?"

The fizzy gurgle of wine filling a glass. I wondered if it was me or the room Jeff Abels was performing for.

"Henry would argue that's innate—a genetically modulated biochemical response triggered by perceptual cues. My view is that it's an acquired pattern possibly rooted in a biochemical predisposition but persisting because of positive experiences with redheads in the past." Jeff gave me an intimate smile and another whiff of aftershave.

"That is utterly frivolous," stated Henry. "If you must air our differences at a social gathering, Jeff, at least have the goodness to do so responsibly."

"My god, aren't we pompous tonight!"

"Cory?" murmured Bruce. "Champagne?"

"I'll pass it around," I murmured back.

I took glasses to Olive and Gloria, which gave me a chance to snatch a few more hors d'oeuvres from the plates Lilah had set on the coffee table. Lilah herself was still circulating. I didn't blame her.

"A slur is no argument," Henry retorted. "Though I

don't suppose someone with your cavalier attitude toward science could be expected to know that."

"Now, now." Olive patted his knee.

"If you want an argument—" said Jeff.

"We don't," said Melinda.

"What *I* want," Lilah said brightly, "is Henry's scientific opinion on what Mary Helen's put into these pastry puffs."

"What about *my* scientific opinion?" asked Jeff.

"Of course. Yours too."

Henry took a judicious nibble. Jeff popped a puff into his mouth. "Animal or vegetable?" he inquired, chewing.

"You're the biologists. You tell me."

"Vegetable," said Henry. "More accurately, fungus. Mushroom."

"No way. Animal! Escargot."

"Henry, dear, bring me one," Olive directed from the sofa. "I refuse to believe any male, even a scientist, knows more about food than a woman."

"Me, too, Jeff," called Gloria. "Toss it right in here." She opened her lipsticked mouth like a baby bird.

"Don't hit the DiChiara," said Bruce.

His hands were in his pockets. "You think a puff pastry will break it?" Jeff asked. "Hey, there's an idea. Gloria, separate the parts and we'll do a controlled experiment."

Gloria lifted the double blown-glass bowl and moved it to the far end of the coffee table.

"How about your wife's portrait?" Jeff took mock aim over the fireplace. "Or are you more hung up on a fairy piece of glass?"

"Jeff, don't," said Lilah. "Olive, I asked Mary Helen to make these artichoke things especially for you. Don't they look yummy? Gloria, you try one, too."

Bruce hadn't even glanced up from the champagne glass in his hand. He was wiping the rim with a soft cloth, no doubt the latest thing in crystal care from Neiman Marcus, content to leave social fencing—for now, anyhow—to his wife.

Lilah stood beside the coffee table holding out her platter. I had a fleeting vision of those iron darkies that used to deck lawns and country clubs, ring in hand.

Jeff, his trajectory blocked, shrugged and ate his weapon.

Melinda's hawklike eyes panned around the circle by the fire, checking for sparks. The clean-up committee, I thought, in charge of shepherding stray conversations back on track.

"Bruce, what's the news on Wayne Glynn?" she asked with the exaggerated heartiness of a TV anchorperson. "Did Edgar retrieve him? Our resident Mountie!"

"What appalling weather for a walk!" Olive shuddered picturesquely. "I take it this Glynn is one of those hardy souls who imagines tramping through the cold and wet is good for the character."

Bruce answered Melinda with a nod. "More like our resident St. Bernard."

"It's not his character," Gloria told Olive through a mouthful of artichoke. "It's his bod. He does Nautilus, too."

"Nautilus?" Henry looked puzzled.

"Who?" said Jeff. "I'm getting confused."

"You remember, dear," said Olive. "Like that shell I brought you from Sanibel, with the compartments."

"Lilah," said Bruce, pivoting, "I wish you'd done as I asked and told Wayne to stay on the plowed walks. You know I don't like anyone wandering around the property unsupervised, especially in snow."

His abrupt sharpness startled her. "But I did tell him. I mean, I must have. I never let anybody—"

"Has everyone got champagne?" Bruce cut her off. "Good. Friends, a toast." He lifted his glass. "To our guest of honor, Professor Henry Howrigan, author of Communicore Higher Ed's flagship project for next year's Spring list. Henry, our deepest thanks for your long hard work."

"Hear hear!" seconded Melinda.

Everyone looked jovial as glasses were clinked and drained. I gathered this was such a familiar ritual that even the right facial expressions had become automatic.

Only Lilah didn't drink. She still gripped her platter of hors d'oeuvres in both hands. Her mouth smiled, but her eyes gazed off into an unfathomable distance.

For a moment I saw her at our dorm Christmas party in college, cross-legged on the rug in jeans and a Grateful Dead sweatshirt, singing heartily of peace on earth. Peace was a priority then. Never mind bottom lines, capital gains, corporate downsizing, mergers and acquisitions. That sort of thing one could pick up later at Harvard or Stanford. The mandate of the NESLACT—New England Small Liberal Arts College Tradition—was noblesse oblige. With privilege comes responsibility. From each according to ability; to each according to need. As graduates of Mount Holyoke, we would solve the social problems of mankind with the sensibility of women.

We'd imagined commencement would fling us out of academia into action like stones from a slingshot. Free at last! Free to go anywhere in the world, to tackle all the challenges our parents' generation had botched. Vietnam, the Soviet Union, South Africa, the Middle East . . . Not boomerang back to New England to toast our former jailers with grown-up rum and coke.

"Speech!" bellowed Jeff Abels.

"Speech! Speech!" Gloria echoed with the enthusiasm of someone recognizing a cue.

Henry shook his head, blushed, and dithered. Olive gave his shoulder a playful punch. Lilah's eyes focused; she nodded encouragement. I tried to look willing, if not eager, and vowed to defer any further philosophizing until I'd had more to eat than three bacon-wrapped water chestnuts and two artichoke hearts.

"Shall I say a few words?" Henry asked Bruce.

"By all means," Bruce replied gravely.

Jeff grabbed a handful of pastry puffs from the coffee table. "Do it, Henry! Rah! Rah!"

With his fingers nervously intertwining, Henry might have been a third-grader called on unexpectedly by his teacher. He glanced at Melinda, then back at Bruce. I wished he'd stop squirming. He made me ashamed for the sharp, capable Nobel contender I'd interviewed half a dozen years ago.

"My friends." Henry sent a self-conscious smile around the room. "I want to thank each of you for being here this evening. And most of all I want to—"

A crash. Jeff Abels clapped his hands over his mouth. Shards of glass skittered across the tiles around his feet.

"Shit!" He doubled over, coughing into his hands. His eyes bulged. His face was scarlet.

Bruce and Lilah converged on him from opposite directions. Bruce thumped his back. Lilah glanced around for somewhere to put the hors d'oeuvres.

"Jeff! What is it?" Bruce demanded. "Tell me!"

"Something—" Another spasm of coughing. "In the goddam—"

Lilah slid her platter onto the bar, grabbed a pitcher and splashed water into a toddy mug.

"Shit, oh, dammit!"

Melinda had moved in behind Bruce, where she hovered, waiting for a signal. Gloria's eyes were as big as manhole covers.

Henry seemed torn between alarm and perplexity. Only Olive, watching Jeff's agonized contortions with her chin on her arm, was frankly fascinated.

Gradually Jeff's coughing fit subsided. Assisted by Bruce, he straightened up. From Lilah he took the mug, gulped water, rinsed his mouth energetically, and spat it out.

With unconcealed disgust Bruce inquired: "Well?"

Jeff stooped to examine the debris on the floor. He picked up a small round object and held it between a thumb and finger.

"You know what this is?" He thrust it in Bruce's face.

"No."

"It's the head off one of your goddam snakes!"

CHAPTER FIVE

In the shocked silence that followed Jeff's announcement, I didn't need to check faces to know what my fellow guests were thinking. *Get me out of here!* And then, as one pair of eyes after another sneaked to the windows: *Impossible.*

Bruce moved first. He picked up the platter of puff pastries and carried it toward the kitchen.

Jeff blocked his path. "Where are you taking those?"

"To the dispos-all."

"No. We've got to—"

Bruce stepped around him. The rigidity of his jaw and his walk suggested his composure was close to cracking.

"—check every one of them— God damn it, Bruce!"

I glanced at Lilah. She was staring at her husband's back as if willing him not to bite off Mary Helen's head in retribution. Or maybe she'd just never seen him carry a tray before.

"What's his problem?" Jeff demanded angrily of the room at large. "It wasn't him who damn near ate the bloody thing!"

"It's his party," Olive Chute observed.

"It was his snake," said Henry Howrigan.

"You might," Melinda said tightly, "have spit it quietly

into a napkin, Jeff, instead of broadcasting it all over the living room."

"Jesus fucking Christ!" Jeff was pacing back in forth in front of the fireplace. "So now Bruce is the victim and I'm the bad guy? I don't fucking believe this!"

Gloria, who'd been cringing beside the chimney with both hands over her mouth, flung herself at him. Was he OK? Shouldn't he go to the hospital? Olive retorted that if he needed treatment, which she doubted, a drink of soapy water would do the trick. Jeff snapped at both of them to shut up. Henry volunteered to seal off the master bedroom in case the snake-decapitator was hiding inside. Melinda snapped at him not to be a fool. Olive ordered Melinda to call the police and Jeff to stop grandstanding. Melinda retorted that the phone was out and she wasn't holding her breath for the repair crew. Lilah looked as though she wished she dared sneak out for more coke.

I kept quiet. Watching façades crumble, maybe I'd learn something—for instance, why Bruce Easton had owned a snake, and who disliked it or him or Jeff or all of us enough to turn it into an appetizer.

"All right!" said Melinda. "I'm calling Edgar to clean up here. Will someone—Jeff?—please open another bottle of champagne, *now!*"

From the foyer came a slap-slapping sound. A pallid, concave young man with a red nose was approaching in oversized corduroy slippers. Above them he wore brown polyester slacks and a sweater ringed with romping reindeer.

"Greetings, all! Sorry my preprandial stroll turned into a peregrination. What'd I miss?"

"Oh, Christ," muttered Jeff.

You could feel a refocusing of attention as all eyes went to the newcomer, and each mind phrased a knockout answer.

"What'd you *miss!*"

Gloria's squeal was fast, but I was faster.

"Hi," I held out my hand. "I'm Cory Thorne, a friend of Lilah's."

The man in the reindeer sweater gave me a fishlike handshake. Olive came in smoothly: "I don't believe we've met. You must be Wayne Glynn? Olive Chute."

"Pleasure." Wayne Glynn transferred his damp, limp fingers from mine to hers. He looked around with wary curiosity, as if he smelled a red herring.

"Jeff," said Lilah with her steeliest smile, "have you got that champagne open? Poor Wayne missed our toast to Henry."

Jeff lifted an eyebrow and went to the bar. Olive settled herself on the sofa. Gloria perched on an arm. Henry stood at the far side of the coffee table, his hands clasped behind him, his back to the fire, rocking lightly on the balls of his feet.

"Welcome, Wayne," he said gruffly. "Afraid you missed a bit more than congrats on the book. Some joker slipped a foreign object into Professor Abels' hors d'oeuvre."

Gloria sputtered, "A foreign—!"

Lilah gripped her shoulder. "Find Wayne a glass, Gloria."

Jeff produced a bottle from under the bar. He wriggled the cork, which blew across the room with a loud pop.

"Nothing poisonous, lucky for me," he told Wayne. "Here you go. Who else needs bubbly?"

Lilah held out her glass.

"Henry?"

Though I'd done my part to restore order, I wondered now if it had been a wise move. Like the champagne Jeff was pouring, we were under pressure. Etiquette wasn't a cork but only a wire cage. Untwist it and sooner or later you'd get an explosion.

Maybe Wayne Glynn's arrival would serve as a safety valve. Certainly the others had been more willing than I'd expected to stonewall him . . .

With a sudden suspicion I sent my eyes around the room. Every face looked blandly congenial. What calculations were going on inside those heads? Ten minutes, maybe fifteen, for Wayne to remove his wet boots. How long did it take to cut off a snake's head and stuff it into a pastry puff?

What did these people know about Wayne Glynn as a possible snake decapitator that I didn't?

But I wasn't here to play detective. My job as Lilah's guest was to help her keep the wire around the cork.

"Lilah." Jeff clunked his bottle down on the bar. "Getting back to unfinished business, I'd like to inspect your room."

She stared at him as if he'd spoken Russian. There it goes, I thought with a sense of futility. The first twist.

"Bruce will take care of that, Jeff."

"Yeah. Sure. But this is kind of a," he paused, "personal thing for me."

"Horsefeathers!" said Olive sharply. "It's no more personal for you than any of us. It could just as easily have been me."

"You weren't asked for your scientific opinion on the filling."

"*I* was," said Henry. "In fact I was asked before you. Whoever put that—that *thing* in there might very well have heard Lilah say she wanted my opinion, and then stuck it where he thought I would get it."

"He or she," said Wayne Glynn. "What are you talking about?"

An editor. Had to be. Who else corrects you first and then asks what you meant?

Gloria, who'd been bursting to tell Wayne all about it since he'd arrived, beckoned him to the sunporch corner and launched a hushed explanation.

Lilah looked pale. "I hope you don't think I had any

idea—"

"Of course not," Henry said stoutly.

"I can't see why you would," said Jeff. "But then I can't see why anybody would. That's why we need data. How can anybody believe anybody till we've at least got a working hypo-thesis on whodunit?"

"I take it for granted that no one *here* did it," Olive sniffed. "Presumably Bruce is questioning the staff."

"Oh, but—" started Lilah, and stopped as the implications hit her.

"I repeat," said Jeff. "I want to inspect your room."

Lilah flung up her head—a gesture of annoyance I remembered well. "Why not?" she retorted. "Let's all go! Come on, Henry. Olive, you too. Come on, everybody! Grab a piece of the action!"

Any action that might have taken place in the Eastons' bedroom was long over. There were no snakes. There were no fugitives in the closets. There were also no clothes draped over chairs, no books on bedside tables, no combs, no brushes, no jewelry boxes. There wasn't so much as a stray hairpin.

The decor, not to my surprise, was off-white. Thick wall-to-wall carpet. Quilted silk bedspread. Curtains. Towels and tiles in the adjoining bathroom. Do they have a whole vocabulary for it, I wondered, like the Eskimos and snow? Bone, ivory, eggshell, cream . . .?

The glass aquarium that had housed Bruce's snake sat on a stand near the foot of the bed. Why he'd chosen such a pet I couldn't imagine. Why he'd kept it here I preferred not to. I'd noticed in spite of myself that with the closet door open, someone in bed would face a full-length mirror reflecting both himself and the snake.

We gathered around the empty cage.

"They're gone all right," said Jeff.

Bruce Easton spoke from the doorway. "I could have told you that."

His eyes were hard and bright as he walked toward us. He's furious that we're here, I thought, and who can blame him?

"How many were there?" Olive asked drily.

"One. A garter snake, ten inches long and quite harmless." Bruce took a stick from the aquarium and stirred the gravel on the bottom. "Much more harmless to us," he added with a cold glance at Jeff, "than we are to them."

"Them," said Jeff. "Last time I was here you had two."

"We lost one."

"Should we look around?" asked Wayne Glynn.

Jeff answered with a mirthless laugh. "So far they're finding us."

"Looking for things is Edgar's job," Bruce said curtly. "Ours, if you recall, is science publishing."

"Today's special, herpetology."

"That's not funny, Jeff," said Olive.

"No," Jeff agreed. "And it won't be funny when you get the other nine inches in your clam chowder, either."

"Jeff—" said Lilah.

"This whole damn thing isn't funny." He wiped his forehead on his sleeve. "Excuse me, Bruce, I need to use your bathroom."

Nobody wanted to talk about grandchildren, Nautilus, the snowstorm, or revolutionizing the teaching of biology until we established how the head of Bruce's garter snake had gotten into Jeff's puff pastry. But what could we do?

Yes, Bruce answered as we regrouped in the living room, he had questioned Mary Helen. No, he didn't believe she had spiked her own cooking. He'd as soon believe Henry would plant errors in his manuscript, or Gloria put typos in a memo. No, he had not checked the other hors d'oeuvres before disposing of them. However, he and Mary Helen together had minutely inspected every dish now under way for dinner and found no sign of tampering. Yes, he'd asked her if she'd noticed anyone poking around in the kitchen, and no, she hadn't. Although most of the guests had passed through at one point or another, Mary Helen had not paid them much attention.

Jeff, leaning against the chimney, inquired, "Did she say if the original filling was mushroom or escargot?"

"I hope," Bruce finished coldly, "we can all avoid troubling Mary Helen any further. We're lucky to have her, and like any artist she's not at her best when she's upset."

He handed the champagne bottle he was holding to Melinda, who stood a few feet away at the bar. "Now, if you'll excuse me, I'll go bring up the wine for our first course."

"I'll help you." Lilah jumped up.

"You can be most helpful, darling, by staying here with our guests." Flicking his nostril with his finger, Bruce walked out.

Why don't you just thumb your nose at her, I thought, you self-centered creep? If any husband of mine ever spoke to me like that—

"Jeff," Melinda asked in her TV-anchorperson voice, "what's the current status of your neurotransmitter project?"

"Moot. We're waiting to hear from NIMH. Or," he glanced at Olive, "for other sources of funding to emerge."

"What are you doing now, then?" Gloria had resumed her seat on the white rug near his feet, where she was jabbing at the fire with a poker.

"Right this minute, a survey." Jeff cracked his knuckles. "Time to ask the question everybody's been ducking, ladies and gents: Who pulled a John the Baptist on Bruce's garter snake?"

"Jeff!" Gloria slapped his ankle.

"It had to be someone in this house. I don't really give a damn who, or even why. We're all half tanked, right? Maybe it seemed like a big laugh at the time. I just want to know that's how it was meant—as a joke, not some kind of," he hesitated, "weird vendetta."

"I agree," said Olive unexpectedly. "I'd rather believe one of us did it as a prank, however ill-advised, than wonder if . . ." She let it trail off.

"I'll go first," said Jeff. "I sure as hell didn't do it, and I don't have any idea who did."

"Nor I," Olive declared.

"Me neither," Gloria said primly. "I can't *stand* snakes!"

"Henry?"

"Certainly not. A damnable trick to play on a man who's done so much for all of us. Bruce, I mean, of course." He glowered at Jeff.

"What about you, Melinda, dear?" inquired Olive.

"It wasn't me."

"I," said Wayne Glynn.

"*You?*" Gloria gasped.

"No. No." Wayne's sallow cheeks flushed. "Melinda said it wasn't *me*, and I said *I*, meaning—"

"We know what you mean," Melinda cut in, "and we all wish you'd keep it to yourself until someone asks you." She looked around as if daring anyone to do so. "Anyway, as I was trying to say before I was interrupted: I didn't do it. And I don't believe for one second that Bruce did, either. Or Lilah," she added as an afterthought.

"Let them speak for themselves," said Jeff.

"I think this is silly," Lilah said.

"But what about the snake?" Jeff persisted.

"No."

She might have been answering, or she might have been

refusing to answer. I decided not to take chances.

"I didn't do it, either. And I don't think we have much hope of finding out who did. Whoever's responsible obviously doesn't choose to admit it. So why abuse Lilah and Bruce's hospitality? Unless they want us to investigate further, I suggest we drop it and enjoy the rest of the evening."

"Hear hear!" Henry hoisted his glass.

"Cory, you're an angel," Lilah said warmly. "You, too, Henry. They're right, you know," she told the others. "Bruce put so much effort into making this a good party—why let one mean person spoil it?"

"I'll drink to that," said Wayne Glynn. "And I'll finish off the question before the house, if Melinda will allow me to speak, by reminding you all that I was outside in a blizzard, so I couldn't have guillotined any snake."

As a denial it was equivocal enough to revive my curiosity about why Wayne had taken so long to rejoin the party after his—what had he called it?—preprandial peregrination. Hauled in by Bruce's resident St. Bernard . . .

"Well," said Gloria, "but what about Edgar?"

"Goodness! A dark horse!" Olive's green-lidded eyes widened with anticipation.

"I don't mean Edgar cut up Bruce's snake—"

"No," seconded Melinda. "I've known him for years, and I can't believe he'd betray Bruce's trust like that."

"He'd have to be crazy," Gloria added practically. "He'd never get another job."

"Even if he could find anybody else who'd put up with him living in that raunchy trailer—" said Jeff.

"RV," Gloria corrected.

"—with that garbage hound of a dog."

"I'm just saying we should ask him."

"Well, but, Gloria." Wayne Glynn stepped into the center of the group with the determination of a man who still isn't sure what's going on but can't bear to be left out. *"He'd have to be crazy* isn't a cogent objection, now, is it?"

He delivered this insight so triumphantly that I itched to punch him in the reindeer. And decided to withdraw before the impulse overwhelmed me.

I slipped out the kitchen door and headed for my room. These people's appetite for blood was starting to turn my stomach. Guilty or innocent, did they expect Edgar to confess? If he didn't, what then? Were we doomed to spend dinner slinging accusations and denials, checking under every leaf of arugula in case the missing corpse turned up mincé or farci?

The radio on my bedside table confirmed that snow was coming down harder than ever. The powers who decide such things had declared it a major storm. Travelers' warnings were in effect. The accumulation ante had been upped to sixteen or eighteen inches.

I lay back on the off-white bedspread and stared at the off-white ceiling. My body seemed to be circling gently in space. Lucky I'd passed up the cocaine. And still two or three wine courses, a brandy course, and Lilah's eggnog to face.

Not to mention whatever warped joke the snake decapitator came up with next . . .

From the radio, a rueful singer reminded me how very far away I was from anyplace I'd meant to be at Christmastime. I wished I'd gone to Seattle with Larry instead of coming here. I wished I could either give up on helping Lilah or think of a plan. I wished—

Someone tapped on my door. I sat up.

It was Bruce Easton, carrying an uncorked bottle of Chateau Nuage '79 and two goblets.

"I saw you as I was coming up from the cellar." He set the glasses next to the radio. "I don't like parties, either. This is the wine I've picked to complement Mary Helen's shrimp bisque. Nice color, don't you think?"

"No thanks," I said as he started to pour.

The inch of liquid in his glass was straw-colored. Perfect, I thought. Off-white wine.

"I'm glad you could be with us this weekend. It means a great deal to Lilah." He sniffed, then sipped. "She's an uncommonly sensitive woman, as you know."

I felt it was time to set Bruce Easton straight on a few things. "I don't really know," I said. "Lilah and I haven't seen each other in years. And as far as your party, I've got nothing against parties per se—I just needed a break."

He swirled his wine and nodded absently. Acceptable. The vintage or me?

"This last year has been a very stressful one for Lilah. For both of us, of course; but Lilah's reaction concerns me. Perhaps she's told you."

It was close enough to a question that I answered cautiously, "A little, yes."

"Paul was my son by my first marriage, but I'm afraid Lilah blames herself for his death. Not that it was at all her fault, any more than the original accident that crippled him. She feels responsible for *that*, I think, because of the timing. I had just told my wife of my intention to divorce her and marry Lilah."

I closed my eyes.

Once on Memorial Drive in Cambridge I saw a motorcycle spin out and the rider go skidding down the yellow line on his back. As I ran toward him I felt myself slowing, moving ponderously as if through water, stretching out the seconds until I reached him. Hoping against all probability that he would stand up before I got there and had to look at the face inside that helmet.

My eyes opened.

"I'm sorry, Bruce, but I don't know what you're talking about."

So—naturally—he told me.

CHAPTER SIX

A late Sunday afternoon in August. The weather is glorious—has been all weekend. Hot enough to swim but not too hot to bask on the sundeck. No mosquitos (the spraying was successful); no major quarrels, thank god, over Henry Howrigan's biology book. Henry has accepted Wayne Glynn as his writer. Melinda is delighted. Bruce too is pleased. Henry doesn't much like Glynn—nobody does except Gloria—but has agreed to cut him in for one-and-a-half percent. Hardly a painful sacrifice when Henry's own royalty rate escalates from fifteen to eighteen-and-a-half as the book's sales rise. Wayne's function is to ensure that sales do rise, Melinda has explained to Henry. He'll generate chapters from your outlines which you can then reshape as you like. You win both ways: speed and expert assistance. After two years of slogging through drafts, Henry's doubts are outweighed by his relief. Bruce and Melinda, in the studio, high-five each other in a rare outburst of euphoria.

Lilah is asleep in the master bedroom. Outside on the deck drowses Paul.

In her darker moments Lilah fears that Paul is God's vengeance on her and Bruce for flouting their marriage vows. Illicit ecstasies in Communicore's private Manhattan apartment while Julia puts Paul to bed in Oxbridge and Numero Uno kills another fifth on East Fourth. We're doing nothing wrong, she would tell her reflection, entwined with Bruce's in the full-length mirror overhead. Is it our fault we fell in love? Still, a burden lifted when Bruce sublet a condo and announced they were moving in together. Numero Uno's hysterics were horrible but short-lived. Julia, silent, shipped her belongings and Paul's to her parents' home in New Hampshire. Before leaving the house where she and her son had spent so many solitary nights, she gouged every window in the glass-walled dining area with her wedding diamond.

Halfway across Massachusetts Julia's car went out of control. A tactful way of putting it, thought Bruce when the police finally tracked him down. By then his soon-to-be-ex wife had been discharged from the hospital and the doctors were all but certain Paul would never walk again.

That he also would never speak again was a twist the doctors failed to predict.

For a while Julia and her parents cared for him. They found a special school—ironically, not far from the scene of the accident. When Julia's mother died, she and her father reluctantly switched Paul from day student to boarder so Julia could get a job. It's not merely that I can't support him properly on the pittance you pay us, she told Bruce. You with your perfect house and your perfect job and your perfect new bride—you can't even begin to imagine what it's like to have no life but babysitting a ten-year-old infant.

Bruce conferred with Julia, her therapist, Paul's therapist, doctors, and teachers. He dusted off his dormant visitation rights. Every few weeks, when their schedule permitted, he and Lilah brought Paul home with them for a day or two. Lilah, sensitive creature, adored the boy. This was fortunate, though not surprising: Even mute and in a wheelchair, Paul bore a striking resemblance to his father.

On this particular August Sunday Bruce left for the

school before his guests arose. Awkward to manage both a business houseparty and a crippled son; but with the Glynn question settled, Melinda can handle the Communicore group, and Lilah will tend to Paul. Olive Chute is due for cocktails on her way home from visiting Chet and family in Short Hills. Jeff Abels may drop in if his Macy Foundation conference in New York wraps up early. It is Bruce's experience that nothing much is ever accomplished on a Sunday, so one may as well socialize.

Lilah has wheeled Paul to the end of the driveway and back—his favorite walk—and fed him lunch. Bruce, Melinda, and Henry have roughed out a schedule for Wayne Glynn's draft chapters and Henry's revisions. Mary Helen's Crab Louis, coupled with a Montrachet from the former Caxton Press cellars, has sent most of the party to lawn chairs for naps. Paul too is tired. Bruce reads to him in a shady spot on the deck till he falls asleep. Then he moves softly past Lilah, her long hair loose, her bathing suit discarded beside her on the bed, and takes the *Times Book Review* downstairs to his office.

A crash overhead jerks him awake. The pond is churning. Up on the deck Lilah screams, over and over, like a car alarm that won't shut off. Through his window Bruce makes out Paul's plaid blanket floating among the lily pads. He dashes for the stairs. Up the hall to the studio, out the glass doors. Melinda is already wading in murky water up to her chest. She grabs the blanket. It pulls away from nothing. Bruce splashes in after her, without regard for his handmade shoes and silk slacks, until he can see around the willow tree beside the deck. Over his head is a chaos of splintered rails— and an empty wheelchair, tipped, one chrome rim glinting as it spins.

"The fire department dragged for the body." Bruce poured himself another glass of wine. "Hauled him out onto the lawn —a wet limp heap of rags on the green grass. I called in exterminators after the funeral to poison the water and dredge out the lilies. To clear the pond of debris, I told them." He smiled, wanly. "Why should fish swim and flowers bloom where my son died?"

Nothing I could say seemed adequate. "I'm so sorry. What a terrible thing for you and Lilah."

He inclined his head. I was struck again—incongruously—by the fine chiseling of his features, the grace of his gestures.

"We've tried to look at it as a blessing in disguise. To remind ourselves that Paul must have hated his life in that chair, hated being a burden. Unable to swim or play baseball or lead any kind of normal existence— And then to look so much like me without any hope of ever matching my activities, my achievements . . ." Bruce's fingertips traced the curve of his glass as if searching for a flaw. "Lilah has taken it very hard, though. I'm almost afraid—" He looked up. "But that's not your problem, is it? I simply felt you should know why she's so moody. And be forewarned in case someone refers to what happened the last time this group was together. It's been pushed out of everyone's mind by this foolish incident of Jeff's, but it might come up later."

For two awful seconds I thought he expected me to reply. How? *So astute of you, Bruce, and so thoughtful, to keep these things in perspective.*

Suddenly I could hardly stand being in the same room with him. It wasn't merely that Bruce Easton radiated attracttion and ego with the indiscrimination of a quartz heater. What made me want to slap that glass out of his hand was knowing he held Lilah just as lightly, just as tightly.

He was saying something about the snow. Possible problems ending the party after the tree-decorating as planned. I nodded and rose. Edgar had been instructed to keep the driveway clear (Bruce stood back to let me precede him), but as for the roads, there was no telling . . .

All through dinner I gazed at the shining black windows behind which lay the now-barren pond, and at Lilah, laughing as her spoon dipped into her shrimp bisque, and I thought about Paul Easton.

Not by choice. I'd hoped to abandon myself to Chateau Nuage, Mary Helen's medallions de veau, and stimulating conversation. Unfortunately Wayne Glynn, on my left, spent the meal telling Gloria about his hike through the blizzard; while Jeff Abels, on my right, debated the biochemical components of sexual preference with Henry Howrigan. Now and then Olive Chute cut in with warnings against homosexuality and other perversions threatening what she called—inaptly—the Family of Man.

So I ate, drank Perrier, blocked my ears, and wondered why Lilah had said nothing to me about Paul's death.

Was she afraid I'd refuse to come to a house so literally cursed? Was the memory too painful to speak of? Had Bruce asked her not to mention it? Dredge up lilies, yes, but not the past! Or had she refocused all her terrors on Lucifer, AKA Tony Cyr?

I didn't know. And until I got more data, I had no way of figuring it out.

Bruce sat at the other end of the table with Melinda at his right hand (naturally) and Henry at his left. For a man who disliked parties he appeared to be enjoying himself. So charming was his smile, so relaxed his manner, that I couldn't help wondering if he had a twin who wandered this house like the Ancient Mariner, telling his tragic tale to passers-by.

Had anyone here mentioned last August? No. Had I hinted that I found Lilah moody and wanted an explanation? No again. Was Bruce such a doting husband he'd try anything to cheer up his wife? Alas, no.

Then why the revelations?

Only one reason struck me as plausible: Bruce must think the severed snake's head in the puff pastry tonight was connected somehow to his son's death.

Why?

I sat back as a white hand removed my dinner plate. The first and worst possibility was that he didn't really believe Paul's fall from the deck was accidental. That, on reflection, I doubted. Murder his own son, maybe; but let someone else get away with smashing the sole treasure in his collection he himself had created? Not Bruce Easton!

More likely he was spooked. Paul's drowning had been horrible and pointless. So was having his pet snake beheaded and fed to a guest. Under the strain of bereavement and cocaine . . .

A small perfect salad slid onto the linen cloth in front of me. Olive was once again pontificating about the sanctity of the family—not awfully sensitive of her. Jeff held his wine glass in the air, awaiting a chance to swoop down on Henry. Loudest was Wayne Glynn, still narrating to Gloria, who stabbed at her lettuce with the methodical energy of a park trash collector.

"Mr. Glynn," said Bruce.

Silence rippled down the table.

"Sir?" Half compliant, half mocking.

"Do I understand you've been trekking all over the grounds this evening? Risking your safety and our peace of mind in spite of my request that you stay on the walks and driveway?"

"That wasn't my intention." Wayne appeared torn between "So sorry" and "So what?"

"He saw footprints," Melinda intervened. "He told us when we tried to pick him up. He left the driveway to investigate."

Bruce was not impressed. "I don't like my guests wandering around the property, especially in weather like this."

Jeff leaned toward me and murmured, "They leave ugly marks on his nice white snow."

"Investigating footprints, or any other irregularity"—Bruce shot a quelling look at Jeff—"is Edgar's job."

I expected him to add that our job was science publishing, but perhaps he realized he'd already said that.

Lilah dropped her napkin on the table. "How about a pause before dessert? Coffee around the fire, anyone?" She stood up. "Olive, would you show me your pictures of Tres?"

If the next two minutes had unfolded differently, so would a lot that followed. In the back of my mind a hazy image was forming. Once—years ago—I'd read something, or heard something, that matched a piece of this puzzle.

What, though? Not science publishing. Not Harvard, or snowstorms . . . Something more unsavory.

Cocaine?

I was rising from my seat, resolving to have a private talk with Lilah as soon as convenient, when Olive Chute shrieked.

Heads turned. Someone knocked over a chair which clanged and clattered on the tiles. Lilah froze with her hand out.

Olive was staggering backwards away from the sofa. Her purse, apparently defying the laws of physics, hurtled in a high arc across the living room. Her scream shattered into a staccato of anguished gasps.

"What the hell?" muttered Wayne Glynn behind me.

Olive stumbled against the coffee table and into a floor lamp. Lilah lunged to catch her.

As Olive crumpled into Lilah's arms, Bruce and Melinda rushed in from opposite sides. "What happened?" Bruce demanded. He supported Lilah from behind, inching her and Olive toward the sofa. Melinda grabbed the swaying lamp. "Olive! What—?"

"See for yourself," Jeff Abels retorted.

He held out Olive's purse: a shapeless leather sack whose mouth gaped like its owner's.

"Olive's solved your problem, Bruce. She's found the

rest of your snake."

Once could be dismissed as a bad joke. *Twice* smacked of malice. This time Bruce headed for the phone, as if sheer force of will might get it working again.

Lilah and I settled Olive on the spare bed in my room over her protests: She was fine, just a little shaken, for god's sake don't let this get around or they'd laugh her out of the Labs. I had to admire her sang-froid. For someone who'd just found nine-tenths of a garter snake coiled on her family snapshots, Olive looked like a travel poster for Palm Beach.

In the hall I remembered my almost-revelation. Not about cocaine. Something to do—wasn't it?—with Bruce's snake.

OK. What did I know about snakes? Cold-blooded scaly reptiles. Sometimes poisonous. Egg-layers that shed their skins. Not much. Nothing related to a spiked hors d'oeuvre, anyhow, or a kid drowned in a pond.

The recommendations flying around the living room were harsher than last time. Get the cops. Search the house. Dust the snake for fingerprints. Too late: Bruce, ignoring both police procedure and Jeff's lecture on scientific method, had already confiscated Exhibit B and sent it the way of Exhibit A. Whether he was more upset about Olive or his murdered pet was anyone's guess.

The worst news came when he returned. The phone line remained as dead as a . . . well, never mind. The radio reported that although the storm was tapering off, the roads were impassable. Listeners should stay inside and keep warm until the snowplows could get through.

"Impassable?" Jeff tapped a silver-tipped cowboy boot against the chimney. "Crap! All of a sudden I'm stone cold sober."

"And no cell phone, either?" Henry asked anxiously.

"We have phones." From Bruce's tone, it was all he could do to be civil. "What we don't have is service."

"Being in a kettle-pond basin of marble and granitic gneiss," added Wayne Glynn.

Henry turned to me. "Cory, how is Olive? Do you think we should risk trying to get her medical attention?"

He sounded so worried that I wanted to pat his shoulder and say *there, there*. Instead I quoted Olive's quip about being laughed out of the Labs. "She promised to join us for dessert. Meanwhile she'll appreciate it if we don't let this incident ruin the party."

Henry harrumphed. "Easy for her to say. Olive enjoys parties. I'd just as soon retire to my room with a book. And I don't," he added, "mean introductory biology."

That possibility was forestalled by Melinda.

During the aftershock she'd changed from her tweeds into a forest-green velour sweatsuit. Robin Hood, I thought. Dressed to gather merry gentlemen around a tree; which was precisely what she had in mind.

We rallied our Yuletide spirit. Jeff and Wayne dragged in the seven-foot Douglas fir. Henry screwed together a stand. Gloria and Melinda and I carried boxes of ornaments. Bruce supervised the laying of a white cloth in the right spot to center the tree's reflected lights in the windows, and to catch any needles it might try to strew on his floor.

Having done my part, I slipped away. I wanted to check on Olive. Even more, I wanted to talk to Lilah about the snake.

The hall was so silent I half-tiptoed. And suddenly missed my untidy front hall at home with its holly branches and bronze Chinese bowl full of Christmas cards. What did Bruce and Lilah do with their cards? Catalogue and file them?

Olive had recovered enough to be enjoying her celebrity. Propped in off-white pillows, her weathered face bloomed like a Christmas cactus. She'd borrowed the book I'd brought, Sara Neustadtl's *Moving Mountains*, and sat flipping pages and sipping tea.

"But I'm anxious to get back," she told me. "Those poor boys—I worry, dear. Fish in a barrel!"

"I beg your pardon?"

"Business is business, of course, I wasn't born yesterday. However! Brilliant as they are—and believe me, they *are*—they haven't a glimmer. The boys, I mean. How could they, stuck up in that ivy tower? *He* wines and dines them, *she* tosses them chunks of money, like zoo animals, and they sign away their best years." Olive's nostrils flared. "I dare not leave them alone, truly I don't! For their own sake and for the future of science."

I construed this scatter-shot speech to mean that Olive didn't approve of Bruce and Melinda's enlisting Henry and Jeff as textbook authors. Not my uppermost concern. I asked her what she thought about the snake episodes.

Well! Surely there was only one possibility. An outsider had sneaked in. Some left-wing radical, Arab terrorist, or homeless person with a grudge against the privileged class who throw Christmas parties. "If I were such an individual, I'd certainly attack us rather than bomb Penn Station, wouldn't you?"

Her half-closed eyes waited to see if I'd buy it. I resisted the urge to ask whether, if she were such an individual, she'd pick a garter snake as her weapon against capitalism.

"You can't think of anyone here who might want to frighten or threaten you personally?"

"Ha!" Olive's laugh seemed genuine. "If they do, dear, they'll have to do better than that!"

"One other thing." I rose. "When did you last see your purse before you went to get those pictures?"

Olive's pause and a slight compression of her lips branded the question in bad taste. Better get used to it, I told her silently. This is just the beginning.

"Before dinner?" She adjusted one of her rings. "I seem to recall not remembering where I'd put it."

"And that was — when?"

"Oh, heavens. How should I know?" But she considered, pushing the ring up and down her thin finger. "I had it in my room. Did I bring it upstairs? I must have." She looked up. "Really, dear, I can't say. The last time I distinctly recall having it in my hands was when Jeff and I came up for cocktails."

I sighted Lilah in the foyer, but I didn't catch up with her till the breakfast room.

No time to talk (she rolled her eyes at the kitchen). Dessert to serve, Mary Helen having conniptions, domestic upheaval, captain to the bridge, all hands on deck.

"Let me help."

"Here, then." She thrust a sheaf of napkins at me. "Put these on the table."

What are friends for? "One question first, though. Where did Bruce get his snakes? There were two of them originally, right?"

She didn't answer.

"Did they belong to Paul?"

A nod.

"When Paul used to—"

"No," she cut me off. "You said one question. I'm sorry, Cory, but that's all I can handle right now."

As she turned away, I caught her by both shoulders. "I'm sorry, Lilah, but that won't do. Listen to me. Somebody in this house is out to make trouble."

"I can't *take* any more!"

"Right. So let's nip it in the bud, OK? Help me figure out who cut up the snake." I didn't add, *before he or she escalates to mammals*. Being a Mount Holyoke grad, Lilah could make that leap by herself.

"I have no idea." But she'd calmed down enough to think. "Somebody who wants to hurt Bruce, obviously. But *why*?"

"Why would you guess?"

"Jealousy?" She shook her head. "It's crazy! He's done so much for them."

"For all of them? How about Olive?"

"I can't see Olive putting that—that *thing* in her purse."

Neither could I. "Who's jealous, then? And of what? His position? His power? You?"

Lilah was getting edgy again. "I don't know! It doesn't make sense. These are perfectly normal people—*nice* people—our friends! Except—"

"Except?" I prompted.

"Well, of course, Wayne. Gloria."

"What about Edgar? Mary Helen?"

"Oh, no," she said positively. "They've been with us for years. They adore Bruce!"

Sure, I thought as I laid out napkins. Everybody adores Bruce! Like the French adored Louis XVI. Like the Russians adored Czar Nicholas.

Frankly, I was worried. Although I didn't swallow jealousy as a motive, I did agree Bruce looked like the snake-killer's target. It was his party; it was his snake. Worse: it was Paul's snake—the last living memento of his dead son.

So I'd guessed right about Bruce associating the puff-pastry incident with Paul's drowning. But where did that leave me? I still had no idea why the snake had been hacked up and its parts passed out like grisly Christmas presents. Much less who'd played Santa.

One thing I did know: Whoever had struck twice at this party wasn't likely to let it end on a note of Peace on Earth, Good Will toward Men.

So I kept my eyes open as I rejoined the decorators. Wayne and Gloria were holding the tree steady on the floor while Henry hacked at its spiky tip and Jeff sawed a section off the trunk. Melinda wiped dust off a papier-mâché angel which I gathered traditionally crowned the top. The tree was shedding a heavenly aroma, pungent and cold, as if its branches carried deep magic from the heart of some wild Northern forest.

Perhaps it was that sharp icy smell that moved Bruce to switch on the outdoor floodlights. Everything behind the tree went from black to white. Fifteen seconds later Lilah appeared, her face drained of color, and pointed at the windows.

"Is it Olive?" I hurried toward her. "What's wrong?"

Her hand wobbled and fell to her side. With visions of Lady Macbeth, I grasped her arm. She was trembling all over.

Jeff's saw stopped. "My god, Lilah, you look like you've seen a ghost."

At that she clutched my shoulder and burst into tears.

"She has," said Bruce in a flat frozen voice.

He wasn't facing us but staring out the dining room windows. Melinda stood behind him with her arms folded and her lips pressed tight.

"Oh my god," breathed Gloria.

Wordlessly Lilah steered me around the tree.

At first all I saw was snow. The storm had let up: most of the flakes whirling past the lights were blowing off the roof. Was that it?

No.

The pond's surface should have been smooth as a bowl of milk. Instead, peaks and holes and hollows had churned it into whipped cream. Footprints—an army of them.

Wayne, you poor sucker, I thought, this means the firing squad.

Then I saw the man standing knee-deep in snow ten

yards from shore.

He faced the opposite bank, hands clasped in front of him like a cop at a shootout. Black splotches between him and the near bank suggested a hat, gloves, and a liquor bottle. Even at this distance I recognized his sheepskin coat.

And his initials—TC—steaming furrows in the snow.

CHAPTER SEVEN

"We can't let him stay out there." Gloria spoke in the hushed, thrilled stage-whisper of a kid at a horror movie. "We'll have to let him in."

"Over my dead body."

Though he said it drily, Bruce's body hadn't stirred. I got the distinct impression he dared not move for fear of turning his run of bad luck into an avalanche.

"Bruce, he could freeze," Jeff objected.

"Too bad."

"No one invited him here," said Melinda. "He can leave however he came."

Tony Cyr, zipping his fly, appeared comfortably oblivious. As he turned around there was a general retreat from the windows.

"Switch the lights off," hissed Melinda.

"No point." Bruce was regaining control. "He's well aware we're watching. He waited for the lights to go on before he started to piss."

"What do you think he wants?" asked Gloria.

"Good question." Jeff slapped the seat of her pants. "Anything to do with snakes, would you guess?"

Gloria gave an unconvincing squeal of protest and rolled

her eyes at him.

Melinda muttered venomously, "Oh, *shit*."

Henry, moving to the bar, poured himself a large Scotch. "But how could he have got into the house? Let alone Bruce's bedroom."

"He used to live here," Melinda answered through her teeth.

"I thought Bruce changed the locks."

"Tony can open doors with a credit card and a hairpin."

"Plus he's buddies with Edgar," Gloria contributed.

Lilah nudged my shoulder and put a finger to her lips. We were on the sunporch side of the fireplace by the Christmas tree. The others, on the dining room side, were drifting toward the bar. Lilah slipped out to the foyer. I followed: through the breakfast area and kitchen, down the hall and into the studio.

On the stairs she turned. "This is where he'll come. It's the only ground-floor entrance on the pond side." And she crossed behind the piano to unlatch the sliding glass doors.

"Lilah, what's he doing here?"

"I don't know." She gave a small convulsive shudder. "But ghosts don't piss their initials, do they? That's got to be real live Tony."

I sat on the piano bench. "And what are *we* doing here?"

Lilah didn't seem to hear me. She was twisting her hair around her hand, peering at the angled shadows outside the glass.

Melinda hadn't kept up the house standard of tidiness. Her skirt and jacket lay on the sofa, her pantihose in a nest-like heap on the carpet. A leather suitcase sat open beside the vase of pink and orange lilies on the coffee table.

She'd had enough human qualities once for Tony Cyr to marry her. Hard to picture that Melinda Doerr—not only thin and in love, but naive enough to cherish the process of publishing more than its politics.

"Lilah," I said, "did you—" Pause. "Is this honestly the first time you knew Tony was here?"

"Cory! Yes! Of course!" She bristled. "Do you think I'd let him in to chop up snakes and god knows what without telling Bruce?"

I lifted an eyebrow at the door she'd unlatched.

"Oh, this is for him. Bruce." She was positive. "What else is there to do? I mean, *look* at all that snow."

I wondered if she meant Bruce didn't really want Tony to freeze to death, or he didn't want any more footprints mucking up his landscape. Either way, she must be right; he hadn't followed us down here.

A remarkably quiet place, this studio. After the cocktail chaos in the living room my ears echoed with silence. I realized I was listening, straining to hear—

Crunching footsteps.

My heart flipped over.

"Don't break the lock," Lilah ordered. "It's open."

Tony Cyr stumbled in like a wet St. Bernard, snow in his hair and on his coat. He'd brought the bottle—cheap Scotch—and one glove. Stone cold, I thought, but far from sober. I prepared a noncommittal smile. Tony's eyes flickered past me without focusing.

"Lilah." In a single word he conveyed appeal, affection, and apology. Stuffing his bottle in his pocket, he held out his arms.

Lilah stooped to pick up his glove.

I could guess how she felt. Once Tony Cyr had been the star editor of Caxton Press. As an ex he'd become the wild man who blew out her windows. Even as a ghost he'd loomed larger than life. This bedraggled drunk must seem as empty an anti-climax as the bottle that had got him here.

"Come on," she told him shortly. "Everybody's waiting for you upstairs."

He managed a watery grin. "Home is where, when you

have to go there, they have to take you in."

I thought I saw Lilah wince as she started for the stairs. I wished I'd asked her—oh, lord, so many questions I hadn't anticipated!

Tony, lingering to survey his old haunts, recognized Melinda's suitcase. With a sigh he pulled the bottle out of his pocket and laid it tenderly among her underwear.

Lilah turned. "I forgot. Cory, this is Tony Cyr. Tony, this is my friend Cory Thorne."

Tony's smile was blank. "Charmed, Ms. Thorne."

"Glad to meet you, Tony," I returned with deliberate irony.

As we walked up the hall I did some quick mulling. Suppose Tony Cyr, drunk on a beach in Corfu, is struck by a fogged idea of coming home for Christmas. He rents a Lincoln so as to arrive in his former style. On the road he runs into a fellow pilgrim, whose car he is sober enough to haul out of a snowbank. When they part he swears her to silence. Three hours later they meet again. Has Scotch blotted the encounter from his memory?

No way.

So why was it so important to him—then and now—for nobody to know about our rendezvous on the road?

No clues from Lilah, striding ahead of us. Nor from Tony, drumming on washer and dryer lids like a kid who's just arrived at Grandma's for Christmas.

If he was expecting a prodigal son's welcome he was in for a letdown. Approaching that circle of unfriendly faces, I couldn't help hoping Tony's brain was blurred enough to soften what promised to be a bumpy landing.

Bruce, standing by the bar, radiated authority. *This is my game*, he seemed to say, *and you'll play by my rules.*

Olive Chute, on the sofa beside Henry, lowered her champagne glass.

"Good evening, Tony." A composed smile. "Are you

well?"

Although she clearly meant it as a probe into the when and why of his return, Tony chose to take it as a social overture. "You bet, Olive! Fit as a fiddlehead." He grinned and swayed. "You're looking tough as ever. How's the Lab?"

Her brows had drawn together warningly, but she couldn't resist the chance to crow. "Thriving," she declared. "Two new six-figure contracts this month."

"Did my ex-colleague Wally Tippett have a hand in that?"

Olive conceded it with a slight nod. "He's done very well for us." Her lizard's eyes flickered at Bruce, then back to Tony. "I appreciate your recommendation."

I thought Bruce's mouth twitched, but I might have been mistaken.

"Hey, Henry." Tony took a staggering step toward the sofa. "I heard you copped a Guggenheim. Congratulations."

Henry looked disconcerted. "Thank you."

Tony peered down at him. "Is something wrong? Wasn't I supposed to mention it?" His eyes swung from Henry to Olive's champagne glass. "Oh! I get it!" He slapped his forehead. "That's what we're celebrating! Right? All your old buddies gathered round— Well, hot damn, Henry! Good thing I got here before the bubbly's gone."

Henry averted his head in embarrassment.

Melinda, who stood facing Bruce across the circle, watched Tony grimly. She looked so angry that I cringed when he wobbled in her direction. Of everybody in this room, she was the one I could easily imagine snuffing any unwary reptile who crossed her warpath.

Bruce—evidently sharing my fears—signaled to Gloria.

"Tony!" She scrambled to her feet and stepped around the coffee table. "Come on over here and sit down. I'm going to bring you some nice hot coffee."

Tony exhaled mournfully and addressed Olive. "For three years she was my secretary, and she never brought me coffee." Then, to Gloria: "You're too late. I don't want it now."

Lilah patted his shoulder. "Come on, Tony. Warm you up."

"I am warm," returned Tony. "The surroundings are cold."

Jeff let out a snort which he quickly stifled.

Nobody else dared to look at each other. It was like that moment in "The Emperor's New Clothes" when the kid drops his brick. All evening we'd been tiptoeing around the Eastons' glacial decor as if one false step might trigger an avalanche. Enter Tony the firebrand; and suddenly you could feel great cracks shooting through the ice.

Only the Snow King showed no sign of thawing.

Perhaps sensing that his footing had grown precarious, Tony bellowed, "And her name is G!" He waved good-by at the door swinging shut behind Gloria. "L! O!" Then he heaved a sigh that became a belch. "She's never liked me," he told Lilah. "She thinks I'm a nut case."

Another muffled snort from Jeff. "And you disagree?"

He cast an amused glance at Bruce and around the circle, confirming our complicity. The Snow King will never thaw, I realized. Why should he? This is his game—his house, his guests, not Tony's anymore.

"Not me. I'm a witless nut. Raaarrgh!" Tony pounded his chest. "Better than a nutless wit, eh, Jeff?"

Henry Howrigan choked back a chuckle.

"Oh, for Christ's sake, Tony." Melinda couldn't contain herself any longer. "Put a cork in it!"

Tony staggered toward her, the grin draining from his face. With both hands he clasped the sofa back between Henry and Wayne Glynn. For a few seconds he stared at his ex-wife. Then his right hand swooped up to hover over

Wayne's head.

"Who's this? Is he with you?" He crouched, peered into Wayne's startled face, straightened and glared again at Melinda. "Is this poor forked creature my replacement?"

Melinda's arms were still folded tight under her breasts. She spoke not to Tony but to Wayne. "I don't believe you've met Tony Cyr, Wayne. He used to work for Communicore."

Wayne swallowed and nodded uncertainly.

"Tony, this is Wayne Glynn. Formerly a *Science* staffer. Now the writer on Henry's book."

In spite of her staccato delivery I wasn't prepared for Tony's reaction. His face blanched and his fists clenched as if she'd punched him. "The— You—" He blinked rapidly. "Oh, Jesus, Melinda."

Meanwhile Wayne was twisting around in a belated attempt to hold up his end. "I'm glad to make your acquaintance, Tony. I understand you were instrumental—"

"Henry!" Tony pivoted like a turret gun. "Don't let them do it! Hire a lawyer! Hire a plane! Leave town with the manuscript!"

Henry shrank into the sofa as if wishing to hide behind the cushions.

I was recalling Bruce's unemotional summary in my room two hours ago: *Henry accepted Wayne Glynn as his writer*. I'd been so caught up then in the story of Paul's drowning that the obvious question hadn't occurred to me: Why did Professor Henry Howrigan, noted Harvard biologist, award-winning researcher, need hired help to write a textbook?

Tony swung around to confront Bruce.

"This is your baby, your malformed changeling, isn't it, you son of a bitch?"

"Hello, Tony." Bruce was unruffled. "Have you eaten? Lilah, perhaps you'd take Tony out to the kitchen. There must be some leftovers you could heat up for him."

"Fuck your leftovers."

"You're welcome to leave."

"Make me."

A faint smile curled Bruce's lips. "That's Edgar's job."

"Oh yeah? And what's your job, you frigging parasite?"

"Tony." Lilah took a firm grip on his arm. "Let's go hang up your coat. And we'd better get those wet boots off you, or you'll catch pneumonia."

She steered him around the sofa, past Melinda guarding the harbor entrance like a hostile Statue of Liberty, to the foyer.

That's it? I wondered, glancing around the room. No parting shots?

"Sad," Wayne Glynn remarked.

"Pathetic," snapped Melinda.

Henry was frowning. "Bruce, I wonder if, ah, you could say a few words in response to the concerns Tony expressed regarding my book."

Melinda turned on him. "In case you failed to notice, Henry, your pal Tony is stinko. You'd be wise to take any *concerns* he might *express* as the drunken ravings of a disturbed personality."

I thought: The lady doth protest too much. Oh, sure, divorce turns princes into frogs and sweethearts into shrews; but what Albee-class horror scenes must have passed between Tony and Melinda to fill her with such fury?

"Who's ready for more champagne?" Bruce intervened. He held up the bottle. "Henry, you're almost empty. Olive? Cory?"

Even coming from him it was such a macabre suggestion—*Cheers! Let's drink to the alcoholic decline and fall of Tony Cyr!*—that I waited for someone to protest. No one did. One after another they held out their glasses.

"Melinda? Come on. Have some champagne."

Like a falcon gentled by her master's voice, Melinda

drew in her talons. "Thanks, Bruce. You're an angel." She crossed toward him. "And you know what else we need here? More Christmas music!" She sent one last hawklike glance around the group. "We've got a tree to decorate!"

The Mormon Tabernacle Choir sang "Angels We Have Heard on High." Gloria returned on cue, with coffee no one wanted. The champagne was carried from the bar to the sunporch corner. Minor arguments reopened: Lights or garlands first? Balls or ornaments?

I thought of those scenes in Shakespeare where they've finally shoved Falstaff or Sir Toby Belch offstage so the serious characters can carry on with the plot; and wondered if Tony Cyr had chosen the role of Fool or had it thrust upon him.

Jeff and I tested lights. He didn't mention Tony and neither did I, but twice I caught him glancing toward the foyer. He seemed edgy, distracted, as if inside that bristly dark head a problem was unraveling which might push him to do something he'd rather avoid. When I pointed at a burnt-out bulb he nodded absently. After a moment I replaced it myself.

Wayne, Henry, and Jeff hoisted the tree into place. "Adeste Fidelis" gave way to "Silent Night." I checked my watch. Tony and Lilah had been gone for eleven minutes.

I found them in the kitchen, sitting on wooden chairs they'd pulled around from the breakfast nook. With coffee cups staining the counter, Tony's coat draped over the open oven door, and Lilah's hair hanging like a curtain from her tipped-back chair to the floor, the place actually looked cozy.

She saw me first and righted herself. "Oh, gawd! Are people having fits? Should we go back in?"

I told her not to worry. Tony, without meeting my eyes, offered to bring me a chair.

"We can't get too comfortable," Lilah demurred. "I've got to play hostess."

"Not yet you don't," said Tony.

Away from Bruce and Melinda and company he didn't look drunk. His hand as he poured me a cup of coffee was steady as the table under it.

"Lilah, did you ask Tony about the snake?"

She nodded.

"Wicked creepy." He wiggled his eyebrows.

"That's all?" I retorted. "And you the house expert on practical jokes?"

"Not snake jokes." Tony seemed neither offended nor guilt-ridden—merely curious, as an ex science publisher should be. "The question I'd be asking if I were you is *why*. I mean, has somebody got it in for Jeff, or Olive, or Bruce, or that snake, or all snakes, or the whole animal kingdom, or what?"

"I think—no." Lilah sighed. "I don't know! Every time I think I have it, I change my mind."

"How about you, Ms. Thorne?"

I wish, I answered him silently, that I could tell which of your personas is an act and which—if any—I can believe.

"I don't know either," I said. "However," I lined up my shoe with the edge of a tile, "I can't come up with any explanation that doesn't put us snowbound in an isolated house with somebody who's either got a screw loose or a very warped sense of humor."

"Yeah," said Lilah soberly.

"Everybody here's got a warped sense of humor," countered Tony. "And probably a loose screw or two, too. Maybe what you want to look for is somebody who's acting abnormally sane."

"Oh, hell!" said Lilah.

"I can't help wondering," I said to Tony, "why you came here."

"Why do the swallows return to Capistrano?" he quipped. "Why do salmon cross vast oceans to swim up the stream where they were spawned?"

I leveled a meaningful look at him. "If this is a game of who can ask whom the best questions . . ."

"Ah, Ms. Thorne, you're a hard woman." Tony bowed his head in mock sorrow. "Here I pass up the chance to celebrate Christ's birth among simple shepherds and fishermen, unencumbered by street-corner Santas in cotton beards, Rudolph the Red-Nosed Reindeer, or Bloomingdale's, so as not to disappoint my nearest and dearest. Am I bitter because no invitation to this party reached my lonely outpost? Did I say to myself, 'Hey, Tony, screw those motherfuckers! Let's crack a bottle of ouzo and get *down!*' No, by god, I did not! I hearkened to the Spirit of Christmas Past—"

"What he's saying," Lilah interrupted, "is he got sprung from the clinic in Corfu and he didn't want to go back to where he was crashing, so he crashed in on us." She gave his knee a not unfriendly shove with her boot toe. "I've got guests to entertain. You're on your own, amigo."

Tony lurched to his feet. "Su casa es mi casa." He held out a hand to help her up. "Your guests are my guests. Anyhow, my buzz is wearing thin."

Not thin enough, I thought, as he shambled after Lilah like a dancing bear bound for the ring. You're good at this game, Tony Cyr. But don't get cocky. I'm not through with you—not by a long shot.

CHAPTER EIGHT

No wagons in a circle. No smiles, either. Everybody was facing in different directions looking blank. Olive stood on a chair beside the tree, shoeless, her hands full of glass balls. Henry crouched at her feet fiddling with a branch. Gloria, on the sofa, tied ribbons onto ornaments and handed them to Wayne Glynn.

Were Tony's ex-colleagues struck dumb by his rabbit-from-hat reappearance? Or had we missed a new bombshell?

Lilah held the door open just a few inches, waiting to see. I peered around her.

Bruce stood behind the tree fastening a wire to a hook in a window frame. A few feet away Jeff whacked a burning log with a poker. Each blow scattered a shower of sparks across the hearth, dangerously close to the white rug.

"That's ridiculous!" Melinda, by the stereo cabinet, rattled a CD case at him. "Pressure you? Just the opposite! We've given you an opportunity which stands to benefit you far more than—"

"Bullshit."

Bruce's voice cut in like a whip: "I won't have that language in my house, Jeff. It's offensive and it gets us nowhere."

Lilah stood motionless with her hand on the door. I agreed this wasn't the moment to walk in—not because we might overhear a private quarrel, but because we might cut one short.

"You kill me, Bruce, you know that? You want offensive language, read my contract." Jeff whacked the log. "*That's* obscene!"

"You were happy to sign it six months ago," Melinda snapped. "You didn't see anything obscene in a ten-thousand-dollar advance check."

Lilah tried to herd Tony and me back into the kitchen, but he thrust his arm past her and barred the door.

"This isn't your business!" she whispered.

"Sure it is." He mimed kisses at her. "Who do you think negotiated that contract? It sounds like your honeybunch and my ex-sugarplum threw in some curves after Jeff and I left the table, though."

Olive, who had continued to fasten balls onto branches throughout the exchange, pirouetted on her chair like a jewel-box ballerina.

"You're digressing," she wagged a finger at Bruce. "My question was not about Jeff's contract but Henry's."

"And here's my answer." Bruce looked up at her. "We're here tonight to applaud Henry's fine work on his manuscript and to celebrate the holidays. If Henry has any concerns about his contractual arrangements with Communicore, the time and place for him to address them is with the legal department during business hours." He turned to Jeff. "The same of course applies to you."

As a put-down it was thorough yet graceful. Olive glanced at Henry, evidently hoping he'd rise to her aid, but he stayed hunched on the floor.

"I'm sure you can appreciate that for our authors' sake we prefer to keep discussions of this type confidential," Bruce added. "Especially given the danger of"—he paused—"hostile eavesdropping."

He must have noticed the door ajar. I braced for him to call Tony out . . .

But Tony didn't wait.

"Thanks, Bruce." He pushed past Lilah. "I will have a drink. No, don't move, I'll get it."

Not wishing our conference in the kitchen to be mistaken for a conspiracy, I headed the other way, along the wall of books behind the sofa.

Lilah started to follow Tony to the bar but changed her mind and veered toward the tree. Of course: Bruce would want a show of loyalty after her huddle with the enemy.

"Tony." Henry heaved himself upright with a grunt. "Bring me a Scotch on the rocks, will you?"

Hmm! Had the worms begun to turn?

I glanced again at Bruce. His lithe body remained composed. Only his thumb plucked at the wire he'd just strung, testing the strength of his work.

Tony, at the bar, tossed ice cubes into glasses. One missed. Another. Four. Six. Ice cubes skittered across the bar's mirrored surface, clinked against bottles, slithered into corners, bounced onto the rug.

Bruce's muscles tensed. Ready to strike? No. He about-faced and resumed checking his wire. Even from here I could see he was twitching it harder than any tree ever would.

A loud clank: Jeff had dropped his poker into its stand. As Lilah passed the coffee table he stopped her with a touch. He murmured something; she laughed. He grinned and slid his arm through hers, leading her toward the fire.

Bruce's wire snapped.

I stifled a smile. Yes, the natives were getting restless!

But did it matter? Already Bruce was unrolling a new strand of wire. After all, he had Jeff signed to a textbook contract. And Lilah, captured by Halsey, in a gold frame over his fireplace.

As for Tony Cyr—

Close to my left ear, ice cubes clinked against heavy glass.

"Dewar's," confided a husky whisper—as if I couldn't smell it.

I wished he hadn't come over here. I wanted him back out there in the arena thrusting at Bruce till Bruce was forced to thrust back.

"In honor of my ex-wife. That's what they used to call us—Seer and Doer."

"Is that why you've got two of them?"

Tony peered into his left-hand glass. "My crystal's fogged," he whined. "I can't see her."

Great, I thought irritably. Word games. Mind games. What happened to the Lone Ranger?

Bruce stepped around the Christmas tree. "Lilah."

The room fell silent. Lilah moved away from Jeff toward her husband.

"You'd better start arranging beds for our guests. It doesn't appear anyone will be able to leave tonight."

Bruce's fingernail scraped the inner edge of his nostril as if to emphasize his privilege of alternately flaunting and flouting the conventions of civilized behavior. I fought down a surge of anger—not only at his arrogance, but at all of us for deferring to it.

"Edgar should have come back by now from walking Mary Helen home—"

Jeff folded his arms aggressively. "If they got out, so can we."

"They had less than a quarter mile to go," Bruce rejoined, "and high boots. As I was saying: Edgar will bring down extra blankets—"

Olive interrupted with unexpected severity. "If this is an invitation, Bruce, I'm afraid I must decline. I have business in Boston tomorrow. I don't suppose my car is heavy enough to get through, but Henry's should be. Henry, dear, if you are going home I'd like a ride. If you aren't, let's trade cars."

Henry had sidled into the niche between the tree and the chimney. He looked from Bruce up to Olive down to Bruce again, visibly unmanned.

"I'll go with Olive," said Jeff. "I'm happy to add my weight to your expedition."

"Delighted to have you, dear."

"Well." Henry shook his ice as if hoping to find more Scotch underneath. "Has anyone heard a weather report?"

Bruce stirred impatiently. "Snow. Look out the window."

"Henry," said Melinda in her corporate-officer voice, "We have a lot of work to do here this weekend. I've arranged my schedule around your promise to stay till Sunday."

"Melinda," said Henry, "you know, I've put in a lot of work on this book already." He set his empty glass on the mantelpiece and faced her. "At least it used to be a book. It was a book when I signed the contract. Now you call it a *project*. Lab manual. Teacher's manual. Slides. Test bank. Software. On and on and on! Where does it end?"

Tony edged around the coffee table and handed Henry a fresh Scotch, growling what might have been "You tell 'em!" or "Rrrrgh!"

"You keep out of this!" snapped Melinda.

"It's Tony's name on the contract I signed." Bolstered by gratitude and/or Dewar's, Henry was warming to his new role as Mr. Forceful. "I agreed to write this book because of Tony. I value his opinion."

"His opinion!" she echoed scornfully. "A drunken, crazy—"

In a single motion Tony gulped his own drink, hurled his glass at the tile floor, scooped up a jagged shard and advanced toward Melinda.

Gloria screeched.

"Don't, Tony," warned Bruce, backing out of his way.

Melinda was scared and furious. "You bastard! You lunatic! Don't you *dare* threaten me!"

Tony cocked his arm. At the last instant he swung left.

"Oh, Christ! No!" screamed Bruce. "Not the *windows!*"

Melinda leaped at Tony. Jeff dived for the coffee table. Tony's shot went wild and smashed against the chimney. Melinda knocked him sprawling on the white rug, inches from Henry's feet. She staggered but recovered and stood over him, panting, as if she intended to tear him apart with her bare hands if he tried to stand up.

Tony rolled on the floor, helpless with laughter.

Bruce, who'd been inching forward cautiously, glared down in disgust. One of his gray Italian shoes prodded Tony's ribs. "Get up," he muttered savagely. "And get the hell out of my house!"

I glanced around. Already everyone was moving back into place, pretending furiously that nothing was amiss.

Were they always like this? Had they clamped the lid on so fast last summer when Paul Easton drowned in his father's pond?

I strolled back to the pile of slivered glass Tony had left on the floor; crouched and sniffed.

As I suspected: ginger ale.

Olive and Jeff were determined now to make a break for Boston. After token protests Henry yielded to Olive's request for his car and Melinda's pressure to stay. Tony didn't mention the Lincoln he must have stowed somewhere nearby. Nobody asked him, including me.

I tried to get near him as we all milled down the hall, but he dodged. Bruce was insisting that Olive should give Wayne and Gloria a ride, too. Since Wayne was bound for New York and Gloria for across town, Olive said no. I wondered why Bruce didn't try packing Tony off to Boston, till I remembered that the last time he'd done that, Tony had picked Hell over Siberia.

The mood was unexpectedly upbeat. I guessed we all shared the same sentiments: If Olive and Jeff could get out, we weren't trapped. The Eastons' jinxed Christmas party could be declared over.

Edgar agreed to ride point on his snow-blower. I'd been curious to meet this man who'd served as groundskeeper for both Bruce and Tony. What little I could see of him under layers of down and wool looked more like a mini-Schwarzenegger than an Easton employee. Ex-Marine? Ex-con?

I watched for signs he and Tony were in cahoots and didn't catch any. If Edgar had hidden Tony's car, unlocked a door for him, or sneaked in himself and beheaded Bruce's snake, he wasn't about to say so.

But then, who besides me was asking?

Stomping snow off his boots, Edgar pulled a radio out of his jacket. The announcer confirmed what we could see through the door: snow was falling again. She sounded huffy, as if the storm had violated a cease-fire. Listeners were urged to stay in until the plows could get through.

"This is foolish," Bruce murmured, helping Olive into her calf-length mink coat. "If the roads aren't plowed . . ."

Melinda agreed. So did Tony. The gratified surprise on Lilah's face at this burst of harmony made my heart ache for her, poor soul, longing in vain for the old days when they were a team.

Henry's Cadillac stuck at the first bend in the driveway. We could hear it better than we could see it: the whining crescendo and decrescendo of tires struggling to spin free. It took Edgar and Jeff several minutes of pushing to rock the big car back into motion.

They crept back to the house like the celebrity float in a rained-out July Fourth parade: Edgar on his snow-blower, and behind him in the Cadillac a daunted Olive and dampened Jeff.

"Well," announced Olive, brushing snow off her coat, "I for one am ready for a nightcap. In both senses."

Nobody else had much to say after that. Not even "I told you so."

The former offices of Caxton Press, now guest rooms, looked like the rest of the house: a few more nubbly pillows, a bit less brass, carpet instead of quarry tile. Lilah and Gloria and I carried armloads of off-white sheets to off-white convertible sofas. Watching Gloria pounce on a striped pillowcase, I could understand Joseph's brothers in the Bible going wild over his multi-colored coat.

My goal was information. No more holding the wire around the cork. Leave that to the folks upstairs. Cory Goodwin, investigative journalist, wanted the scoop behind Bruce Easton's late snake—now, before I spent the night locked up with the decapitator.

But Lilah wouldn't cooperate. Drunken pranks, she insisted cheerily. Too many toddies. Here we are, old friends, Christmas, nicest people on earth. Forget it! Enjoy!

I guessed from the fresh sparkle in her eyes what had changed her mood. Not much I could do about that but hope it made her talkative.

She'd decided Olive and Wayne would sleep down here and Jeff in the room next to mine. Gloria was assigned to my spare bed.

"Not that she'll use it." Lilah unfolded a sofa-bed. "Bruce wanted to fire her when Tony left because of that."

"Oh?" I prodded.

"Well, not *just* because of that. The whole way she *is*." Lilah grimaced eloquently. "Tony only hired her because she's local. You can see she's not the publishing type."

"*Because of that*, meaning what?"

She flapped a sheet across the mattress. "Rumor has it Gloria provided services outside the normal nine-to-five for a couple of Tony's authors, including Jeff."

Well, well! "Was Tony, ah, aware of this?"

"Probably." Lilah laughed. "He'd have figured it was a piece of luck—so to speak—for both of them. Since he and Melinda were in the same boat."

"Why would Bruce care, then? If he didn't about Tony and Melinda."

"Oh, come on, Cory." Lilah's arched eyebrow reproached my lapse in taste. "A secretary screwing an author? Anyway, Bruce wanted to leave Gloria here when he moved the rest of Caxton Press to New York, but Melinda wouldn't let him. She said, for god's sake!—the girl types eighty words a minute, she takes dictation faster than I can talk, plus she's the only person on the planet who understands Tony's filing system."

And since Tony's files were now the backbone of Communicore's science list, I completed silently, Bruce cast taste to the winds and kept Gloria on the payroll.

"What about Tony?" I asked Lilah.

"Oh, gawd. I don't know where to put him." She tossed me a pillow. "I wish more people in this house were sleeping together. We're running out of space."

For no good reason my cheeks flushed.

"When I thought he was a ghost I stuck him in with Melinda. Less trouble!"

I tucked in corners and reminded myself that Lilah didn't know—couldn't know—about my confrontation with the real live Tony while she was busy with linens and cocaine.

It had looked like the perfect opportunity. He'd stepped out to use the bathroom. I'd cut through the kitchen to the guest wing and waited in ambush.

My plan was to lure him across the hall to my room for a brief interrogation. Instead he'd grabbed my wrist, pulled me into the bathroom with him and shut the door.

I mustered my wits while Tony spread a thick white bath mat over the tub's porcelain rim.

"Sit down."

It was either that or go on facing him like a dance-class partner. Up close his eyes looked tired: the lids puffy, the skin underneath pouched and bruise-colored. Deep grooves around his mouth . . . Yet he radiated a disordered energy that made me want more space between us.

I sat.

"You don't know these people."

"Only Lilah. But—"

"So fuck 'em!" He waved his arms. "Scram! Vamoose! Get out while the getting's good!"

I caught a whiff of sandalwood—aftershave? or the soap in the marble scallop shell behind him? "While the getting's good?" I countered, trying for a note of humor. "You just saw—"

"Head for the hills!" Tony wasn't in a humorous mood. He was pacing, insofar as one can pace in ten square feet. "Blow this frigging pop stand!"

As often happens on subways, my eyes were level with his crotch. His tan corduroy slacks bagged around his hips and legs as if he'd lost weight. His thigh muscles when he turned, though, looked remarkably tight for someone who'd spent half a year drinking.

I moved my knees out of his way. "How?" I asked him. "And *why*?"

Tony halted and faced me. "This house is not a safe place, Ms. Thorne. Things die here." His gaze shifted to the white shower curtain above my head. "Water lilies. Snakes. Sometimes people."

Snakes again. A shiver ran up my neck. "What are you getting at?"

"Have they told you what happened to Bruce's son

Paul?"

I didn't like the turn this tête-à-tête was taking. Paul Easton had drowned during Tony Cyr's supposed Mediterranean exile. How—and how much—did he know about that tragedy?

"What does Paul have to do with you?" I asked.

"What's Hecuba to him or he to Hecuba, that he should weep for her?" Tony quoted to the shower curtain. "I knew him, Horatio; a fellow of infinite jest, of most excellent fancy; I have borne him on my back a thousand times. *Hah!*" He jabbed a finger at my face, mocking my surprise. "Yes, Ms. Thorne, I can tell a hawk from a handsaw when the wind is southerly. And I'm telling you: Get thee to a nunnery!"

His abrupt change of key startled and then angered me. For a moment there I'd been touched—not only by his sentiments but because he must have scoured Corfu for a *Hamlet* script to clothe them in. "Or else what? I could be next? What is this, a threat?"

I took it for granted he'd say no. Instead he clasped his hands behind his back. "It's one point four miles to the Mobil station. There's cross-country skis in the hall by the studio. Jeff'll go with you—he's got a thing for redheads, as he's probably told you. You can wear Lilah's boots—"

"Forget it. Lilah's a six double-A and I'm an eight B." I was shivering, no doubt from the cold bathtub I was sitting on. I stood up. "Knock it off, will you? If you're so hot to get rid of me, why didn't you leave me in that snowbank? Or give me your car while the roads were still passable?"

For the first time Tony's eyes met mine, with the deep considering gaze of a madman or a lover. "I didn't know then you'd be dangerous."

Dangerous? I tried to break off staring back at him and couldn't. In my mind we stood alone again in a frozen glitter of headlights and snow; and his hand was sliding around my neck, pulling me into—what? A kiss? A stranglehold?

Footsteps in the hall. The current between us crackled and dissipated. I was marooned in a strange house, standing in the bathroom with a strange man I didn't trust as far as the towel rack.

Up the hall a latch clicked. Tony reached past me to open our door. His arm pressed my shoulder for an instant . . . a warm spot contrasting with the cold tub against my legs as I backed away.

"I'm out of here," he told me.

"Tony, wait a second. I've got to know—"

"No," he echoed, and gestured at the white terrycloth and porcelain around us. "You wanted to be next? All yours, Ms. Thorne."

CHAPTER NINE

Lilah chattered away as we folded and unfolded convertible sofas, pulled sheets around mattresses, and dropped pillows into cases. Amazing that a pinch of powder could cause such animation. I half expected the Seven Dwarfs to march down the hall singing "Whistle While You Work."

Well, better to have her happy and dopey than sleepy and grumpy. And full of information! Yes, Chester Chute had left his wife a controlling interest in Chute Labs. Olive had persuaded the board to fire his successor the day before Thanksgiving and taken over—temporarily, everyone hoped—as CEO. Lilah thought Olive had the hots for Henry, but Bruce disagreed. Anyhow, Henry had shown no interest. His only known non-scientific activity was collecting Princeton memorabilia. Jeff Abels was divorced from a dancer in New York; no children. Gloria collected Danielle Steel novels, lived with her parents, and was dying to get married. Bruce thought she had the hots for Wayne Glynn, but Lilah said not even Gloria was that desperate. Besides being a nerd, Wayne had lost his last job for plagiarism. He was pathetically grateful to Bruce and Melinda for giving him a break.

When Lilah paused for breath, I slipped in the question I'd wanted to ask her since dinner.

"Were all these people here last summer the weekend Paul died?"

"Yup. All but you and Tony."

"Do you have any idea how Tony heard about Paul's accident?"

She hesitated. "I told him."

Seeing my surprise, she added defensively, "I wrote to him in Corfu. And, no, I didn't mention it to Bruce."

I stowed a cushion behind the bed; and turned to see Lilah hugging a pillow as a child hugs a teddy bear.

"They were pals. Tony used to take Paul on nature walks —wheel him or carry him through the woods, teach him the names of birds and things."

Hard to imagine. But hadn't he told me himself? *I have borne him upon my back a thousand times . . .*

What did that imply about the rest of Tony's ravings?

"We weren't sure at the beginning if Paul even cared; but then Tony rigged up a little portable computer where he could type out words and sometimes he'd say thanks for the walk or remind us of something we saw last time. So I thought Tony would want to know," Lilah laid her pillow on the bed, "and I got his address from Gloria and wrote him a letter about it."

"Did he write back?"

We flipped up the foot of the bed into sofa position. Lilah shook her head. "I never heard a peep from him till he showed up here tonight."

"How did Bruce react to Tony's making friends with his son?"

"Oh, he was glad." She nodded vigorously. "He's always so busy . . . and Paul wasn't an easy kid to relate to, not being able to talk or walk or even move except for part of one side. Bruce appreciated everything anybody did to help."

We moved into the hall. I imagined a small boy running through this house when his family first moved in; sitting on these stairs while his mom waited up nights for his dad to come home; rolling soundlessly over this carpet in a wheelchair after the divorce. Not an easy kid to relate to. Who would be, with Bruce Easton for a father?

A father who'd been glad to share the burden of his imperfect son. But only for an afternoon. If Bruce knew someone in his entourage had caused Paul's death, his vengeance would have been swift and nasty.

But suppose he didn't know. Suppose he only guessed. How would he make sure? Invite the suspects back, perhaps? Stage a mini-reenactment of the crime, as Hamlet did, to shock the culprit into self-betrayal?

I'd assumed Bruce wouldn't sabotage his own party. That his role in the snake incidents was victim. Now I wondered if I'd gotten it backwards.

And if it were sheer coincidence Tony Cyr had picked *Hamlet* for his quotations about Paul.

Again that elusive piece of flotsam about the snake bobbed into my brain. Something creepy. Scary, even. Like the head in the puff pastry. A man eating a snake? They did—rattlesnakes, in the Southwest. Not weird enough. A snake eating a man? You're groping, Cory. Anyhow, if it really were the missing link, surely you'd remember it . . .

Lilah was heading for the stairs.

"How has Bruce coped with Paul's death?" I asked her. "Is he recovering OK?"

Her stiff shoulders told me she didn't want to discuss it. "He was very upset at first. Of course. He's better now."

"What's your take on his mental health?"

"Oh, gawd!" She laughed shortly. "Ask his shrink. Ask him. Ask Melinda, Gloria, anybody. Don't ask me. Mental health is *not* my strong point."

The Christmas tree in its glass-paneled corner looked so dazzling, so splendid, that for an instant I forgot everything else. The whole right end of the room—branches, windows, french doors—twinkled with tiny stars. In the far corner someone had lit candles on the dining table, tall white tapers which spread a warm glow all the way to the kitchen door.

"Star of wonder, star of night! Star with royal beauty bright!"

I thought of candlelight church services when I was growing up; and closed my eyes to wish that the peace of childhood Christmases would carry us through this night.

Bruce Easton, keeping watch over his flock as usual, stood at the bar pouring eggnog. Melinda sat nearby on a chair she'd commandeered from the dining table. Olive, Henry, and Wayne occupied the sofa; Jeff leaned against the chimney. Gloria sat on the hearth rug, a vivid splotch of aquamarine against white fur and russet tiles . . . and there was Tony, lounging half under the goatskin-marble coffee table. He seemed subdued. I hoped it would last. More particularly, I hoped he wouldn't shatter this truce by dropping his phony Scotch into Bruce's DiChiara.

Lilah outlined the sleeping arrangements. "Tony," she finished, "since we haven't got enough beds, you'll have to either wing it here on the sofa or make yourself a bed in Gloria's old cubbyhole from the cushions downstairs."

Tony lifted his glass approvingly. "And they wrapped the babe in swaddling clothes and laid him in a manger, because there was no room for them in the inn."

Bruce paused with a cup of eggnog in each hand. A faint frown crossed his face, but he didn't speak.

Gloria did. Her cheeks were ruddy, her voice resonant with rum. "And there were shepherds abiding in the fields—right? Jeff! Isn't that right?" She tugged on his trouser leg. "Oh, you don't know, you're Jewish. Forget it. Henry! What comes next?"

"Gloria," said Melinda sharply, "shut up."

"I believe," answered Henry, smiling, "it's angels,

Gloria, isn't it?"

"Right! Right! And lo, the angel of the Lord came upon them, and the glory of the Lord shone around them, and they were sore afraid!"

Bruce interceded. "As much as one savors its melodious language, one can't help feeling the Christmas story *qua* story would be more effective with fewer *ands*."

Tony's head tipped back. "Too bad Matthew, Mark, Luke, and John didn't publish with Communicore," he remarked to the ceiling. "Tighten that sucker right up."

"You should know!" blurted Melinda. "That's your specialty these days, isn't it? Getting tight?"

Tony wriggled around to look at her. Melinda sat with her legs crossed and her arms folded. If ever anyone radiated tightness, I mused, thar she blows.

"Sweet Melinda, the goddess of gloom." From Tony's wry tone I guessed he was recalling another lifetime when they'd shared that song. "Or is it doom? Good old Dylan, I wonder if he's got enough brain cells left to care. Any more than me."

Neither Melinda nor anyone else knew what to say to that. Eventually Jeff broke the silence: "Lilah, where does your name come from? I thought you were born with it, but Gloria tells me it's a nickname."

I cringed. Wrong question!

"Hah!" Tony leapt to his feet. "Best goddam drinking song in the book!" And he bellowed: "My, my, my, Delilah!"

"Oh, my lord," murmured Olive.

Tony snatched the poker from its rack by the fireplace and banged his beat on the stones.

Henry, pricking up his ears like a retired racehorse who's heard the Call to the Post, declared, "I'm familiar with that song." In a rusty but true tenor he joined in: "Why, why, why, Delilah?"

Bruce had to raise his voice to be heard. "This party appears to have reached its logical conclusion."

Gloria and Melinda stood up simultaneously. Wayne Glynn glanced around for guidance and then got hastily to his feet.

"Sorry, Bruce," said Jeff, trying not to laugh. "How could I know?"

Tony and Henry and the poker stumbled through the lyrics but hung on tight to the beat. Olive departed for the stairs, with Wayne close behind her. Melinda, head down, stalked past Bruce and shoved the kitchen door out of her way.

"La, la, la laughing . . ."

Gloria shifted her gaze from Wayne's disappearing reindeer sweater to Jeff; glanced at Bruce and back to Jeff.

"La la la la la la hand, la-la la la more!"

Lilah slipped her arm through her husband's. "Let's go to bed, darling, shall we?"

"Whoever's up last," Bruce said tersely, "turn out the lamps."

As I followed Bruce and Lilah toward the foyer I heard Gloria, flirting over the din like a Tom Jones vamp: "Jeff, be a sweetheart and pour me one of those."

Coolness of clean sheets on an unfamiliar bed. For a moment I couldn't think where I was. Then I remembered worrying I wouldn't be able to sleep . . . because—ah, yes!—Gloria might come in . . .

I looked. She hadn't.

What was I dreaming about? Music. A Christmas concert. The Mormon Tabernacle Choir. That was what woke me: crashing cymbals.

Alcohol has a mean-spirited habit of knocking me out and then pumping me full of adrenalin four or five hours later. I wasn't a bit sleepy. On the contrary, my nerves were taut as wire. All around me I sensed people—ten feet away, twenty feet away, separated from me only by walls, people snoring or muttering or lying awake staring at a smooth white ceiling like this one.

Maybe Gloria and Jeff, or Lilah and Bruce, were coiled at this moment in the sweaty intensity of love-making. Maybe others—Olive? Wayne? Tony?—wished they dared tap on certain doors and join the silent orgy.

Oh, hell. There were two choices: I could lie here for another hour waiting for the rush to fade; or I could go find some hair-of-the-dog to snuff it with.

I crawled out from under the covers, slipped on my quilted bathrobe and slippers, and padded down the hall.

In the archway I halted. Someone had knocked over the Christmas tree.

The sunporch corner looked like a planetarium whose stars had fallen off the walls. The tree lay angled across the floor, big and bunchy, strewing light at random toward the sofa.

I thought distractedly of water in the stand, electrical wires, a short circuit; and moved closer.

With no illumination but those pinpricks of white, it took me a moment to sort out what I saw. Tree, fallen. Glass ornaments, shattered. Of course—the cymbal crash. Lights, still on. OK. But what was that odd pale shape under the last zigzag of lights?

My throat tightened. I stumbled around and groped for the wall.

There was no switch. The Eastons did not go in for overhead lighting. With a dull thud like a headache I remembered Bruce's parting directive to turn out the lamps.

Finding one of his brass objets d'art near the end of the sofa, I turned it on.

Parting directive indeed. For there lay Bruce with his

head among the branches, his arms and legs splayed across the tiles, and a diamond choker of white lights around his neck.

CHAPTER TEN

Thanks to summer camp and gym class, I know basic first aid. I also knew before I touched him that first aid could not help Bruce Easton. He was too still, too helpless sprawled there in his silk robe—too many things Bruce would never have allowed himself to be while alive.

I rolled him over anyway. And regretted it when I saw his face, garish and swollen.

I thrust the thought of CPR out of my mind. For a long time, at least ten seconds, all I did was tell my stomach to hang on. I took deep breaths. I tried to erase the gruesome picture burned on my mental screen.

My brain was still balking at the next step like a horse at a muddy ditch when a small voice came from the sofa.

"Cory?"

I turned. Lilah sat with her arms hugging her knees, her face as pale as her robe, trembling so violently I could see it from here.

The living I could deal with. Had to. "Lilah, for heaven's sake, what—?"

I pulled her against me on the cushions and felt her body shaking harder and harder till sobs rasped from her throat. Her chin dug into my shoulder. Her hair was everywhere, wet with tears. I drew it out of her face and patted her back ineffectually.

What can you say to a woman whose husband is lying twenty feet away with Christmas lights twisted around his throat?

She said it before I did. "The lights." Barely a croak. "Cory, oh, please. We've got to get those fucking lights off."

And somehow we did. I yanked the main plug, and then we disentangled Bruce from the tree and those horrid rattling little bulbs and wires from his neck. The rule about not touching anything connected with a murder crossed my mind, but only briefly. Most urgent right now was keeping Lilah from going the way of the glass balls splintered around her husband's body.

We rolled Bruce back over and put him as close as I could remember to how I'd found him. I sent Lilah for a sheet while I checked in vain for a pulse.

She staggered back in like a sleepwalker with her arms full of bunched ivory linen: the sheet off their bed.

That was a gesture I understood so completely that my throat lumped. More than anything she could have said, that sheet convinced me Lilah Easton hadn't killed her husband.

She was brushing the shattered glass away from his bare leg. "Don't, Lilah. Just cover him up. We've got to call the police."

I beckoned her toward the sofa.

"But—who did this?" Her eyes looked empty. "Who would want to hurt Bruce?"

Who indeed? I thought. "I don't know," I said, sitting. "I didn't see anybody. Did you?"

Lilah shook her head. "He's dead, isn't he."

"I'm afraid so." I patted the sofa. "Come on, sit down."

She kicked off her slippers; tucked her feet up under her.

"What's the first thing you remember?"

She thought about it. From her lack of expression I

wouldn't have been surprised if she'd forgotten the question; but after a moment she said, "Bruce on the floor with those awful lights."

"And where were you?"

She touched the sofa. "Here."

"How did you get here?"

"I don't know."

No embarrassment. No regret. Just the blood-chilling simplicity of a woman who'd been sheltered by her parents, her schooling, and her husband till she literally didn't know the meaning of responsibility.

And to think I used to wish we could trade places.

Well, too late now. Too late to become her, or change her, or give up on her.

"Try to remember, Lilah. Why did you come out here? Did you and Bruce get up together? Or did something wake you—"

I stopped. She was shaking her head again. "I don't know," she repeated dully. "I can't remember anything." She looked at me in appeal. "Bruce gave me a couple Valium, like he always does when we've been tooting, and I went to sleep. Then I woke up and I was out here. That's all."

I squelched the urge to tell her she was going to have to do better than that for the police, or that she must be incredibly self-destructive to drug herself up and down like a seesaw. I was about to suggest that she go sleep off the Valium while I tried to reach the cops, when a corner of my eye caught something moving in the shadows around the kitchen door.

My insides froze. Suddenly I was horribly aware of being unarmed and in my bathrobe a few yards from where someone had just strangled Bruce Easton.

The seconds ticked past like a nightmare. Here sat Lilah, drug-dumbed and oblivious, with her head full of undeveloped film that might send the killer to prison for life. I wanted to act—to leap up and confront the intruder, or, failing that, to scream—but I couldn't budge. I couldn't even squeak.

"Hey." The shadow spoke. "What are you two chit-chatting about in the middle of the night?"

From the darkness stepped a familiar silhouette. "Tony!"

Lilah, who hadn't reacted until now, turned her head a few inches.

"How long have you been there?" My heart was pounding like a bongo drum.

"Just long enough to see who I was interrupting."

I watched his face as he came close enough for a good look at Lilah. His expressions were right: surprise, concern, suspicion.

"What's happened?"

"Stay back!" Lilah warned him. "The police are coming!"

Tony's eyebrows went up. "What the hell's going on?"

"It's Bruce," I said. "Strangled with Christmas-tree lights."

He didn't believe me. That was right, too. He strode over to the sheeted shape on the floor; lifted a corner, then a whole side. I heard a muttered exclamation.

Lilah curled up tighter on the sofa. "You hated him. Are you glad?"

"Hell no," Tony answered curtly. "I don't want him dead." He was still staring down at Bruce's body. "I wanted the bastard to *get it*. To understand how bad he fucked up every damn thing he ever touched."

He dropped the sheet and faced Lilah. "I wanted to watch him dig himself a hole so deep he couldn't get out."

And that's why you came here? I thought.

I said, "He can't get out of this one."

None of us spoke for a while after that. I gazed at the

snow whirling past the single floodlight still on outside the dining room windows and wondered distantly if it were falling again or only blowing. And if Tony had rescued his hat and glove or left them out there as hostages to whatever purpose really did bring him home for Christmas.

Journalists' Rule #2: *When in doubt, find out.*

"Lilah," I said, "why don't you try and rest in my room. You won't get much chance once the cops show up."

She didn't want to. Tony asked how I planned to reach the cops without a phone. Good question. I had no idea. On TV they just appear: body, jump cut, cops.

Lilah was hunched up among the cushions again, looking shell-shocked. I decided not to mention the Valium in front of Tony. If they'd been partying together since Bruce took over at Communicore, he should recognize the symptoms.

And apparently he did, because it was he who convinced her she needed sleep—though not in my room, she insisted, but her own. That too I could understand. Once she left the bed she'd shared with Bruce, she'd have to admit he was never coming back to it.

"One small point before we split," said Tony. "I expect it's occurred to both you ladies that when the cops do come, they're bound to wonder why we all showed up here at this particular moment." He glanced from Lilah to me. "In my experience, they have a low tolerance for glitches in the laws of probability."

"So do I," I said.

"I'm not asking for your alibi, Ms. Thorne." Tony hooked his thumbs in his pockets. "I'm just telling you the Oxbridge police aren't likely to buy Lilah waking up beside her husband's murdered body with her mind and her conscience a blank slate."

"Well, I'm asking for your alibi." I folded my arms. "What are you up for, or up to, in the Eastons' living room in the middle of the night?"

"Professor Plum with the lead pipe in the conservatory?" returned Tony. "Sorry, Miss Scarlet, no cigar. I came up here looking for a place to sleep. You want evidence, go downstairs and try draping yourself over the cushions in that cubbyhole." He wriggled. "Like being the prize in a box of Crackerjack."

Lilah spoke faintly from the sofa. "Tony, they'll have to buy it, because it's true."

"What are you suggesting?" I asked him. "That we invent an alibi for her?"

"That she, or you, keep her mouth shut—and I'm talking *clam*; I'm talking name, rank, and serial number—until she's got something coherent to say."

A laggard wind rattled the french doors and sprayed the windows with a hiss of snow. Maybe, I thought. Maybe he wants to help her. Maybe he wants me to think he does. Or maybe he's afraid she'll spill a crucial clue before he can shut her up for keeps.

There being no way to know, I decided the question on its merits. "Lilah, he's got a point. Are you OK with that? Stay in your room, keep the door locked, and don't talk to anybody till the cops get here?" I held out my hands to haul her onto her feet. "I'm going to go try my cell phone, just in case."

"It won't work, but—sure."

"I'm going to see who else is up," said Tony with a glint in his eye.

I didn't care so much for that idea. "Wait a minute and I'll come with you."

"You can't do everything, Ms. Thorne," he retorted. "Stick with Plan A." Blowing Lilah a kiss, he started toward the kitchen. "Don't worry, I'll give you a full report."

And with that I had to be satisfied.

As I ushered Lilah to her room I ran a mental instant replay of Tony's arrival on the scene. Looking for a place to sleep . . . It could be true. Lilah *had* offered him the sofa. His impulse to check on the other guests seemed natural . . . but then, if he'd killed Bruce, wouldn't he have worked out a plausible set of actions and reactions in advance?

Did that mean that in order to verify his authenticity I'd have to figure out what he thought I'd expect from him?

Forget it, Cory. That way lies madness.

Lilah burrowed under her duvet. No, she didn't need a sheet. Yes, she'd be fine here. With the covers pulled up to her chin, her chestnut hair echoed the note of color struck by the small oriental rugs on the carpet and the pillows on the window seat.

An ironic complement to the off-white mound outside on the red quarry-tile floor. Compliment, too: *Here lies Bruce Easton, whose decorator grip even death could not break.*

Giving the room a quick check before leaving, I paused at the empty glass aquarium. Get that thing out of Lilah's sight . . . But no. It was evidence now. The first link in a chain of events that, in retrospect, I felt my journalist's intuition should have foreseen as soon as I walked into this house.

My journalist's intuition was rustier than I knew. There was a lot more retrospect ahead, if I'd only realized.

In the living room every lamp was lit. The whole household was up and semi-dressed, charging around asking each other how to get hold of Edgar.

"Henry." I caught his arm—unexpectedly skinny through his terrycloth bathrobe. "Why Edgar?"

His ruddy face was wide with dismay, like a baby's the instant before a howl. "Bruce is dead," he said as if he couldn't believe it.

Melinda paused to add shortly, "The phone's still out." She wore a long blue flannel robe with red piping and looked intense but controlled—much as I imagined her at the office. "I've asked Wayne to hike down to Edgar's trailer and call the police from there."

"Melinda, that's dumb," Gloria objected. "Edgar's phone line is on the same poles as this one."

"Oh, gawd, Gloria, don't be an ass!" tossed Melinda as she hurried on her way.

Her blatant borrowing of Lilah's pet word startled me. Neither Henry nor Gloria seemed to notice. I found it very disquieting.

"Ass yourself!" Gloria called after Melinda. She tugged primly, smugly, at the hem of an oversized sweater which I took to be Jeff's. "I don't have to put up with that! You're not the boss here!"

Henry and I both glanced in spite of ourselves at the sheeted shape beside the Christmas tree.

Then he shook himself like a horse shivering off a fly and marched out to the foyer.

Gloria moved toward the kitchen. When she pushed the door open I caught snatches of a muted but heated discussion, which faded in and out as the door swung. "Cory's here," I heard her report.

But to whom? Who *was* the boss, with Bruce gone?

Rather than stand around waiting for somebody to tell me, I decided to go find Tony.

If anyone had asked me then whether I thought Tony Cyr had murdered Bruce Easton, I don't know what I'd have said. On the one hand, this whole situation still felt utterly unreal. The president and publisher of Communicore's college textbook division strangled with his own Christmas lights? Too, too tacky! On the other hand, during the odd moments when I managed to grasp that this wasn't a farce but a tragedy, I had to admit Tony was the most likely suspect. Circumstantially he had everything: motive, opportunity, a screw loose.

Yet I balked at casting him as villain. Tony Cyr had hauled my car out of a snowbank. How could he have killed Bruce Easton?

I found him sitting halfway down the stairs with his chin in his hands.

"Quick work, Paul Revere," I said, tightening my bathrobe around my knees.

"That Melinda." He mimed a cringe. "Must have been a four-star general in a previous life. I should have left her till last."

He told me he'd started his bed-check with Melinda for geographic reasons. That I doubted. More likely he'd wanted to be the one to break the bad news . . . but to soften the blow or to gloat? As closely as I scrutinized him, I couldn't tell.

Dammit, Tony Cyr, how do you feel about your ex-wife's defecting to your ex-boss? The answer to that question, it seemed to me, could be the loose end to unravel this whole tangle. Are you angry? hurt? bitter? Did you crave revenge?

Of course, it depended how far he thought she'd defected. Personally, I didn't believe Bruce and Melinda had had an affair. *A*, Lilah wouldn't have allowed it; and *B*, not even my extravagant imagination could picture Bruce Easton's slim manicured fingers caressing the folds of fat beneath Melinda's velour waistband.

But did Tony concur? Or did he assume the man who had destroyed his career and co-opted his authors must also have seduced his wife?

"She sounded so cocky about the phone being dead," he was saying, "I came down here to see if she might've snuffed it."

That got my attention. "Any sign she did?"

Tony's eyebrows and shoulders lifted. "No pliers in the wires."

"Does that mean—"

"What do I know from telephones?" He stood up. "How's Lilah?"

With our faces on a level he was suddenly formidable again. "OK as can be expected," I said, resisting an impulse to back off. "Under the circumstances."

He climbed past me up the stairs. "You shouldn't have left her. She's upset."

"That's why I left her, remember? So she can sleep."

"Sleep isn't what she'll go for if she's holding Bruce's stash."

My heart clenched. "Why didn't you mention that before?"

"Didn't think of it."

Tony knocked on Lilah's door. No answer. He knocked again, louder. Nothing again.

He took a billfold out of his back pocket and an American Express gold card from the billfold, which he slid into the crevice.

Melinda wasn't kidding, I noted distractedly. He *can* unlock doors with a credit card.

Lilah sat huddled in her duvet, watching the door as if braced for Fate's next dirty trick. She looked too burnt out to care about chemical stimulation. Her mouth relaxed a centimeter when Tony and I walked in—not enough to tip the balance. I realized that, whatever my opinion of Bruce Easton, I'd like to strangle his murderer for doing this to Lilah.

She held out her hand and I squeezed it.

"People have been banging and yelling to come in," she said tiredly. "I locked the door and ignored them."

I sat on the bed beside her. "Good."

"Who?" asked Tony. "What did they want?"

Lilah shook her head and made a face. "They think I must know something."

"And you don't?"

"No. I told Cory, I can't remember."

Up close her eyes were bleary, her skin pale and papery. Except for her hair she looked more like Whistler's mother than his mistress.

"Where's Bruce's stash?" Tony asked her.

Lilah didn't appear to understand.

"You said he bought five grams of blow yesterday. Where is it?"

She tilted her head. "Why do you care?"

"I want to ditch it before the cops get here."

"Do you think that's wise?" I asked him.

"Obstructing justice," Lilah chimed in. "You could be an accessory, Tony." She giggled faintly. "What a funny word. Like a purse, or jewelry."

"Plus they'll expect it, won't they?" I said. "They'll find it in his bloodstream."

Tony leaned against the door. "If there's coke in the house, she'll toot it."

Lilah was nodding. I grabbed her wrist. "No," I told her. "You won't. You're not that stupid, Lilah, and you're not that helpless."

She twisted to face me: mouth trembling, eyes brimming with pain. "You don't think so?"

"No." I forced myself to speak evenly. "Like Tony said before: It's not you that's messed up, it's the surroundings." I released her wrist but held her eyes. "This is a rotten situation, Lilah. What we've got to—"

A fist pounded on the door.

"What?" barked Tony, snapping to attention.

"Lilah?" called Melinda. "Are you in there?"

"No!" said Tony. "Go away!"

"Yes," said Lilah. "What do you want?"

"We're all getting together in the living room to discuss what to do till we can get through to the police. We'd like you to be part of the decision-making process."

Lilah shrugged off her duvet. "Oh yeah?" she retorted with unexpected spirit. "This is my house, Melinda Doerr, not yours! If you want to have a meeting you can *ask* me, not tell me!"

She looked surprised and pleased by this flash of her old self. Tony was hiding a grin. Outside the door Melinda launched a conciliatory counter-statement. Lilah rearranged the black fringed shawl she'd draped over her ivory satin robe. "I should go, don't you think?"

"If you're up to it," I agreed.

"Will you come?"

"Sure."

We found her slippers. Tony unlocked the door with a mock bow.

"You're in this too," Lilah told him. "And stop smirking. You're the one who dragged these bozos into my life."

Lilah's bravado carried us as far as the foyer. There she halted, and drew her shawl tighter around her shoulders.

"Are you all right?" Henry inquired anxiously.

He'd been hovering in the hall when we came out, gallant and solicitous as Gatsby waiting on his Daisy. Even Tony had to concede that Henry's arm (the terrycloth robe now replaced by a tweed jacket) made a more suitable support than anything we could offer. His courtliness was oddly touching—a tacit declaration that all would surely end well if everyone behaved properly.

"I can't go in there," Lilah stated.

Henry patted her hand. "Now, now, m'dear."

"I *can't*, Henry. Not with Bruce—"

She sagged. Henry's eyes rolled in panic, but he hung on manfully. "Now, now. There, there. Jeff and I took the liberty, to spare you further distress, that is, we removed, ah, so as to respect the delicacy of your feelings, and of course all of our feelings—" Henry bobbed as he stammered out this speech, reminding me vividly if uncharitably of a chicken.

"Where'd you put him?" Tony broke in.

Henry harrumphed. "I don't think we need go into that now."

"Are you planning to tell the cops you moved the body, or let them figure it out?"

"When the police arrive, I'm confident they will appreciate that as biologists, Professor Abels and I, tenure at Harvard and so forth, are qualified to evaluate the, ah, position and the condition, and take initiative on that basis." He gave Lilah's hand another flurry of pats. "Are you bearing up, m'dear? Shall we go in?"

Tony, standing aside for me to precede him, murmured, "Tennis, anyone?"

I shook my head. Not at Tony—he was watching Lilah's and Henry's entrance—but at the summit conference about to take place.

Bozos, Lilah had called her houseguests. Yet there she went, sailing into their midst as if to the bosom of her closest friends. Once again, civility prevailed. Olive smoothing the lapels of her mink-trimmed bed jacket; Jeff straightening his collar; Gloria fluffing her hair . . . Rearranging deck chairs on the Titanic.

Melinda, re-veloured, had taken over Bruce's old post at the bar. Big and dauntless as she was, she'd be in over her head if she tried filling his shoes.

But I with mournful tread
Walk the deck my Captain lies,
Fallen cold and dead.

I pushed Whitman out of my mind. I didn't want to think about sitting here a few hours ago listening to Bruce Easton recite Robert Frost.

Anyway, this was no time for poetry. What we needed

wasn't books, but action.

Are you volunteering, Cory?

Of course not! I answered myself. I have no fish to fry here. The ball is not in my court. Tomorrow the phone will be fixed, the road plowed. The police will come ask us questions and take away whoever scores lowest. Meanwhile, Melinda can play King of the Hill all she likes. Not me. I'm a journalist, not a detective. Anyhow, I'm on vacation.

But I could tell from the quickening of my pulse that I was lying.

CHAPTER ELEVEN

In the artificial light of brass lamps and exhaustion, everyone in the living room looked capable of killing Bruce Easton.

I wondered if they'd reached the same conclusion. Nobody was talking. The Christmas tree had been hoisted back into place, without lights, and the broken glass around it swept up. Logs and twisted newspaper filled the fireplace. Evidently we weren't expecting to go back to bed any time soon.

I looked at my watch: Quarter past one.

Earlier than I'd thought. When had the party broken up? Eleven? Then the murderer had allowed less than two hours for us all to fall asleep. Risky...

Henry was asking Lilah where she wanted to sit. I'd hoped someone would react to her arrival—jump up screaming, maybe—but no luck. Jeff nodded and smiled at her. Olive, on the sofa, gave her a smile with no nod; Gloria, cross-legged by the fireplace, a nod with no smile.

The logic of the cautious: *If I go rushing up full of condolences, that means I know she didn't do it, which could be taken to mean I did.*

Henry deposited Lilah on the other end of the sofa from

Olive. Jeff held a match to the paper stuffed under the grate. A breathless instant . . . and then it caught in a crackling *whoosh* of flame.

"I assume we're all agreed," Melinda said a little too loudly, "on the need to decide together how best to present this tragedy to the police."

"*Present?*" asked Jeff. "Don't we just *tell* them?"

He lowered himself onto the white hearth rug next to Gloria. Like most of the others, he'd dressed for daytime. Olive and Lilah and I were the only ones still *en peignoir*.

Deference to convention? Or had some telltale trace on a pajama leg spurred the guilty party into changing clothes? Not blood—there hadn't been any. Pine needles? Splinters of glass?

Impossible to say without a laundry round-up . . . which no one here was likely to suggest. Not even Bruce Easton's murder, I suspected, canceled his taboo against airing dirty linen in his living room.

I glanced at Tony, perched beside me on Olive's arm of the sofa. Beige cords, striped earth-tone sweater, brown socks. I thought I remembered the slacks and socks from when he'd joined Lilah and me at the scene of the crime. Nothing suspicious clinging to his cuffs . . . not, of course, that that let him out . . .

"Really, Jeff." Olive sniffed. "As a scientist you must know it's hardly so simple. How much do we volunteer to the police? Do we mention the snake? In what terms do we describe Tony's surprise reappearance, and his relevance to this party?"

She might have been grilling him for a top-security slot at Chute Labs. Jeff stood up and dusted off his trousers.

"I may be a scientist, but I'm also a regular old red-blooded American. I say we let the cops ask whatever they need to ask, and we answer with the truth, the whole truth, and nothing but the truth."

"I must agree with Olive," said Henry. He stood close to Lilah, hands clasped behind him. "You're being a tad naive, Jeff, don't you think? Any report is necessarily selective. If we leave the police to choose the questions, what will they find out? Very little, I dare say, beyond the simplest facts."

"What *are* the simplest facts?" Lilah interjected. "*I* don't know, and I was here! At least, it looks like I—"

She stopped, too late, and cast a distraught glance down the sofa at Tony and me.

Melinda pounced. "You were here?"

"I don't remember. I was asleep." Lilah's chin went up defiantly. "So I wish you'd all tell me as much as you can, because otherwise the cops are liable to think"—her voice broke—"god knows what."

Melinda quickly surveyed the room and made her decision. "Of course. But let's address one problem at a time." She paused, too briefly to allow anyone else to cut in. "First, for those who haven't heard, Wayne is hiking down to Edgar's trailer."

"RV," Gloria corrected.

"*If* his phone is working," Melinda ignored her, "*and* he can get through to the police, they'll still have to wait for the snowplows. That means arriving tomorrow morning soonest. Wayne and I decided he'll say nothing over the phone except that someone is dead, apparently by foul play."

"Good luck, sweetheart," muttered Jeff.

"Not even that it's Bruce?" Lilah, startled, sat up. "But, Melinda—"

"No," said Melinda positively. "Not until I can notify Bill Ballantine and he can inform the Board."

"And his *mother!*" cried Lilah.

"Certainly." Melinda's head inclined a fraction of an inch. "But let's not forget that this tragedy has wider implications than the personal. Bruce Easton is—or was—the president of Communicore's Higher Education Group." Again she sent her eyes around the room, as if she expected someone to deny this. "We must look beyond our own grief, anger, suspicions, et cetera, to the impact on the corporation."

"The corporation!" Tony guffawed. "My god, Mel! You're incredible!"

"That is precisely the attitude we would expect from whoever murdered Bruce," she snapped back. "If you've got even half a brain left, Tony, you'll keep your mouth shut."

"Before your foot shuts it for you," added Gloria, evidently completing a familiar formula.

"Oh, baloney," said Tony, unimpressed. "Who here gives a flying fuck about Communicore but you?" He lifted his shoulders. "Henry? Nah. You've got him chained to your galleys when his heart's in his lab. Lilah? No way. God meant her for finer things than playing geisha to a bunch of yahoos. Olive? Hah! She's only here to steal your best authors. And one of 'em at least is begging to be stolen— aren't you, Jeff? As far as Gloria, you must know she ranks textbook publishing up there with hooking and pushing."

Tony slid his arm through mine too fast for me to get away. "Ms. Thorne doesn't care either, unless she's a closet stockholder. Are you? No, I didn't think so."

"You—" Melinda attempted.

"Wayne Glynn, your pet hack," Tony overrode her, "maybe, except I'd bet a fifth of Chivas you and Bruce and your *corporation* have been screwing him on money." He dropped my arm. "See, Mel? Save your sob song for Billy Bally and the board."

"Oh?" Melinda's hands were on her hips. Her voice was scathing. "And what's it to you, Tony? Why do you care so much what we tell the police? Could you possibly be afraid they'll wonder, as we all do, why you showed up uninvited right before the murder? Flew here from *Corfu*, for god's sake? Are you scared they'll figure out you blamed Bruce for the mess you've made of your life? Might they guess your one and only reason for coming here was revenge?"

"Sure," said Tony promptly. "They might. Especially with you making sure they don't miss any counts in the indictment."

"Stop it, both of you." Lilah's hands clenched into fists on her lap.

"In fact I'll give you a couple of points. Would I enjoy watching Communicore go down in flames? Baby, I'd lick my chops! Bill Ballantine is a greedy asshole who's got no business touching anything as vital and delicate as the dissemination of knowledge. Let him burn!"

"Will you *stop*?" Lilah pounded the sofa in soundless fury. "I don't want to *hear* this!"

"Am I weeping over Bruce's death? No sirree! Look." Tony pointed at his eye. "Not a tear." Then his finger swung around the room, jabbing at each of us. "Not, one, damn, tear."

Lilah buried her face in her hands and sobbed.

"Tony," said Henry severely, "this is shameful!"

"Oh yeah? Making Lilah cry, you mean? Whose fault is that, Henry? Me or the scumbag who offed her husband?"

Tony stood up to address everybody in the room. "I make no secret of my feelings about Bruce Easton. Whoever wrung his neck has my deepest sympathy. But do I hide the nasty remains from sight?" He stamped his foot. "No! Do I fuss about potential impact and proper sequences of notification? Do I sweep sand over the stink as if it were cat shit? *No*, god damn it!"

He jumped onto the coffee table, which cracked and buckled. "You want to know what to tell the cops? Zip. Nada. Niente. You know why? Because one of you poor suckers croaked him." Tony's finger wagged around the circle. "Fine! The bastard deserved it. But the minute you start being helpful, filling in the blanks, rolling the old thumbs over the old ink pad—brother, they'll nail your ass."

He stepped off the coffee table and walked across to his ex-wife. "Murder is not a civilized business, Melinda. What are you going to do about that?"

What we all did, in the aftershock of Tony's jolting performance, was vote to investigate Bruce Easton's murder.

Melinda took charge. She moved that we follow parliamentary procedure. Gloria seconded. I abstained, being busy trying to gauge whether Tony was miffed or licking his chops.

The ayes had it. Henry moved that in deference to Lilah's feelings Tony leave the room. Lilah moved that people stop speaking for her. Melinda ruled Lilah out of order. Jeff told Melinda to ease up, this wasn't a court of law. Melinda ruled Jeff out of order. Jeff moved that Melinda shove her gavel where the sun don't shine. Gloria seconded.

Then Olive said if we were going to squabble all night she wanted a drink; to which Henry replied that Bruce had locked the cupboard; whereupon Tony produced the key he'd picked up in the bedroom.

I had to hand it to Tony. Under that lunatic exterior lurked a born organizer. Without once acting either calm or sober, he managed to transform nine yapping foxhounds—or, more accurately, eight foxhounds and a well-disguised fox—into a hunting pack. He didn't so much take over from Melinda as work around her. Henry and Jeff became our collectors of facts, Olive our judge-commentator. Lilah, who I feared might get stuck as defendant, landed the part of helpless bystander. That freed me as her sidekick to poke in wherever I liked. Gloria chose barmaid and comic relief. Melinda was dragged by her short hair into the role of Greek chorus.

Tony himself stood at the edge of the field and yoicked when anyone strayed off after a rabbit. An unusual management strategy, but effective. If he'd run Caxton Press like this, I could see why Bruce found him dangerous enough to fire.

I say nine foxhounds instead of seven because Wayne and Edgar showed up midway through our meeting. Without his coat and hat Edgar looked more than ever like an extra for *The Terminator*: beat-up leather jacket, camouflage pants, Army boots with matching haircut. He walked with that hulking simian gait my husband calls Rolling Rock. I could picture him revving a chopper or drumming in a Somerville bar easier than pruning the Eastons' hydrangeas.

Edgar reported that he'd snowshoed up to the ridge with his cell phone. The cops had been called and would come in with the first plow that could get through. Unless the snow picked up again, he figured he and the blower could clear the driveway down to the road by mid-morning. Wayne had confessed Bruce was dead—otherwise, I gathered, Edgar would have told this geek to shovel his own way out—but the Christmas-tree lights were news. He was clearly disappointed when Tony said no, we hadn't photographed the body before unplugging it.

The lights, Jeff and Henry reported, were extraneous. A dramatic flourish. On the basis of a necessarily superficial examination of the body, they concluded that Bruce had been strangled with something wider and softer than a bulb-studded wire. Were they positive he was dead? Oh, yes. Beyond all hope? No doubt about it. Henry gave a somewhat technical summary of their examination of the body which I understood to confirm that Bruce was already past resuscitating when I found him. That took a load off my mind.

Jeff's part of the briefing centered on the murderer's modus operandi. Judging from the type and degree of bruising, it appeared that the killer ("whom we shall call X," Henry interposed) had looped his or her weapon around

Bruce's neck from behind. Caught by surprise, Bruce grabbed at his throat, abrading the skin; but lack of oxygen would have knocked him out within a minute.

That scenario drew several protests. Melinda, looking pale, objected that human beings can stay conscious longer than a minute without air. Not when they're fighting for breath, countered Jeff. Olive didn't believe any of the women here were strong enough to, ah . . . Henry rejoined that strength wouldn't have been all that significant, given the advantage of surprise.

"But how could X have surprised him?" asked Lilah. During Jeff's recitation she'd wilted into the sofa. Now she stif-fened up again. "Whoever did it must have come in our room, woke Bruce up, talked him into putting on his robe and going out to the living room—"

She stopped, as if she was on the brink of recollecting something; then she sighed and shook her head.

"He might have come out here for some other reason," Olive suggested. "Perhaps he saw you weren't well, dear, and got up to fetch you something—milk, tea, brandy— He ran into X and they quarreled. Meanwhile you realized Bruce had been gone for some time and came looking for him. You stumbled; Bruce leaned over to help you; X grabbed his opportunity—"

"Possible but unlikely," interrupted Henry. "Jeff may disagree with me, but as I reconstruct it, Lilah was most probably not involved in any way." He reddened. "Cory found her on the sofa, yes?—whereas Bruce was over by the tree. I should guess that Lilah came on the scene after Bruce was dead, having heard the struggle; saw his body, and fainted."

Melinda said scornfully, "Women don't faint at the drop of a hat in this day and age, Henry."

"My husband is not a hat, Melinda Doerr!"

"You know, all this is pure speculation," said Jeff. He

was chipping with his thumbnail at a stray blob of mortar on the fireplace. "These floor tiles are great for scuff marks, OK for footprints, and hopeless for cloth-soled slippers or bodies dragged around in bathrobes. So, yes, Henry, I disagree with you, in that I see no empirical basis for drawing any conclusions about who was where when."

I sidled around Henry and sat on the sofa beside Lilah. "Well, wait a minute," I said to Jeff. "Lilah and I had to pull Bruce away from the tree in order to get the lights off his neck. Right?" She nodded. "Before that he was on his stomach with his head in the branches—"

Melinda interrupted. "Are you saying Bruce was under the tree? That the tree fell on top of him?"

"No." I wished someone would give this woman a Valium. "On the contrary. If you want me to speculate, I'd guess that Bruce fell on top of the tree. Either that or he was dragged over there after he was unconscious so that X could wrap the lights around his neck."

"Scratches!" Olive sat up excitedly. "Henry! Did you find scratches on his face from the needles?"

"We didn't examine the face," Henry admitted, shifting uncomfortably. "It wasn't, ah, I should say, that is, our intention was not to establish mode of death, et cetera, but merely to document the state of the body before moving it."

"Tony did take pictures then," Gloria assured Edgar.

Edgar, who had assumed a military at-ease stance in front of the dining-room table, smiled at Gloria and winked at Tony.

"So you walked in, saw the tree, Bruce on the floor, Lilah on the sofa," Tony addressed me, "and then you and Lilah cut him loose from the lights. Right?"

"Right. Approximately."

"Why, Ms. Thorne? What got you out of bed?"

"Oh!" Another puzzle piece I'd forgotten to contribute. "I heard a crash—I thought it was part of my dream, but when I came out here and found the tree down, I realized it must have been that."

Melinda cut in. "How long from when you heard the crash to when you entered the living room?" She flicked a glance at Tony as if daring him to challenge her right to ask questions.

"I'm not sure. Twenty minutes, maybe?"

"Long enough," nodded Jeff.

"Barely so, I should think." Henry, rocking back and forth on his feet, sounded dubious. "For X to strangle Bruce, drag him across the floor, pull the lights off the Christmas tree and wrap them around his neck, make sure Lilah was unconscious, and return to his room?"

Olive cocked her head at him. "As Wayne pointed out *re* that wretched snake, dear, one is presumably not dealing with the sanest of minds. X must have been desperate, which could have made him reckless."

"*Him?*" Wayne, encouraged by this citation, stepped forward from his post by the kitchen door. "Do I hear reverse chauvinism? Now that the chips are down the ladies embrace the hitherto objectionable male pronoun?"

"The other possibility," Melinda said evenly, "is that X didn't go back to her room."

Jeff, leaning against the fireplace, craned around Edgar. "Is that an accusation, Melinda?"

"No." Her chin jutted. "It's a datum."

Lilah's lips pursed, but she didn't speak. I looked past her to Tony, half-sitting on the sofa arm next to Olive. He was staring at his ex-wife with an expression I'd hate to have anyone direct at me. Beside me, Henry recommenced rocking on the balls of his feet.

"I," declared Olive, "am exhausted! Even if I believed we could finish this before the police arrive, which I don't, I'm sure I'd be snoring long before the finale." She yawned and stretched her bony arms. "Tony, am I just a tiresome old creature? Or may I move that we adjourn until, say, seven-thirty?"

"Second," nodded Henry.

"Third." Gloria shot a covert smile at Jeff.

"Wait!" Lilah glanced around distractedly. "I don't want you all going off to bed thinking I killed Bruce!"

"Don't be silly," muttered Henry. But he didn't look at her.

Melinda arched an eyebrow. "No one's said you did, Lilah." She squared her shoulders; surveyed the group one last time, and wheeled toward the kitchen door. "But if you're not too sleepy, you might try and remember how you got from your room onto that sofa."

CHAPTER TWELVE

The snow had stopped. From Lilah's bedroom windows I could see across the pocked, wind-blurred pond to a row of evergreens, humped under their white burden like bearers in a halted safari. On the near shore, the floodlit willow tree cast spidery shadows across the deck. Lilah had rushed around switching on every lamp in sight—as a memorial to Bruce? a hex against further evil?—till I persuaded her it was enough to light up the outdoors.

So still and silent the world looked out there. *All is calm, all is bright.* Like a Christmas card. Not in here. I could hear the gurgle and clunk of plumbing, occasional muffled voices, footsteps, doors shutting . . .

Was Lilah asleep yet? The lump under her duvet hadn't moved in several minutes. Give her a few more. The way things were going, I wasn't eager to leave her.

I'd asked Henry what he and Jeff did with the body. Wrapped it in a sheet, he answered solemnly; duct-taped it into two large garbage bags, and laid it in the snow outside the sliding door to the studio.

Did Melinda know? Yes. She didn't mind? Henry shrugged: Evidently not.

She must not have seen what I saw, then. That grotesque

crimson-and-purple gargoyle where a face should have been. That throat I'd first heard quoting poetry, gouged by its own clawing fingernails.

And by a garrote held tight around it till Bruce Easton no longer had breath to fight whichever of his guests had strangled him.

Whom we shall call X. That's right, Henry. Let's make this a textbook example of scientific inquiry. Keep biology's guts and jolts where they belong: in the lab. Let's focus on identifying X in this equation, so we won't have to think about that stiffening bundle on Melinda's doorstep.

But that was unfair. Identifying X wasn't Henry's idea, it was all of ours.

Or almost all. Not Edgar and Wayne, who weren't there then. And not Tony.

I let out a sigh which clouded the windowpane. Too many calculations in this problem led to Tony.

Despite his manic flair for leadership, our investigation hadn't yielded much. Everybody swore they were asleep when Bruce was killed; nobody could prove it. Gloria had murmured blushingly that sleep in her and Jeff's case wasn't exactly . . . at which point Jeff declared that he'd been dead to the world—oh, *sorry*; out like a light—for at least an hour before the, ah . . . you know.

No one had thought that discrepancy worth poking into, including me. But then my fellow detectives were reluctant to turn over any rock that might have creepy things underneath. Up to a point, I sympathized: As colleagues, friends, and guests of Bruce Easton's, they still couldn't believe he was mortal, much less dead. However, they also couldn't get over thinking they were the kind of people to whom this kind of thing simply doesn't happen. Professionals. Scientists. Supporters of democracy, civil rights, the free market, and public television. Even Henry and Jeff, who'd handled the body, didn't seem to link it with the interesting logical problem Fate had dropped in their laps. As for the others, they'd gone off to bed confident of having done their bit for truth and justice by providing a forum in which to deny any connection with the, ah . . . you know.

Consequently, Lilah had left the room convinced that everyone in it believed she'd murdered her husband.

Never mind old friends, Christmas, nicest people on earth. Never mind the law or burdens of proof. Secretly they all ("except you, Cory") agreed with Melinda. And the only way she could ever face them again would be with evidence to the contrary.

I was too weary to be tactful. "How are we supposed to come up with that?"

She burrowed under her duvet. "I wish I knew."

"Lilah," I tried again, "this is nuts. Everybody knows you loved Bruce."

Silence.

"Did you hear what Gloria told Edgar when we were leaving? 'That side door is never locked. Any tramp off the street could have come in . . .'"

That drew a snuffly giggle. "The Old Mill Road bag ladies?"

"With snowshoes." I patted a lump that looked like a shoulder. "Let it go, OK? In a few hours it won't matter anyway—the police will take over, and you'll be—"

"—their top suspect. That's what I'll be."

"No you won't. Come on, Lilah. They're experts— open-minded, not like your friends out there. Really, things will look better tomorrow. Just sleep off those Valium—"

"Experts? The Oxbridge cops?" She curled away from my comforting hand. "You don't know them."

This was not an argument we needed to have right now. I switched back to her need for rest, said good-night, and moved to the window seat. Now I watched a gust of wind snake under the eaves and dance across the deck in a twisting veil of snow.

She had a point. How could she convince anybody she was innocent except by finding out who was guilty?

In spite of my vow not to get sucked in again, I considered. Candidates for X? Everybody in the house. Crossing off Lilah and me, that left seven suspects. Motives? At least one each. Tony's list of reasons why nobody cared about the impact of Bruce's death on Communicore had made that clear—and not, I thought, by coincidence.

Who would want to hurt Bruce? Lilah had asked. More realistically, *Who wouldn't?*

I closed my eyes and pictured the living room as it had emptied out. Olive and Wayne ambling downstairs to their rooms; Henry splitting off toward the guest wing, carrying the last of Bruce's Armagnac. Jeff had lingered to put out the fire and avoid flaunting his arrangement with Gloria. Edgar hulked toward the kitchen for another beer before striking out again through the snow.

Melinda had waited beside the bar for Tony to lock it and leave. When he kicked off his shoes and curled up with an ostentatious yawn on the sofa, she'd about-faced, narrowly missing Edgar with his Heineken, and marched off to her suite.

Tony again. If revenge hadn't brought him here, what did? Was he really tossing and turning on lumpy cushions downstairs when Bruce was strangled? Where had he been during the snake episodes? Assuming his drunkenness was an act, for whose benefit? Why didn't he want anyone to know we'd met on the road? What was the full story behind his nervous breakdown?

Could anybody in this house vouch for any statement by or about Tony Cyr since the day Bruce fired him?

I wiped the mist off the window with my bathrobe sleeve. *When in doubt, find out.*

"Lilah?" I whispered. "Are you awake?"

The mound on her bed heaved, thrashed, and produced a quantity of curly red hair. "Yes," said Lilah. "My head's absolutely killing me. Would you be an angel, Cory, and get me a pain pill?"

"I'll get you an aspirin," I said firmly.

But when I walked into her bathroom I forgot Lilah, drugs, Tony, and everything else.

Someone had smashed the medicine-cabinet mirror. Across the cracked glass was soaped a message in shaky capitals. Squinting, I read: "MYOB OR U 2 ->"

Under the arrow, curving around the point of impact, ran a long squiggle with a forked tongue. Its severed head dripped white blood.

Even as my stomach plummeted, my eyes scanned. There was a flat spot on the scented oval bar reposing in the marble soap dish. Nothing else had been disarranged. Whatever the message-writer had used to invite seven years' bad luck, he or she must have taken it along when s/he left.

Now what?

Now—too late—I remembered the puzzle piece I'd been groping for all night. *A warning*. That's what the beheaded snake was. More precisely, a threat. From a story I'd written years ago for *Phases*. A man in Chelsea who'd done unspeakable things to his niece had shut her up by chopping the head off her kitten. *See? Tell anybody and this is you.*

So X had warned Bruce Easton. And Bruce either didn't get the message or didn't choose to listen.

I opened the door gingerly, not wanting to jar loose any broken glass. Amid a vast array of prescription pill bottles I found aspirin. I filled a cup with water, thinking hard.

Whatever killing the snake was meant to scare Bruce into or out of, it failed. Was this threat a final notice, then? MYOB: mind your own business. That could fit. Suppose Bruce dis-covered it after we'd all gone to bed. Suppose he wasn't scared but angry; slipped into his bathrobe and went looking for the writer.

Maybe that was X's plan: not to intimidate him, but lure him out to die.

Who wanted Bruce's nose out of his or her affairs urgently enough to commit murder?

That I couldn't guess. Jeff and Gloria? Olive? Henry? Edgar? Wayne? Melinda? None seemed likely, but none were inconceivable. Offhand, Lilah and Tony—top suspects to an objective outsider, which I wasn't—looked least probable.

"Cory, are you lost?"

"No." I closed the door. "I'm coming."

As I handed Lilah her aspirin I asked her, "When were you last in the bathroom?"

She pondered. "Before bed, I guess." She swallowed. "Why? Is it a mess? Oh, crap, look at this! Now I've gone and spilled water on the duvet. Bruce will—"

She stopped. I caught her hand just in time to keep the cup from toppling completely.

When I'd set it on the bedside table I saw she was crying again, slumped in a heap of linen with her hands on her cheeks and tears running down her fingers.

One reason I skipped news reporting and went straight to writing features was my unwillingness to poke microphones into the faces of grieving survivors. Well, Cory, Fate sure nailed you on that one.

I went back to the bathroom for tissues; climbed up beside Lilah and hugged her till she calmed down.

"Listen," I said. "I have some news which isn't exactly good but may help us solve this thing."

I told her about the mirror. Her face contorted as if to cry again, but she didn't. She wanted to see the message. No, Bruce hadn't mentioned it to her.

"I don't use this bathroom much," she explained, sliding her feet into slippers. "I mostly use the guest one, since it's closer to the living room, except when I get up and go to bed. This is more his bathroom."

"Do people know that?"

"Oh, gawd! I don't know."

Though she didn't speak when she saw the broken mirror, I could see she was upset. After staring at it for a long moment she reached for a towel.

I stepped in front of her. "Don't even think of it."

Lilah glared. The least she could do for Bruce's memory was erase that disgusting thing. Of all forms of destruction, the one he'd hated worst was broken glass—as the person who wrote this obviously knew.

Through my head flashed an image of Tony hurling his smashed shot glass at the dining room windows. "Does anybody in particular come to mind?"

"No." She lunged again at the mirror.

I grabbed her in a wrist lock. "Forget it! We've already destroyed our quota of evidence. What do you think the cops will say when they get here tomorrow and find the entire scene of the crime has been tidied up?"

"I know what they'll say if they see *that*," she said passionately. "They'll say I wrote it! They'll say I was the only person besides Bruce who used this bathroom, and when Tony showed up and I let him in, I knew Bruce would suspect there was something between us so I threatened him. And when that didn't work I killed him."

I stared at her. So many questions were jostling in my head that I didn't know which to ask first.

"You don't believe me?" she challenged.

"Believe you?" With my free hand I seized her shoulder and pulled her around so we were facing each other. "Where's this coming from, Lilah? You told me you let Tony in because Bruce wanted you to. Why would he suspect there was something between you?"

"He wouldn't. He didn't," said Lilah. "I'm just telling

you what the cops will say."

"But why would they say that?"

"That's how they think! It's a gotcha game for them. Don't you watch TV?"

I was in no mood to debate the American legal and/or entertainment system. "Lilah," I let go of her, "please give me a straight answer on this. One: Was there anything besides friendship between you and Tony? Two: Did anybody in this house, or in this town, have reason—right or wrong—to think there was?"

"No, no, no!" she shook her head. "Ow! That was dumb, with a splitting headache. Of course not! I've got to get some sleep, Cory. Can we finish this later?"

I pushed, but Lilah was adamant. Reluctantly I agreed to come back at quarter past seven. Meanwhile, as a precautionary measure, would she please keep her door locked? If X was the type of killer who returns to the scene of the crime, at least s/he wouldn't get in here without American Express.

I found Tony where I'd left him, on the sofa talking to Edgar.

And not apparently about murder. Edgar lounged among the pillows with a beer bottle in his hand and two more on the floor beside him. He'd taken off his boots and leather jacket, exposing large wool-socked feet and a T-shirt that gave a new meaning to off-white.

When he saw me, his voice shut down in mid-laugh.

Tony twisted around. "Hey, Ms. Thorne! You want a beer? We're not keeping you awake, are we?"

"No," I said. "I'm not breaking up a party, am I?"

He grinned and waved dismissively. "Nothing important. Women talk. Speaking of which—Edgar, have you met this one? Cory Thorne, Edgar Palumbo."

We clasped hands sixties-fashion over the back of the

sofa. "You seem to be taking Bruce's death in stride," I remarked to Tony.

"Antidote." He flourished a half-full glass. "In the noble tradition of several major cultures, we drown our grief in laughter and libations. Here's to Breece! May he rest in puce!"

Edgar, guffawing, lifted his bottle.

"We honor our host by toasting his taste and tasting his toast!"

I fixed Tony with what my husband calls my Queen Victoria stare. "More ginger ale?"

His grin was unrepentant. "The better to leave a full bar for the widow."

"Tony dried out while he was away," said Edgar. "He's on the wagon."

"That's no wagon," I said. "That's a Trojan horse."

Edgar squinted at me as if I'd spoken Greek. "Say what?"

"Why act like a lush if you're straight? What do you accomplish but to alienate everybody and guarantee they won't take you seriously?"

"I give up. What?"

"You want to get in where you've been kicked out, you don't come charging up the drawbridge like Sir Lancelot. On the contrary: you dress like a beggar and infiltrate."

"Oh." Edgar's frown dissolved. "Gotcha! You know, when you said Trojan—"

Tony interrupted. "Is she a sharp one or what? Edgar, what'd I tell you about Mount Holyoke girls?"

"You said they've all got—"

"I said they're paragons among women," Tony cut him off again, "and I was right." He mimed me a kiss. "You do look fetching in that robe, Ms. Thorne."

I could either cringe and blush or thank him, so I thanked him. "There are a few additional points I'd appreciate your clearing up."

His eyebrow twitched. "Take a number. Line forms to the rear."

"Try again." Holding my robe closed, I slid onto the sofa arm behind Edgar where I could face Tony. "Let me remind you of a few facts. A, given that I never met Bruce Easton till a few hours ago, I'm the one person in this house who's guaranteed clean. B, I don't believe Lilah killed her husband, and I don't think you do either. C, as she may have told you, I moonlight, or rather daylight, as an investigative journalist."

"I sense a message." Tony leaned his head back, eyes shut, fingers to his temples. "It's getting clearer. You're telling me you're trustworthy, you want to help Lilah, and you want me to help you."

"Not exactly." His eyes opened again. "I'm telling you this goose chase you started isn't going to stop without a goose, and I don't fancy Lilah as anybody's Christmas dinner."

"So let's volunteer Tony?"

"If the shoe doesn't fit, why squawk?"

"What if it does?"

I gave the flap of my robe an unnecessary tug. "Then you can either give yourself away by refusing to cooperate, or humor me and hope I'm not as sharp as I think."

One corner of Tony's mouth curled. "I'd hate to stake my freedom on that possibility, Ms. Thorne."

"Wait a minute, man." Edgar pointed his beer bottle at Tony. "I don't get this. If what she wants is some kind of partner thing, like, you know, what's-their-names—"

"Holmes and Watson?"

"Mulder and Scully, right?—then how come she's picking on you? I mean, no offense, but you're not exactly Mr. Clean."

"He's got you there," Tony nodded. "If the idea is to save the goose, why send in the gander?"

"Because I have to trust somebody," I rejoined, "and you rescued my car."

So Tony Cyr and I became partners, after a fashion, for the second time that night. My statement about trusting him was an off-white lie, but he knew that. What I did trust was his self-interest. Tony stood to gain as much as Lilah from finding another goose. We could trade items from our fact collections; and if his weren't necessarily true, at least I could use them to triangulate.

He'd already refused to answer one big question: Why did he warn me "things die here" three hours before Bruce's murder? So I took an indirect approach. Two can play Trojan horse.

"To start with, Tony, why did you ask me on the road not to say I'd met you? That's the kind of thing the police are bound to wonder about. If you weren't coming here to have some kind of confrontation with Bruce—"

"Surprise!" Edgar broke in eagerly. "That's why we hid his car. Right, Mr. T? Keep it quiet you're on the premises so you can go anywhere and do anything without them knowing it's you."

"Give that man in the checkered suit a kewpie doll!" Tony raised his glass. "Ms. Thorne, looks like you've got yourself an A-1 sidekick."

I smiled back at him. Then I turned to his proud accomplice. "Nice work, Edgar! But weren't you on your way home ages ago? With that long driveway to clear in the morning . . ."

He didn't like it, but he went. Nor did Tony try to stop him. We all bid each other good-night. Edgar remembered his beer bottles, came back and carried them to the kitchen. We said good-night again, less warmly. I waited till I heard the distant slam of a door.

"Returning to Square One." I wriggled into a comfortable position in Edgar's corner of the sofa. "The proposition that you flew across a very large ocean, rented a very large car, and drove through Connecticut in a very large blizzard so as to surprise Bruce for Christmas. I can accept that. So, I'm sure, will the cops. The question remains, however: What kind of surprise did you have in mind?"

Tony stood by the fireplace sipping ginger ale. "You tell me, Ms. Thorne."

"All right. *A*, you planned to kill him. *B*, you thought it would be fun to track footprints all over his nice white snow and get him so pissed, pardon the pun, that the party would be in shambles by the time you made your entrance. Any votes so far?"

Tony shook his head.

"*C*, you came back to the U.S. for other reasons, and hit the Eastons' Christmas party on impulse." This one I was handing him as a favor, a goodwill gesture to seal our bargain. "Suppose you got to Oxbridge thinking you were just passing through town. Then you met me, and it seemed like the hand of Fate tipping the scale. Suddenly you wanted to keep your options open; which meant making sure I kept my mouth shut. Plus, dammit, you can't resist a chance to be cryptic."

A nice touch, the left-handed compliment. Journalists' Rule #4: *Convince them you're harmless.* Which I was, unless Tony had killed Bruce Easton. His true reason for coming here I didn't know. But giving him a plausible motive now was my best shot at getting the real one from him later.

The corner of Tony's mouth twitched. "You don't need me for this, Ms. Thorne. You've got it all figured out."

"Not quite. I'll tell you one thing I haven't figured out: Why the melodrama in the bathroom? If you weren't planning then to kill Bruce, why try to scare me off?"

"Scare you off?" Tony kicked at one of the goatskin-marble curlicues from the fallen coffee table. "Not much chance of that, was there, with a quarter mile of snow between you and the road?"

"That's one reason why I'm asking."

For a moment he didn't answer. I noticed his shoe was leaving black smudges on Bruce's erstwhile table.

"I wanted you to lower your profile," he said finally. "Stop asking other people the kind of nosy questions you were asking me. Obviously, as it turns out, somebody here didn't want anybody poking into his or her affairs."

"Sorry, Professor Plum, no cigar."

He looked up from his foot to me.

"Oh, come on," I said. "Your threats put me on guard, but they sure didn't stop me asking questions. Just the opposite. What you did was point me in a new and rather alarming direction; and I want to know why."

Again that twitch at the corner of his mouth. "You're some interrogator, Ms. Thorne."

"So?"

"So, when I realized that," he raised his arms in a lengthy stretch, "I said to myself, Tony, the great gift shop in the sky has just sent you a special delivery. Look at this woman!" His arms lowered as if to embrace me. "She's got everything you lack: privileged access, credibility, feminine wiles— Will you waste such assets? No, by god!" He folded his arms. "We shall go truffle-hunting together, Ms. Thorne and I, among the roots of academe!"

I fought back a smile. "And has your special-delivery pig dug up any truffles?"

"What she appears to have dug up," said Tony, "is a big fat amanita mushroom."

A chill slid up my spine. "The angel of death. Thanks a lot."

"Don't thank me. Spit it out! Phlwuck! Ptui! The cops will be here tomorrow, God and Edgar willing. Let them eat it."

I sat on the sofa arm. "I'm afraid Lilah may be off the

deep end by then."

"Like her stepson," said Tony.

The chill settled in the back of my neck. "That's my other question," I said. "Exactly what do you know or suspect about Paul Easton's drowning?"

"What I suspect is moot at the moment. What I know is this." He swallowed the last of his ginger ale. "Once upon a time there was a father named Bruce Easton who had a crippled kid. In keeping with his policy of treating Paul as much like a normal boy as possible, Bruce decided he should have a pet." As he spoke, Tony strolled toward the bar. "Now, Bruce is not fond of animals. They have a nasty habit of shedding or shitting on his decor. Ginger ale? Cognac?"

"Cognac, thank you," I said. "A small one."

He poured. "So Bruce bought Paul a pair of snakes. Clean, odorless, noiseless, low maintenance—perfect! Paul seemed to like them OK, although if he went so far as naming them he never told anybody. They lived in a glass aquarium in the studio, which was where he slept when he stayed here."

"This was after you and Melinda moved out?"

"Last summer. You got it." He handed me a snifter. "Then came the evil Sunday when Paul took his dive. That same weekend, Snake Number One departed for parts unknown. No luggage, no postcards, no forwarding address."

I stood up. "They searched the house? They didn't find it?" Thinking: Is he on the same track I am? "Tony, how do you know this?"

"Letters," he said succinctly. "When you're beyond the pale, people tell you all kinds of things."

"And what's your conclusion?"

He gave me a twisted smile. "My conclusion, o sharp Thorne, was that the interests of truth and justice required me to dry me out and hie me home in time for the annual Christmas party."

While one of me registered that I'd finally got an answer

to my original question, another one yearned to wring Tony Cyr's neck till I squeezed out the other revelations he was hiding in that devious brain.

Feminine wiles, Cory, remember?

"So here you are," I said brightly. "Just in time for Snake Number Two to join Number One, and Bruce to join Paul."

"Of the two, I'd say the snake is the greater loss." Then Tony's sardonic detachment collapsed with a sigh. "If you're asking do I blame myself?—sure. Mea culpa! What if I'd shown up sooner, or not so colorfully, or told somebody I was coming? Did I maybe even trigger this mess? Turn up the heat too high too fast? Scare X, or inspire him, into offing the creep?"

"Does it matter?" I returned. "Whoever killed Bruce got the idea long before tonight. You and Lilah make some pair of suspects, beating your breasts when what you need is help from Harry Houdini." Wondering if he guessed I was struggling with my own mea culpas. "Let's get back to the bottom line. One: Who did it? Two: Is Paul's death connected to Bruce's, and if so, how?"

"The big truffles." Tony set his ginger ale on the bar. "I don't do lines, bottom or otherwise, but I dig dirt."

I set my snifter beside his glass. "Then let's hit the trenches."

CHAPTER THIRTEEN

Twenty minutes later Olive Chute, smoothing the mink collar of her bed jacket, said, "Well, really, dear, what can one expect from a person of that ilk?"

She sat in a captain's chair in a corner of Henry Howrigan's room. For a widowed lady caught visiting a single gentleman in her nightclothes, Mrs. Chute's composure was impressive. Henry, wearing slacks and a beige polyester turtleneck but no jacket or shoes, perched uncomfortably on the foot of his bed. I made do with a dressing-table bench. We scoff at luxury in the trenches.

This meeting was one of those flukes that gives you faith in the patron saint of investigators, whoever she or he is. My bravado with Tony notwithstanding, I hadn't expected to accomplish much before morning. We'd quickly emptied the bag on Paul Easton's drowning. Tony told me he had read and reread the letters he'd received—from Lilah, Henry, and (oddly, I thought) Olive; he'd compared their versions of the story, and searched between the lines for clues. His sole conclusion was that something smelled fishy. When I asked if he could identify the fish he retorted that he was a publisher, not an ichthyologist.

"You do think, though, there's a relationship between

Bruce's death and Paul's?"

"Two'll get you five," he nodded. "Actually in this case two'll get you four—I don't see the reptile mortality rate as a coincidence."

"What's the connection?"

"Beats me." Tony's eyebrows wiggled. "Are you angling, Ms. Thorne, or have you got a nibble?"

I didn't believe he'd spent four months on this problem and come up with nothing. However, I preferred not to strain our fragile partnership by saying so.

"Try a hypothesis. You know *Hamlet*, right? Suppose Bruce thought somebody here pushed Paul off the deck. Maybe he's got a suspect, maybe not. How conceivable is it that he'd use Snake Number Two as the victim in a mini-drama to catch the conscience of the killer?"

"Hmm." Tony mulled it over. "It's neat, it's elegant . . . but conceivable? No."

"Why not?"

"Because, as dedicated as Bruce was to getting his own way, he never dirtied his own hands. Take Henry's intro bio text. That book could sweep the majors market, given half-decent editing. Bruce could do it—should, in fact. I would have. But he wants a bigger splash, sooner, without the work. So he hires that hack Glynn to water the book down and speed it up for the nonmajors. That way he can buy instant visibility—color photos, DVD, big PR campaign—and he doesn't get ink on his fingers. Solve the problem by throwing money at it, that's Bruce's M.O."

I said, "How does that bear on my hypothesis?"

"If Bruce thought somebody killed Paul, he'd hire a detective. He'd make a big donation to the Police Benevolent Fund. He'd spare no expense; but he would not, believe me, cut up anything that might bleed or get scales on his shirt cuffs."

All right, I thought. Maybe. Or maybe I did have a

nibble and you don't want me to know.

I told him about the smashed bathroom mirror. Tony looked suitably startled. Like Lilah, he focused immediately on the broken glass. The snake parts in Jeff's puff pastry and Olive's purse were open to various interpretations; but that mirror was meant for Bruce.

"You should've seen him when Julia—his ex-wife— gouged the dining room windows with her diamond. God, what a pinnacle of poetic justice! He was hysterical— literally aching for revenge. But since he'd already screwed her over with Lilah and the house and kid, there was nothing left he could do. And then she smashed up the car, and Paul nearly died, and that took his mind off his precious windows till they could get the glaziers in."

"I take it Julia's, ah, farewell performance inspired you when it was your turn to move out."

He nodded cheerfully. "I used a pistol, since the prick never gave me a ring."

"Did he get hysterical then, too?"

A reminiscent grin. "Tried to get me committed. Told the cops it was a failed suicide attempt—that I missed my head, went nuts and shot the windows. Hah! Actually I *was* missing most of my head then, but that was his fault, not mine. The lawyers worked it out so I left the country and Bruce took the windows out of my severance pay."

As a motive for murder it was more than adequate. If I hadn't been sitting on the sofa listening to him, I'd have sent him up.

"But I wouldn't break a *mirror*," said Tony. "Hell, you could get glass all over yourself."

That, I thought with an inward sigh, is why I don't believe Tony Cyr is X. I can imagine him strangling Bruce; but I can't see him choosing such a bizarre way to warn him off.

I asked if he saw the dead snake and the soaped one as carrying the same message. After considering for a moment,

Tony said it looked like it. If not, this place was turning into General Delivery.

What message?

The corner of his mouth curled. "Why ask me? On a general level, it's obvious. Especially with hindsight. And on a particular level, your guess is as good as mine."

"Are you saying you have no idea who was trying to get Bruce to do what?"

"No," said Tony. "I'm saying too many people had too many reasons to get him to do practically anything else besides what he was doing."

OK. What did he think of the possibility that the soaped note wasn't just another threat, but bait for X's fatal trap?

Tony's eyebrows went up. Yes. Very possible indeed.

Encouraged, I took one more shot at the bottom line. Who in this house could he picture using broken snakes and glass as modes of communication?

Since he couldn't picture anybody here having the balls to croak the bastard, replied Tony, guesses about tactics would be pissing into the wind.

He's getting punchy, I thought. Me too.

I went to the bar and poured myself a ginger ale. I started to put the cognac bottle in the cabinet and remembered Bruce wasn't around anymore to care.

"Dammit," I scowled at my reflection, "there's got to be a lead! How can two people and two snakes die in the same house and not leave a clue?"

"We don't know Snake Number One died," Tony reminded me. "Missing in action."

"Where do you think it went?"

He shrugged. "Answer that and you know everything. Or, answer that and you still don't know anything."

"Like every other thread in this goddam ball of wax." I held up the ginger-ale bottle inquiringly.

"No thanks. Too much drinking and thinking." Tony

looked at his watch. "I'm due downstairs for a conference with my subconscious in cushion-land."

He stood up, stretched and yawned. "We've got plenty of clues, Ms. Thorne. The problem is linking them up."

Plenty of clues? One man strangled, one boy drowned. One snake's head in a puff pastry; one snake's body in a purse; one snake disappeared. One broken mirror with a soaped picture of a snake. And Tony off to cushion-land to piece them all together. Was he hoping for a revelation like the snake-biting-its-tail dream that led Kekule to discover benzene rings?

We'd agreed to meet back here at seven unless something major happened sooner. I sat on the sofa arm so as to defer my own conference in cushion-land till my subconscious and I reviewed the agenda.

Point One: suspects. Tabling my *Hamlet* hypothesis, assume X killed both Bruce and his snake. Who looked likely?

Nobody.

Everybody.

Well, not Lilah. Maybe not Gloria, if she really was afraid of snakes. Cross off Mary Helen—she'd left before Bruce was murdered. Edgar too? No; he'd turned up fast enough when sent for.

What if I assumed that whoever beheaded Snake Two had also abducted Snake One? That left out Tony . . . Not a valid assumption, though. Snake One might simply have crawled away. Anyhow, look at Bruce's dining room windows—destroyed first by Julia, then by Tony. X could have snuffed Snake Two after watching how obsessively Bruce searched for Snake One.

Next question. Suppose—as I was inclined to do—that the head in the puff pastry, the remains in Olive's purse, and the threat on the bathroom mirror made up a matched set of warnings to Bruce. Did Paul's so-called accident fall in the same category?

No. Not credible. If Bruce thought his son was murdered he'd have struck back, not knuckled under. Besides, the sequence was all wrong. Abduct Snake One, push Paul off the deck, behead Snake Two, and finally write a threat on a bathroom mirror?

Odd that X's only explicit message should be the last. *MYOB* . . . Other than Jeff's affair with Gloria, what business here was so private and urgent that Bruce's interference posed a problem, let alone a threat serious enough for murder?

Answer that and you know everything, I thought. Or nothing. Either way, I can't.

Point Two: clues.

In the great unsorted morass of events, any odd or end might be a clue. What items was Tony counting that I wasn't? The Christmas lights around Bruce's throat? The tree toppled on the floor? "We Three Kings"? Puff pastries? Hot toddies? Bruce's fanatical neatness? His bleached decor? His coke habit?

Bingo.

My drowsy brain awoke like a Customs dog that's scented a false-bottomed suitcase. Somewhere in this house Bruce Easton had stashed five grams of cocaine. Maybe it was relevant, maybe it wasn't; but finding it was something I could accomplish before morning.

My eagle gaze swept from the fireplace to the half-bare Christmas tree to the foyer archway. I doubted Bruce troved his treasure in the bedroom, or Lilah would have been in and out of there all night. She'd taken her mini-Cuisinart from . . . where?

In the cupboards I found vases and floral clay. Placemats, linen napkins. Magazines. Racks of CDs and DVDs.

An enormous flat-screen TV on wheels. An amp, a CD/DVD player . . . and a polished rosewood box.

I carried the box to a lamp. No lock. Good. Inside was the coke grinder . . . but what on earth was a man's tie doing here? A common stripe, too shiny for silk—not Bruce's, clearly. Coiled on top of a paper packet (eureka! the coke!) just like that snake in Olive's purse.

My skin shuddered like a snake at shedding time. Caught in the hemmed tip of the tie was a pine needle.

Something wider and flatter than wired Christmas lights. Another pinnacle of poetic justice: *College Publisher Strangled with Old School Tie.*

My first impulse was to run downstairs and find Tony. But wait. What if this was his tie? Despite my doubts that Tony Cyr was X, I dared not ignore the possibility—however slim, however repellent—that his taste in ties ran to institutional stripes.

OK, Cory. What we need here is somebody with low odds of owning the thing and high odds of recognizing it.

Lilah.

No. Not at the cost of waking her.

Gloria?

Worse. All too easily I could picture Jeff Abels wearing this rumpled object—or bragging about the one-and-only tie he kept rolled up in his pocket in case of an accidental encounter with a semiformal occasion.

Olive . . . but I didn't want to wake her, either.

Clearly the best course was to remove the whole box to my room till I decided what to do next.

Using a copy of *Vanity Fair* as a tray so as to preserve any fingerprints, I carried the box across the foyer. I was turning my doorknob when I heard voices.

My spine stiffened. A break-in chez Lilah? What if X wasn't finished after killing Bruce?

No. Henry's door was ajar, a pale stripe of light in the

dim hall.

I let out the breath I'd been holding.

And recalled that Henry hadn't worn a tie this evening. According to Bruce, he seldom did. The other voice (I satisfied myself by tiptoeing closer) was female. Probably Olive.

Stow the box under my bed; and then knock.

I heard the hurried rustle of people who weren't expecting an interruption. "Yes?" called Henry. "Who is it?"

"Cory Thorne."

A pause, and whispers.

The door opened. "Come in, dear," said Olive. "Neither of us could sleep. Would you like a cup of decaffeinated tea?"

She'd actually brought a china teapot from the kitchen, with a trivet to prevent it from scarring Henry's dresser and a cozy to keep it warm. I smiled. "Thank you, no."

"Henry, dear," Olive said more sharply, "surely you have seen women in dressing gowns before."

He blinked. "I beg your pardon."

Not wishing to become a focal point for the wrong reasons, I apologized for disturbing them and explained that I'd come to ask their help. "I couldn't sleep either. When I heard your voices I thought, Well, if they're awake, too, maybe they'll welcome a distraction."

Henry harrumphed and declared himself only too delighted to assist a lady in distress. Olive gave me an encouraging but noncommittal nod.

"I found a tie," I said. "Polyester, with red, blue, green, and white stripes. Any idea who it might belong to?"

Henry looked at Olive. "Sounds like the one Jeff Abels lost last summer. Wouldn't you say, m'dear?"

"I haven't the least idea." Sitting, she crossed her legs. "Jeff lost a tie?" Her eyebrows implied disbelief. "When?"

"That wretched Sunday when Bruce's boy fell in the pond." Henry stared down at his clasped hands. "Dreadful thing. Just dreadful. Police everywhere— And then Jeff comes hot-footing across the lawn with two more of 'em at his heels. They'd cordoned off the drive to keep out rubberneckers, wouldn't let him in, so he parked his car around the field behind Edgar's trailer and sneaked through the woods. Dragged Bruce out of his grief to come vouch for him. Then, once he's in, he makes a nuisance of himself wanting to know who was where when. Pestering Lilah for beer and sandwiches." Henry shook his head. "Finally they let us all go—it must have been midnight—and there's Jeff blocking the door, buttonholing everyone to help him find his damned tie."

He looked over at Olive again. "You don't remember?"

"Mm," said Olive thoughtfully. "Now that you remind me, I do recall Jeff being more than usually Tiggerish." A quick self-conscious smile. "I had arrived late myself, just an hour or so before the accident, as I'd been visiting my grandson in Short Hills. I took him a set of Winnie-the-Pooh for an early birthday present. Not even three yet, that bright little sweetie, and by the time I left he was saying, "Gramma, more Pooh! More Pooh!"

She beamed. Henry looked embarrassed.

I said, "Do you remember Jeff asking about his lost tie?"

"Oh, yes," said Olive blandly. "I'm sure I must. If Henry— Yes. Certainly."

"Did anyone look for it?"

"Jeff must have," said Olive. "I didn't. Did you, Henry?"

"For a bit," he nodded. "I left before it turned up. *If* it turned up."

"Jeff is the person you should ask," Olive told me.

"I will."

"If you can pry him loose from Gloria," said Henry. "That young woman seems to have a grip on him like a C-clamp."

An uncharacteristic slur on a lady from the gallant Professor Howrigan. I inferred he hadn't said it for my benefit but for Olive's, and wondered why.

That was when Olive remarked, "Well, really, dear, what can one expect from a person of that ilk?"

The inclination of her head signaled a disapproval beyond class prejudice. My curiosity mounted. "Just what ilk do you mean?"

Olive's bony, ringed fingers went on stroking her fur collar. "I don't consider it telling tales out of school, dear, to say that this is the second of Bruce Easton's secretaries who have functioned in a very unprofessional capacity vis-à-vis Communicore authors, apparently with Bruce's full approval." Her lips pursed. "One gathers he selects a certain type of girl precisely for that purpose."

I was startled and—yes—shocked. "I find that hard to believe," I said. "From what Lilah's told me, I'd have thought that if Bruce suspected anything between Jeff and Gloria, he'd have stopped it."

"Lilah," said Olive, "is under a misapprehension."

It didn't take much arm-twisting to get her to part with the particulars. According to Olive, everyone plugged into the Communicore grapevine knew about that poor wretched girl who'd played the role of carrot to induce a well-known physicist to write a textbook; got pregnant, and became a stick. "Bruce's contract proposal was this," said Olive with flared nostrils. "You do the book, with the abortion charged to your manuscript preparation grant, and I'll see that your wife and children don't find out."

"Now, Olive," tut-tutted Henry, "that is pure undocumented gossip! I'm ashamed to hear someone like you—such unkind, unfair accusations—poor Cheryl, and Bruce bending over backwards to help her—"

"Rubbish! My land, Henry, why do you stand up for that man? He'd have done the same to you, you know he would, and yet you speak as if he were a saint, instead of a bum, which is what he was, to quote dear Tennessee. Wake up and smell the coffee!"

The flush on Henry's face deepened. "Olive, I don't think you ought to say such things."

His meaning was obvious. Olive barely hesitated before replying briskly, "Don't be foolish, dear. I've never refrained from speaking the truth about a person just because he was dead, and I see no reason to make an exception for Bruce Easton. In point of fact," she turned to me, "I was the one person here who got along well with Bruce."

"That's true," Henry nodded. "Aside from myself, Olive got along with Bruce better than anyone."

"I would go so far as to say that Henry and I have more cause than practically anyone in this house to regret his untimely end." Olive arranged her hands in her lap and assumed a modest expression. "We had intended to make an announcement this weekend which we very much wanted— we know Bruce would have—"

Her voice broke; and I didn't think she'd faked it.

"He would have wished us every happiness," Henry completed. Launching himself across the room, he proffered a handkerchief. "Now, now, m'dear. No tears. There, there."

Olive dabbed her eyes. Through her woe a smirk was emerging like the sun from behind a cloud. I recognized it instantly. I'd seen that same metal-melting brightness on the faces of more women than I can recall as they poised on the threshold of joint tax returns, monogrammed flatware, and his-and-hers towels.

"We had hoped," said Henry with awkward dignity, "that Bruce would stand up with us at our wedding."

Only a herculean feat of self-control kept my smile in place while I groped for a suitable response. "Well, congratulations," I managed at last. "I'm so sorry."

"The saddest thing is that he'll never know." Olive sighed poignantly. "It would have meant so much to him to see us both so happy."

My smile quivered dangerously.

"As far as standing up with us, I can't say I was quite as convinced as Henry of the appropriateness. Bruce was so," her brow puckered in a tiny frown, "*cavalier* about the bonds of marriage and family."

"That reminds me," said Henry. "We're keeping Cory from following up her leads on that tie."

Olive leaned her head against his arm. "Yes. Sweet of you, Cory dear, to be so patient with two old fogies in love. And I know you won't mind my asking you to keep our news to yourself for the present, will you?"

It was less a question than a command. "Of course." I stood up. "Henry, why did Bruce's cavalierness about marriage and family remind you of my finding a tie?"

He looked blank. "I don't know."

"Word association, perhaps," Olive suggested. "The ties that bind."

"Perhaps," Henry agreed.

"Well," I said, "best wishes to both of you, and thanks for your help."

"You know—" said Henry, and stopped.

"Yes?" prodded Olive.

Henry's right heel kicked abashedly at his left toe. He used the hand Olive wasn't monopolizing to scratch his ear. "Nothing. Sorry. Never mind."

"Nonsense," said Olive. "Whatever it is, dear, spit it out."

"Really, it's nothing." Henry looked unhappy. "I just— ah, that is, I don't—Honestly, I shouldn't have brought it up."

"Henry, for heaven's sake!"

"Oh, goodness." He was blushing again. "I only thought, since Cory— I mean, you were asking— Not that I'm suggesting any relationship beyond a simple correlation; as I said before, there are no data to my knowledge that would indicate—"

Olive pinched his arm. Henry let out a yip of pain.
"I think," he blurted, "you should speak to Jeff Abels."

CHAPTER FOURTEEN

Well, well! I mused as I crossed the hall. Biology certainly does make strange bedfellows! First Tony and Melinda, then Jeff and Gloria, and now Olive and Henry. Who's next? Edgar and Wayne Glynn?

I intended to follow Henry's suggestion, if only to find out why he'd prefaced it with so much hemming and hawing. I was debating whether to interrupt Jeff *in medias gloriae*, so to speak, when I saw that my door—which I'd shut after stowing the rosewood box—was ajar.

I froze. The implications of what I'd been doing hit me like a tsunami. This was no journalism assignment. The questions I'd fired at the Eastons' guests weren't research, but serious threats to someone who had already killed one person, maybe two.

How would X react to my truffle-hunting? By going back to sleep? Or by waiting behind my door with a weapon?

And here I stood like a rat in a maze, guessing which path led to the cheese and which to the electric shock.

When in doubt, find out.

I drew in a breath and flung the door wide.

The room looked exactly the same as I'd left it, with one exception. Someone with curly golden locks was sleeping on my spare bed.

No. Not sleeping. She was sobbing into her pillow.

Lurid visions ballooned in my head: Gloria finding the box, recognizing Jeff's tie, throwing it on the fire. Gloria showing Jeff the tie and Jeff throwing it on the fire. Gloria tearfully repenting. Cops grilling me under lights for blowing a murder investigation.

I looked under the bed. The box was still there.

With a silent thank-you to the patron saint of investigators, I slammed the door.

Gloria jerked like a frog on a dissecting table. "Jeff?"

"Guess again."

She rolled over. "Oh. Cory. I hope you don't mind. I just— Jeff and me—"

She dissolved into a fresh howl. I checked to make sure she'd found the box of tissues on the night table, and wondered what to do. I didn't want her here. Why couldn't she trot her emotional crisis down the hall to Henry, who liked helping ladies in distress?

The main thing was not to let her tell me her troubles. Having been on both sides of the confessional fence, I know asking a jilted woman to be brief is like asking the federal government to unpad its budget. Time was short. Whatever sympathy I might feel for Gloria, bawling into fistfuls of wet tissue, heedless of her unzipped pants and inside-out sweater, her cheeks streaked with mascara, her messy hair, her bare feet—

"Gloria," I sat on the edge of her bed, "what happened?"

I pulled up the bedspread and tucked it over her feet. Those quarry tile floors are *cold*.

"He said— He—" She hiccuped. Her shoulders heaved. She tried again. "He said horrible things to me!"

"Why?" I patted her leg. "Do you know?"

"It's— He said mean, horrible things!"

"Mmm," I nodded.

Gloria sniffled and groped for more tissues. "Such awful things, you wouldn't believe!"

Once more and I might agree with her. The evasiveness in her whine, not to mention her replies, was starting to strain my credulity.

"That's a shame, Gloria. What did he say?"

She blew her nose. "We were cuddled up together and I—I asked him, with Bruce gone, would he still see me? And he said—" Her whine became a wail. "He said, It depends whose secretary you are next!"

She crumpled again. I went over to my dresser and got out jeans, a heavy sweater, and a pair—no, two pairs—of socks.

This time Gloria's tears didn't last long. When she spoke again, anger was taking over from injury. "And *then* he said, What if they don't find out who killed him? And I said, Well, what? And he said, You wouldn't want to go on fucking somebody who might be a murderer, would you? *I* sure don't." She blew her nose again. "Can you believe he said that to me?"

I murmured something sympathetic and tossed her socks. Gloria, I suspected, had got cold feet in more ways than one. Considering how calculatedly she'd climbed into Jeff's bed, I couldn't see her fleeing it semi-dressed and weeping over a few insults. Not with knee-deep snow outside and half the night still to go.

"Practically *accusing* me!"

Wriggling into my jeans, I asked carefully, "Do you think he could have been trying to protect you? Like, maybe he's expecting the cops to give him a hard time for some reason, and he doesn't want you getting hurt?"

"Him? Hah!" Gloria thrust a foot into a sock. "What I think about Jeff Abels is he's a selfish prick. I don't know why I even bother with him. He's not that great a lover. He's too stuck on how long and how many times and positions and that stuff to have *fun*."

I was glad my head was inside my sweater. Out of the mouths of babes ... Tough luck, Jeff, old stud.

When I emerged, Gloria had the other sock on and was combing her hair with her fingers, disheveling it evenly all over. I said, "So did you get the idea he's afraid of you, or covering his ass, or what?"

Her palms went up: Who knows? "How could he be afraid of me? He can't possibly believe I killed Bruce. I'm such a softie I can't even smack my cat when he jumps on the kitchen table." She hugged her knees. "You know what? I think his brain got scrambled when he almost ate that snake's head. Jeff, not my cat. No joke, I really think that did something to him."

Here was a topic I was willing to talk about. "Why?"

Gloria was incredulous. "Why? Because it's *gross!* I mean—*ecchh!* I just about heaved right there in the living room."

Half the purpose of asking a question like *why?* is to see which way the subject takes it. Gloria's naïveté sounded genuine. I said, "I meant, Why do you connect the snake incident with the strange way he's acting now? What did he do or say to give you that idea?"

She considered. "No one special thing," she said finally. "He's been kind of weird all night. Like flirting with Lilah when we were doing the tree. Did you notice? He used to jerk Bruce's chain like that when Tony worked here, but not lately. And even before that, he seemed"—she bit her lip in concentration—"different. Wrought up. Like, mad, maybe."

"Do you think— Could the snake's head have reminded him of last summer when Bruce's son died and the other snake disappeared? Along with Jeff's tie, right?"

"Oh, boy." Gloria flopped onto her back across the bed. "That's an idea. Except I bet Jeff doesn't remember the tie. He's no clothes horse, to put it mildly. I bet he forgot about it the minute he left here."

"After badgering everybody in the house to help him look for it?"

"Where'd you hear that?" Gloria rolled onto her elbow. "Henry was the one who raised a fuss. He was all over Jeff that day like a cheap suit. Yelling at him about sneaking in the back way, getting the cops PO'd, disturbing Bruce when Henry thought he shouldn't be disturbed— Which Bruce could've cared less; he was too wacked out about Paul to notice if Jeff had danced down the driveway naked. That was scary," she added. "I've seen Bruce obsess about stuff before, but never like that."

My mind was spinning like a lettuce dryer. Henry was the one who raised a fuss? Jeff wouldn't remember losing his tie? Was this a case of two people recalling the same events differently, or was somebody lying?

"This tie," I said. "What did it look like?"

"Striped. You know. The kind they figure goes with everything. Guys like him who think they're too important to bother, they're so busy saving the world, sticking needles in white mice, they keep one tie in their lab in case they have to go schmooze with the money people at some fancy restaurant."

"The money people," I said casually, though my nose was twitching with the scent of truffles, "you mean, like Olive?"

"Yeah. That must be some life, huh? Every hot-shot scientist in Boston kissing her ass. And she didn't even have to work for it." Gloria was drawing indentations on the bedspread with her fingernail. "Marry a rich guy with a research lab— I'll tell you, I'd be her secretary in a minute! Move out of my folks' house, get a nice little apartment in Allston near my sister . . ."

"Have you ever talked to Olive about a job? Do you know her very well?"

"Nah. You even want to be a receptionist at that place, you need a Ph.D. But I was thinking, if Jeff works it out to quit Harvard and go to Chute Labs, I'd see if he could get me in."

She blew her nose one last time; wadded up her tissues and tossed them in the basket between our beds. Under one eye a smudge of mascara had dried like a bruise.

Gloria, I thought, you are turning out to be an unexpectedly fascinating young woman.

"So is Jeff—what would you call it?—courting Olive? How's the romance going?"

"Hah! Maybe that's what's bugging him. Olive's not falling for the 'Hi, babe, I'm God' schtick. He was pretty PO'd at Tony, I'll tell you, for broadcasting that he's hoping she'll steal him. Last thing he wanted her to hear! Or Bruce and Melinda, either. Jeff's been playing both ends against the middle. Sign the book contract for money, and then lobby like mad to get bought out by Chute Labs before the manuscript's due."

"You mean, he got an advance against royalties for his proposed textbook which Olive would have to pay back if she hires him and he doesn't deliver the book?"

"Not *have to*," said Gloria defensively. "I mean—well, legally, sure; but they don't always. A lot of academics sign contracts just to get the advance, you know?—with no intention of writing a book. Usually if they stall long enough, the publisher gives up and writes it off. That's something Bruce was changing, was taking them to court for the money. At least you have to give Jeff, he's trying to do the right thing."

I refrained from pointing out that wooing Peter to pay off Paul wasn't everyone's idea of the right thing. Nor that fear of a lawsuit might be a motive for murder.

I stood up. "I'm going to go talk to him."

Gloria was alarmed. "About me?"

"About Bruce."

The rosewood box I'd leave where it was. Who'd look under the bed next to an angry, sniffling, half-dressed Gloria?

In the doorway I paused. "Just for the sake of argument, if you had to pick someone in this house as the killer, who would it be?"

"Nobody." Gloria was positive. "It was a tramp. You know that side door's always unlocked—"

"Oh, come on. Humor me."

She debated. In her twisting mouth I saw the house policy of see-no-evil, hear-no-evil, speak-no-evil warring with personal inclination.

"OK," she succumbed. "Just for the sake of argument—Melinda."

"Melinda! That's interesting. Why?"

Gloria's mascara-smeared face took on a crafty expression. "Look what happened when Bruce made her choose between staying married to Tony and becoming a vice president."

"She opted for the VP?"

"You can bet she was on the phone to a divorce lawyer before Bruce walked out the door."

"What's that got to do with . . . ?"

"She swore before God to stick with Tony in sickness and in health, for richer or poorer," Gloria replied vehemently. "If she'd sell out her wedding vows to get a promotion, what's she going to do to Bruce when she sees him letting the division go down the tubes?"

I felt a familiar tensing in my gut. "Down the tubes? That's not what I've heard. Just the opposite."

"Well, sure," said Gloria. "What do you think, they're going to shout it from the rooftops?"

"But—" I frowned. "Do you have evidence of this?"

Bad choice of words. In the silence that followed I could hear the catlike tread of the Oxbridge police—Gloria's former schoolmates, perhaps, now guardians of the town in which she lived with her parents—marching up Bruce Easton's driveway: *You got evidence for these accusations, Gloria? You want to go to jail for slander?*

"I only said it for the sake of argument." Gloria glowered at her toes. "I'm not accusing anybody of anything."

"Of course not." I resisted the urge to grab her shoulders and shake her. "Anyway, we're not talking about classified information. If you're right, the cops are bound to get onto it; and if you're wrong, why should I care?"

I walked over to the dresser. Gloria's head came up. Her big smudged barn-owl eyes followed me as I rummaged in my purse.

"Naturally, Melinda being your boss, I can appreciate your not wanting to say anything she wouldn't like."

"Screw Melinda," retorted Gloria with unexpected energy. "You think I'm afraid of her? Honest to god, if they make her head of the division, I'll be out of here so fast she can eat my dust."

I found my notebook and slid it into my back pocket. "Then why not tell me—"

"Uh-uh. Nope. I can't." Gloria wiggled her toes in my second-best socks. "If they don't promote Melinda, I'm going to need all my brownie points with Billy Bally." Her eyes rolled. "You wouldn't believe how hard it is to find an executive secretary job in Oxbridge, Connecticut."

Had we but world enough, and time, I reflected on my way up the hall, *This coyness, lady, were no crime.*

Maybe the cops could unclam Gloria. As for me, it appeared my only hope of finding out if she'd told me anything actionable was to open up another source.

Who else had access to Higher Ed's bill of health? Melinda, obviously. Scratch that—she'd be as foolish to tell me the truth as I would be to believe her. For if Gloria's allegations were correct, Melinda Doerr had a peach of a motive for killing her boss. Picture the headline: *Madame Machiavelli Murders Mentor!*

But that was a knee-jerk journalist's reflex. The question wasn't, Could I create a plausible case against Melinda? Of course I could. The question was, Did she do it? Did overweight, overzealous Melinda, who could scarcely look at Bruce Easton without genuflecting, sacrifice him on the altar of ambition?

Unthinkable.

But then so must Queen Elizabeth's courtiers have felt up to the moment the axe felled her boy-toy Essex.

By the time I reached Jeff's room I'd settled on two working hypotheses. One: If Melinda hadn't strangled Bruce to save Communicore Higher Ed, Gloria had choked him for sticking pins in her diaphragm. Two: Freelance journalism must be the best background in the world for detective work, since you learn not only to think while sleepwalking but to tolerate a degree of chaos that would send lesser mortals screaming for cover.

Jeff's door was closed. However, he was not alone.

"Hey, Ms. Thorne." Tony waved at me from the far side of a queen-sized bed. "Come join the party."

I hate being scooped, even by a partner. What wee-hours revelation had dragged Tony out of cushion-land to this room? How had he known Jeff would be interruptable? Or didn't he care?

I stepped in past Jeff, who'd put on a sport jacket over pajama bottoms and wore the haggard look of a man whose paramour hadn't quit without a fight.

Tony patted the bed invitationally.

No way, I thought.

I said, "You're mighty chipper for somebody who was half asleep twenty minutes ago." I turned back to our host. "Has he always been like this? Mr. Perpetual Motion?"

"Yeah." Jeff didn't even try to switch on the old come-hither glint. Apparently the most his eyes could do was stay open. "We used to do our best work on my book at two in the morning."

"I gather your book's been less fun since you started doing it with Bruce and Melinda during business hours."

Jeff groaned. Tony grinned. "Now, don't go throwing red herrings at us, Ms. Thorne. Professor Abels and I are digging truffles. Sure you won't have a seat? OK, then. Where were we?"

Jeff, sinking onto the bed, grunted, "The snake."

He kept both feet on the off-white rug and gripped the off-white bedspread with both hands. I propped myself against the wall halfway between him and Tony.

"Right." Tony nodded. "Tell Ms. Thorne what she missed."

Jeff gazed up at me. "We were talking about Paul, Bruce's crippled kid who drowned in the pond last summer. Tony wanted to know what happened to his other pet snake. And I said, How should I know? Paul could have been playing with them. Maybe he thought he'd take one for a ride in his chair, and when he fell overboard, so did the snake."

"The railing was broken," I said. "By whom?"

"Nobody I'd ever heard of," said Jeff. "Some friends of Bruce's. They were gone before this crowd arrived."

Tony got to his feet. "Is this drowned-snake scenario a virgin hypothesis or did you test it?"

"Test it?"

"That's right, professor. Conduct research. Ask questions. Who was in Paul's room that afternoon besides Lilah and Bruce? Did somebody take that snake out of its cage and give it to him? That's where they were kept, don't forget—at the far end of the house, not ten feet from the deck like they are now." He was pacing as he'd done during our conversation in the bathroom. "If somebody did remove the snake from the aquarium, why? How did he or she know Paul wanted to play with it? Mental telepathy?"

"Do you know how Paul got from his room to the deck?" I interposed.

"Yes," said Tony. "Bruce put him into the chair and wheeled him to the kitchen for lunch. Lilah took him from there to the deck. In between they each made one trip to the bathroom. Neither Bruce nor Lilah said anything to the cops, and Lilah said nothing to me, about seeing a snake on Paul's lap, finding a snake in his pockets, or having any snake-related exchanges on his computer."

Jeff gave a weary shrug. "OK, so it was a dumb idea. So sue me."

He didn't seem surprised by the speed and thoroughness with which Tony had dissected his theory. I was. I had a vivid vision of Rik Green at *Phases* whipping his blue pencil through a manuscript I'd thought was airtight. The kind of editor a writer would gladly kill . . . or kill for.

Was that how Jeff—and Henry, and Melinda and Gloria and the rest of them—felt about Tony Cyr?

"Now, now. No sulks, professor." Tony paused opposite Jeff, cocked his head and wiggled his eyebrows. "The double helix wasn't built in a day."

No wonder they let him in after his performance on the pond, then. Even after his breakdown, firing, and exile. To his authors, a good editor is more than a partner—he's an alter ego.

"If the data don't fit the theory, let's put our heads back together like Frankie Crick and Johnny Watson and think up a theory that fits the data."

Tony the Fool. Tony the window-blaster, house-haunter, snow-pisser, Lone Ranger. This must be how the Victorians felt, I mused darkly, watching apes at the zoo and cursing Darwin.

"Jesus Christ, will you give me a break?" Jeff's elbows

were on his knees, his fingers buried in his black hair. "Let the cops generate their own hypotheses. I've got other things on my mind right at the moment besides a bunch of shit that happened last August."

"And her name is G!" Tony warbled. "L!"

"Shut up!"

"What have you done with the body, anyhow? I deduce from the items of feminine apparel on the floor that she was here recently. You haven't—god forbid—mislaid her?"

"Back off, dammit." Jeff staggered to his feet. "You've got no goddam business giving me crap about women."

He looked almost mad enough to take a swing at Tony if provoked any further. Before push came to shove, however, we heard a flurry of fists on the door.

"Jeff!"

A woman, all right, but not Gloria.

The door flew open. "Jeff! Cory!" gasped Olive Chute. "And Tony! Thank heaven!" She panted for breath. "What's happened to Lilah?"

CHAPTER FIFTEEN

Tony and I nearly collided in our rush around the bed.

"What? Is she hurt?" He grabbed Olive's shoulders. "Where is she?"

"Gone! I went to look in on her—just to make sure— The door was open. I can't find her anywhere!"

"Anywhere?" drawled Jeff. "Tony here's a stickler for accuracy. Did you try—"

But Tony had already bolted down the hall.

I took Olive's arm. "She's bound to be OK. She must have gone to get something—or maybe there's someplace, when she needs privacy—"

We caught up with Tony in Lilah's room, where he was thrashing through the clothes in her closet.

He stuck his head out. "Not a trace."

"Did you check the studio?" I asked Olive.

She shook her head. Tony backed out of the closet and loped off without a word.

Surely, I reasoned, Lilah must have gone to get a sheet, another pillow— Or a drink, a magazine— Whatever she does when she can't sleep—

The rosewood box.

If she looked in its usual place and didn't find it, what

would she do?

Depends what she wanted. Valium? Sleeping pills? Plenty in her medicine cabinet. Cocaine? The murder weapon? The box itself, as a memento mori? Search the house, probably.

Olive was gazing out the french doors to the deck, twisting the rings on her fingers. I touched her shoulder. "Which guest rooms did you check?"

"All but Melinda's." She turned to me with worry and appeal in her eyes. "I woke everyone. No one's seen her." With a vestige of her old spirit she added, "Gloria has moved into your room. One bit of good news, anyhow."

Easy for you to say, I thought. "Where else could Lilah have gone? Does this house have an attic? A basement?"

"The basement door is padlocked. The way up to the attic is through there." She pointed at the closet from which Tony had just emerged.

"Where else could she—?"

Olive's eyebrows lifted expressively. "Nowhere."

Nowhere. Unless she was after a bigger memento mori than the rosewood box.

"Olive," I steered her toward the door, "where does Lilah keep her coats?"

In the front hall closet we found my wool tweed, Olive's mink, Melinda's green-and-silver down, Gloria's fake fur, and a dress-up Persian lamb. We thumbed through raincoats, jackets, shawls, and slickers. What we didn't find was the black-and-white tweed ("very much like yours, dear") that Olive recalled Lilah wearing to Chute Labs a month ago.

I slung my coat over my shoulder. "We'll need a search party. Why don't you go find Tony while I get my boots."

"Wait." Olive's gem-encrusted fingers were heavy on my arm. "Let's take advantage of all these fine windows first, to see what we can see."

What we could see from the living room was a maze of

shadows. Wind and snow had blurred Tony's footprints on the pond to ripples. While it didn't appear anyone was out there now, a marching band could have passed ten minutes ago and we'd never know.

The far shore looked the same as it had from Lilah's room: a dark crescent of snow-laden trees, behind which rose a wooded hill. To our immediate right the willow's bare black branches veiled a big wedge of pond; and the deck hid the rest.

I grimaced. "Black-and-white tweed, huh?"

"Not even dear Jackson could be sure of spotting her," Olive concurred sadly.

Behind us a distant clamor broke out. Abruptly I remembered Tony dashing toward the studio, sleeping quarters of his ex-wife.

As I ran through the kitchen the shouting became distinct: Tony bellowing, Melinda shrieking.

I yanked open the studio door. Melinda stood behind the piano, eyes flashing, blue bathrobe flapping, brandishing the bottle Tony had dropped in her suitcase. He was advancing in a karate crouch, both hands poised edgewise. Every few seconds he'd slice the air and roar. Melinda had her back to the sliding glass doors, as if to defend them with her last furious breath.

But the war cries they hurled at each other were like no curses I'd ever heard.

"Pullins et al!" yelled Tony. "Nonmajors intro!"

"I signed that!" Melinda yelled back.

"I set it up!"

"I'm developing it!"

With a hop Tony rounded the piano. Melinda swished her bottle in a threatening arc. One step back and she'd shatter that eight-foot pane of glass.

"Yuhasz! Prep chem!" Tony shouted.

"Saturated market!"

"Breakeven only six K!"

"Not with two colors!"

"Don't need two colors!" His hand slashed the diminishing space between them.

"Pepper's got four!" hollered Melinda, slashing back with her bottle.

"Pepper's a dog! A lame" (chop!) "limping" (chop!) "bow-wow!"

Oh, fine! I thought dazedly. They've both gone smack out of their minds.

Tony took a jump which landed him opposite the piano bench. I ran down the wide carpeted stairs. "Stop! Hold it!"

Tony's hands dropped. Melinda lowered her bottle.

"She won't let me out there." Panting, he jerked his head at the glass doors. "Afraid I'll desecrate the corpse."

With his knees unbent he looked barely less crazed. "Did you—" I started; and redirected my question to Melinda. "Did he tell you we can't find Lilah?"

She nodded shortly. "The lights are on. You can see for yourself she's not here."

There under a floodlight lay the plastic-bagged package Henry had described. If Lilah had come near it, one of them would have noticed.

"Her coat's gone," I told them. "I thought too she might be looking for Bruce's body."

"Well, if so, she hasn't found it," said Melinda, as if that settled that.

I turned to Tony. "You know the grounds, don't you? Why don't you round up some help and get a search party going? In pairs, for safety."

Tony went with a speed that suggested he was as glad to leave Melinda as she was to see him go. I remembered that para-marital claustrophobia, when just being in the same room makes you writhe like two fish caught on one hook.

Not that I wasn't doing my share of flopping. I hated to

waste time here with Lilah missing; but I couldn't pass up the chance to ask Melinda if Communicore Higher Ed had thrived or dived under Bruce Easton.

"Are you OK?"

"Oh, yes." She set the bottle on the piano and moved toward the sofa, stately now as the QE 2. "Tony's always been prone to these outbursts. It's just worse since . . ."

"This must be rough for you."

"It certainly is," she said vehemently. "Besides being a dear friend, Bruce is the finest publisher I've ever worked with. Here we are on the verge of our best year ever— Oh, I just can't bear for him not to see that!"

If she was lying, she was doing an expert job. I said, "That's odd. I'd heard the division had fallen off since Bruce took over."

"Hah!" Melinda's eyes blazed like Bunsen burners. "Look at our sales, up six point eight percent over last year! Look at our profits, up eight point two percent! Look at our upcoming Spring list, the biggest ever! And then look at whoever told you that garbage, and ask yourself where they were when some—some *bastard* murdered Bruce!"

She looked ready to leap up and grab her weapon again. "OK," I said hastily.

"Who said it?" she demanded. "Tony?"

I replied that a lot of people had said a lot of things, all of which I took in confidence and with a grain of salt. "And in that spirit, I'd appreciate anything you can tell me about who might have killed Bruce, or why."

Melinda shook her head emphatically. "It's preposterous! Who would? Who *could?* Everyone here owed him so much! Of course, trust Tony to twist that, with his innuendoes, drunken gossip, jealousy—"

"I'm not sure what you mean," I cut in.

"Oh, you remember." She tossed her head impatiently. "That rot about Olive stealing Henry and Jeff for Chute Labs.

Harvard professors!—think they're God's gift to science. If they wanted to break their contracts, would they come here for a Christmas party? No! They'd have their lawyers on the phone to our lawyers!"

"But someone killed Bruce, Melinda. How do you explain that?"

Her chin went up. "I don't have to. I'm a publisher, not a policeman. And if anyone here appreciates it or not, I'm also a corporate officer, which means I have a responsibility to keep this situation from causing any more damage."

Meaning, I understood, no opening up to the media, however harmlessly disguised as a houseguest.

"Not an easy job," I agreed. "I guess you'll have your hands full long after the police have come and gone. Taking over a thriving division . . ."

The Bunsen burners flared again. "That is not a foregone conclusion. The Board will decide. I may very well—more than likely—be stuck as caretaker while they interview outside. I have nothing to gain and everything to lose from Bruce's death, if that's what you're asking."

"Thanks for your help." I started up the steps. "We can use a hand looking for Lilah as soon as you're dressed."

The living room was empty. Tony must have gotten a search organized.

In my room I found, not Gloria, but Olive, crouched on hands and knees peering under my bed. Her cashmere-clad derriere loomed two feet from the rosewood box.

At my exclamation she backed out. Her face, to my relief, was dusty but incurious.

She and Tony (said Olive), the self-dubbed Committee of the Interior, were searching every person-sized cranny in the house. Henry, too, though he'd fixated on finding the key to the basement padlock. Wayne Glynn had valiantly struggled back into his wet boots to go fetch Edgar, as well as Edgar's dog, snow-blower, and industrial-strength flashlights. Jeff, less valiantly, had volunteered to look outside each door for footprints, aided by Gloria. Olive's lips compressed: One couldn't help feeling—so graceless—distressing lack of judgment—

I reported that Melinda would be along shortly. Now, if Olive would move her search to the next room . . .

The box was untouched. All the same, it needed a better hiding place. I stuffed my feet into almost-dry boots and the box under my coat.

The night was bitter but not nose-puckeringly brutal. Windblown snow stung my face and hissed around my legs— the only sound in this eerily muffled landscape. From the side door down to the parking area there were tracks I could walk in. Wayne's? Too bad to leave a record of where I'd come . . . but the wind would soon fix that.

I locked the box in the trunk of my car.

The footprints continued down the driveway, now scalloped with soft peaks like some exotic dessert. Did Edgar recall how Lilah used to wheel Paul up to the road? Would he guess she'd headed that way?

I had no reason not to head that way myself but a hunch. I went the other direction, around Melinda's studio, past the kitchen, below the dining area, and swung downhill toward the pond.

My first step away from the house took me into a drift above my knees. Except for the snow's cold weight I could have been a bather groping for a sand bar, praying the next wave wouldn't wash over my head. I began to realize how foolish this was, charging through eighteen inches of fresh powder alone in the middle of the night. Should I go back and get Tony? No . . . but be careful. Although I'd wound a bright red scarf around my neck and borrowed a house flashlight, neither would save me if I fell outside the floodlights.

As Lilah might have done twenty minutes ago . . .

"Lilah!" I shouted. "Lilah, can you hear me?"

No answer. No sound at all but my heaving breath and the soft squeak-crunch of my boots.

Down here the shadows along the pond's rim looked like a designer hallucination. All this high-contrast was jangling my nerves. Too easy to picture Bruce on the far side of the River Styx, blotting out colors in death as he had in life . . .

I told myself not to be fanciful. There were enough crazy people up there behind the lights.

Cold was starting to numb my toes and fingers, thanks partly to the snow that kept sliding into my boot tops. The scarf around my face was sticky with frost; my mouth tasted of wet wool. And this was the easy leg of the trip.

"Lilah!"

To my right the willow tree cascaded overhead like a frozen fountain. Behind its trunk, blackness. The deck beyond it cut off the light. I thought of Bruce plunging down this slope into murky water, squinting up at the wheelchair caught in the splintered railing.

I called in exterminators to poison the pond and dredge out the lilies. Why should fish swim and flowers bloom where my son died?

Surely this was where Lilah would look for her husband. The corpse in the garbage bags? Empty. Let Melinda have it. Only to her, who couldn't seduce him while he lived, was Bruce's castoff body precious. What Lilah sought was his soul; and that had gone after Paul's.

"Lilah!" Chilled air seared my lungs. "Lilah!"

I paused, gasping, a few feet above the bank. No sign of footprints. Blast this snowstorm! I hadn't a hope of finding her unless she answered.

Then I heard a noise.

It didn't sound human. A trick of the wind, more likely,

whining through the willow branches. Or the deck creaking on its pilings.

There it was again. Coming from—where? That black cave under the deck?

I switched on my flashlight: useless at this distance.

Bruce had said he'd waded around the willow. So the shoreline must run just below it. Hard to tell through these drifts. I opted for a land route on the uphill side. Haul one leg out of its snow hole and thrust it down again. Then the other leg. My last legs.

"Come on, Lilah." I wiped my wet nose on my wet coat sleeve. "Give me a goddam break."

And suddenly the drift sloped away, and I was stepping through a mere six inches of snow.

I pointed my light up and saw the planked floor of the deck.

Then something smashed my arm so hard I dropped the flashlight. Pain jolted through my whole body. I stumbled; tried to turn. A second blow caught the side of my head. My brain seemed to explode. I fell backward. The snow came up to meet me: deep, strong, sucking me in like an undertow.

My last thought was amazement that drowning in snow didn't feel cold.

I woke to a throbbing headache. I couldn't find my arms or legs. Wet leaves clung to my cheek. I tried to get up and blacked out again.

When I came to, I felt so cold that at first I wasn't sure I was alive. My hands, my feet, and one side of my face were numb. My head still hurt, but not quite so violently as before. I opened my eyes: nothing. Was I blinded? No. There were gradations in the darkness which gradually became shapes: a paint bucket, heaped leaves, a ladder.

I was lying on the ground. Forcing my mind into motion,

I rewound. Someone had jumped me. Whacked me on the head. X, presumably. Which meant I was lucky. He or she must have meant for the snow to bury me. Instead it had spewed me out under the Eastons' deck.

My stomach felt queasy from the pain in my head and arm, but the rest of my body was beginning to respond to orders. I rolled up to a sitting position and, wincing, scanned around. Whoever had knocked me down wasn't evidently here now.

The musty earth and leaves smelled pungent after snow. There was my hat. I shook it off and pulled it back on my head. Oh, good—and my flashlight. In its watery beam the objects around me looked bleached and unreal, like strange sea creatures from a depth where no sunlight penetrates.

How had X managed to surprise me? If anyone had followed me down from the house, I'd have noticed. X must have slipped out another door—evaded the others in the search party; got a head start—

Something rustled. I whirled around, flashlight raised.

Nobody there.

I hauled myself upright, leaned against a post and waited for the throbbing in my head to subside. The noise hadn't come from behind me, but from somewhere under the deck.

My light skipped over rubble and leaves and fell on black-and-white tweed.

Lilah huddled in the far corner. Her face was smudged with dirt, her hair a tangle of dust and twigs. She shrank away from the light.

"Lilah! Are you OK?"

She answered with a small wordless nod. Then her hunched shoulders unclenched, and her face lifted toward me. "Are you?"

"Yes. I think so. What— Did you— What happened?"

At first she didn't reply, just gazed at me across twenty feet of debris-strewn slope. I hoped she would come out to where I was. I didn't relish crawling in after her.

"Did you see who hit me?"

She nodded. "Bruce."

Oh. Terrific.

"He thought you were me. Your coat. And your hair."

"But— Lilah, what gave you the idea— I mean, I don't see how Bruce—"

"He wants me to come with him. To be with him and Paul," she said simply. "Our family together again."

I shuddered. Here in this snow-walled subterranean cave it didn't sound implausible. I could almost feel Bruce Easton's hands—those thin cold collector's hands—reaching for his wife across the frozen water, luring her to join him in Hades.

Pull yourself together, Cory!

"Lilah, whoever attacked me, it wasn't Bruce. It was someone alive."

She shook her head. "I saw him."

"What exactly did you see? How did you recognize him?"

"I can't— I know it was Bruce!"

She drew herself tighter into the corner. This won't do, I thought. I've got to get her up to the house. If X comes back, we could be history—both of us.

"You dragged me out of the snow?" I said.

A tiny nod.

"You saved my life. So help me again, Lilah. We need to go inside. Now."

She pressed both fists against her mouth.

"You can't wait here for Bruce. He's gone." Pause. "Was that why you came down?"

Lilah's fists inched down to her chin, then her chest. "I had the dream again," she whispered.

"What dream was that?"

"I couldn't stop it." Still a whisper—hoarse, as if her

voice wouldn't come out any louder. "I couldn't save him! I couldn't cut the rope!"

Through my mind flickered images of the safe sane world where I'd lived until yesterday. Christmas presents. Jingle bells. Sprinkling colored sugar on frosted cookies. Writing messages on Unicef cards: *All's well here!*

"OK," I said with forced cheerfulness. "Let's go up to the house. I'll make some tea, and you can tell me—"

"No!" That was no whisper. She shrank into her coat again, pulling in feet and hands like an alarmed turtle. "You don't understand!"

I tried to keep the pain in my head out of my voice. "How can I understand anything when we're freezing our butts in the dirt?" Wrong approach. Try again. "Listen, Lilah. If you think this is some kind of secret rendezvous spot for you and Bruce, wait a few minutes. The search party is on its way here right now."

Her mouth quivered as if she were about to cry. Progress, I told myself optimistically: her own emotions this time, not drugs or hysteria. I waited. And finally Lilah moved, scrabbled around to a sitting position and slid across to meet me.

As we started up the hill I let out a frosty sigh. Every part of me ached. The snow dragged at my boots, heavy, wet, and cold. But the worst was over! Soon I'd be climbing into a hot bath, then a warm dry bed. In the morning the plows would come, and the police. Reason would take over; and I could point my VW out of Oxbridge, Connecticut.

Lilah was right. I didn't understand.

CHAPTER SIXTEEN

Half an hour later Lilah and I sat cross-legged on the twin beds in my room, sipping cocoa and pretending to be Mount Holyoke girls again.

Olive had called off the searchers by banging on an omelet pan with a wooden spoon. Jeff and Gloria arrived first, not from outdoors but downstairs, where they might or might not have been looking for Lilah. Then Melinda and Henry—he with a fistful of keys, none of which (he regretted to report) unlocked the basement. Wayne and Edgar straggled in from the driveway, followed by Tony.

I checked shoes and pants cuffs and confirmed that Wayne, Edgar, and Tony had been out in the snow. Jeff, Gloria, Henry, Melinda, and Olive had either stayed indoors or changed clothes.

OK. So now we tell everybody about X's attack, propose combing the house for wet garments, counter the inevitable protests . . .

But luck intervened. Lilah, with the eerie clarity of a woman on the verge of a nervous breakdown, found Bruce's coat and boots in his bedroom closet, clotted with snow.

So we switched to Plan B. Lilah apologized to her guests: aftershock, nightmare, thank you all so much. I scrutinized faces, more out of habit than hope, and learned only that everyone here would be glad to get back to bed.

"It wasn't Bruce after all," Lilah said now, cupping her mug in both hands. I couldn't tell if she was glad or sorry.

"Down there? No."

She spoke to her cocoa. "It was whoever killed him. Wearing Bruce's things."

"Looks like it."

"He did come for me, though. I was right about that." Her eyes lifted to meet mine. "You got there just in time."

"So did you, for me."

She shuddered. And jump-shifted into reminiscences: Wasn't this cocoa better than the skin-coated stuff at school? Remember cooking Jiffy-Pop on hot plates? You bet. And what's-her-name who wore pajamas with feet? And the snoring sophomores? Sure. And those saggy dormitory mattresses? Yup. And midnight fire drills? and sneaking in after curfew?

From Lilah's shaky nostalgic smile I inferred her real reason for this charade: to rewind time, in hopes of erasing the tape.

About X's attack she couldn't tell me much. Her nightmare had woken her. Terrified, groggy, she'd fled from a monster that came charging at her out of the jungle. Plunged downhill through swamp and underbrush. Crawled into a cave to hide.

"Not to meet Bruce?"

She looked puzzled. No; in the dream Bruce stayed behind. "I didn't even know he was there until . . ."

"Until what?"

Lilah frowned, pursed her lips, shook her head. "Until I saw him, I guess."

"Do you remember seeing him?"

"No."

"About that nightmare—"

The door latch clicked.

I put down my cocoa and slid off the bed. "Who is it?"

"Your partner," came Tony's muffled voice. Three seconds later the door opened and he entered, twirling a credit card in his fingers.

"Can't you knock?" asked Lilah.

"You wouldn't have let me in."

I was standing in his path. He maneuvered around me. "Right, Ms. Thorne?"

"Right." And for good reasons, I added silently. One, your pants cuffs are wet. Two, I haven't forgotten that Lilah's first words when you appeared at the murder scene were *Stay back! The police are coming!*

She didn't look afraid of him now, though. On the contrary: her expression, even her posture had visibly unclenched.

Tony sat on the window seat across from her bed. "Face it, ladies, you need a bodyguard."

A thin smile crossed Lilah's face.

"On my honor, I'm armless and harmless. If you don't trust me, search me."

I sent Lilah an inquiring look. With the twigs combed out of her hair she could have modeled for Scheherezade: lacy black shawl over white satin shoulders, fingers toying with the fringe, and sad eyes to melt a sultan's heart.

"Maybe he can help," she said. "Do you think?"

What I thought was that I had yet to hear why she was so sure the Oxbridge police would believe she and Tony were lovers who'd collaborated to kill Bruce.

"Thumbs up or down," said Tony, "or I'm going out to the lobby for popcorn."

"Yeah," I said. "Maybe he can."

Lilah turned to Tony. "I was just going to tell Cory about my nightmare."

He nodded and settled into the cushions. I wished I'd

had more sleep. Or that we'd made coffee instead of cocoa. Or that I'd brought my tape recorder. If Lilah's nightmare held the key to X's identity, would I even recognize it?

"It starts," said Lilah, "with Bruce and me on a jungle safari with a bunch of other people. We're hiking through this thick rainforest, vines and snakes." She sketched in the air. "And pretty soon we realize something is trying to kill us."

Tony started to speak. I shot him a warning glare and he subsided.

"We keep running into traps. Like when you step on leaves and fall into a pit full of spikes, or it grabs your foot and swings you up in a net." Lilah's tone stayed determinedly narrative. "By now I'm so scared I can hardly keep walking, but I have to because of Bruce. But these people, our friends, keep disappearing into the traps . . . and later we find their skeletons in a cage with the clothes still on . . ."

She faltered. Tony stirred, as if to reach out to her, but he stopped himself.

Lilah took a breath and continued.

"We come to a clearing. We all know this is the most dangerous place. Everybody's terrified except Bruce. It's like it's his job to secure the area and make camp. And part of me thinks, Well, thank goodness he's in charge; but another part can't understand why he's so calm when we're probably all about to die.

"So it gets dark, and I'm lying in our tent under mosquito netting, waiting for Bruce to come to bed. And I hear sounds like somebody crying. I look outside and there's Bruce and another man, the head native, standing at the edge of the clearing, talking. And then the native chief goes away, and I see what Bruce is doing. He's tying a baby goat to a tree by a long rope. It's the goat that's making this pitiful noise. Even from here I can see it's paralyzed with fright because it knows it's the bait for whatever's out there waiting to kill us."

Lilah's eyes slid from me to Tony. "So Bruce goes away, and I'm still watching this goat. I can physically feel its terror." She shuddered. "I can't believe they did this — that there isn't some other way to save the camp besides putting this poor baby out there to get ripped to pieces. And I start walking towards it. I'm thinking, This isn't fair! The monster is after *us*, not the goat! And I'm halfway across the clearing when it hits me: The goat isn't the bait. *I'm* the bait. This whole thing is a set-up."

Again Lilah faltered, but she resumed quickly. "They knew I'd see the goat and come out to cut the rope, and that would lure the whatever-it-is out of the jungle. And as soon as I figure this out, I know it's already here. It's hiding in the shadows between me and the baby goat. The goat is jerking at the rope, crying and struggling to get away, and I think: I'll run up fast and cut the rope, and run back before it can catch me. But then I realize I don't have a knife. So I start back toward the tent, and there's this horrible roar, and I look around and the goat is screaming, I can't see it, just this huge shadow, and blood is gushing out, and I run to the goat but I'm too late. Its insides are torn open, and one little foot is kicking . . . And then, and then I remember I was supposed to be the bait, only I wasn't there, so it's my fault—"

Lilah stammered to a halt. "And somewhere in there I wake up."

She glanced at each of us, her eyes brimming with tears.

I reached across the gap between beds for her hand. No wonder she'd said yes to Bruce's drugs. Spending days alone in this house fighting the horrors in her head— Climbing into bed every night knowing they were poised to pounce— Oh, hell, Lilah!

Tony spoke. "You've had this dream before?"

Lilah, clinging tight to my hand, nodded. "Five or six times."

"Starting when?"

"A couple of months ago. Labor Day weekend was the first. We had some people here and Bruce cooked out lamb shishkebabs. I thought that might have triggered it."

Apparently his staccato questions were having a calming effect. She gave my hand a squeeze and let go.

"Were you high?"

Lilah nodded.

"Coke to party, Valium to sleep?"

"You used to do it too, Tony."

"And still would," he agreed, "if that prick bastard hadn't canned my ass."

I stepped in. "Lilah, were your guests Labor Day weekend the same ones who're here now?"

"No." She shook her head. "None of them. I checked. I made lists."

"Good. OK." I strolled over to the dresser where she'd parked the cocoa pitcher. "So what do you think? Any ideas about what all this means? The monster? The goat? Bruce and the chief setting you up?"

Lilah looked at me, then at Tony, then at me again. "You already know what I think, Cory." She held out her mug. "I think it's about him. You, Tony."

"Oh yeah? Which am I, the goat or the monster?"

It was the first time I'd seen him caught off guard. So that's how he reacts, I noted with interest: He blusters.

"Don't be mad. I'm not saying—"

"Or am I the traps? Or the snakes? Or the native chief? Is the whole dream about me, or what?"

"Watch it," I murmured as I poured him cocoa.

He sat back in his chair and muttered something that might have been an apology, but probably wasn't.

Lilah smoothed a fold of satin over her knee. "You could be the goat," she said. "Or you could be the monster."

"Pardon me for asking, but how do you figure that?"

"Oh, stop acting so huffy! Do you think I have

nightmares on purpose? Do you think I want you crawling all over my subconscious like—like *cockroaches*?"

"Hey." Tony raised his mug as if it were a cross and she were a vampire. "Easy there!"

"Can we stick with our inquiry, please?" I climbed back onto my bed. "Lilah, how is it that you see Tony as maybe the goat and maybe the monster?"

"Well," she thought about it for a moment, "the goat, I guess that would mean I think of him as . . . hmm . . . not *helpless*, exactly, but—used. Taken advantage of."

"Screwed," Tony supplied. "Fucked over."

I wondered if she hadn't got hold of the wrong end of the stick. Contrary to psychoanalytic custom, Lilah seemed to be deducing her real feelings about Tony from her dream feelings about the goat.

"No." She shook her head. "You're saying I think Bruce set you up, but I don't. He didn't. It was more . . . oh, you know, balance sheets. You just can't publish as effectively if you're not in New York. He always said so. Even when they first moved us to Boston—"

"And you still believe that crap?" asked Tony. He sounded more sorry than angry. "What, do you believe every crapola line he ever fed you?"

"Stop it," I told him.

"You're so wrong about him, Tony! You talk like he hated you, when really he was your biggest fan. I heard him tell a whole roomful of people once that you were a natural at publishing. Don't you know that? He said you'd never stay down for long because you're so good. So how could I think of you as fucked over or helpless?" She folded her arms. "I didn't. I don't."

Tony frowned at the rug and said nothing. I wondered if he was stunned by the irony of Bruce's having tossed him overboard in the confidence he'd swim . . . or if part of him needed to hear this, needed to believe even now that his faith in their partnership hadn't been entirely misplaced.

When he finally spoke, his voice was brusque. "So that's the goat. What about the monster?"

Lilah swirled the cocoa in her mug. "I don't care to go into it."

"Then I'll go into it for you." Tony leaned forward in his chair. "I shot out your windows. Right? I wrote to the Board of Directors trying to get your husband fired before he could sink Caxton Press and me along with it. Oh, yes—*and* my marriage. When he beat me three-zip, I didn't accept defeat like a gentleman and go work for reference books. Nooooo! I squawked, and I kept squawking, and some of my authors jumped ship and a couple of them sued, and from Bruce's viewpoint I managed to make quite a mess before his lawyers finally booted me out of the country."

Lilah drew herself up with dignity. "That's your opinion."

Tony broke out laughing as if he honestly couldn't help it.

I'd been waiting for an opening, and this looked like the best I was likely to get.

"Question," I addressed Tony. "What shape did you leave the company in financially, and what shape is it in now? Do you know?"

"Why?" Lilah bristled at me. "What's that got to do with my dream?"

"Maybe a lot," I told her. "Here's the problem: Source Number One claims the Higher Ed division has nose-dived since Bruce took over. Source Number Two claims profits are up, and they're about to publish their best list ever. Which is it?"

"Both," said Tony.

"Explain, please?"

"He's just being flippant," said Lilah scathingly.

"No I'm not, as you should know, Mrs. President Easton.

How long have you been a dinghy on the S.S. Bruce? Six years?"

"Tony," I cut in ahead of Lilah, "I really would appreciate the shortest and straightest possible answer."

"Sure." He settled back in his chair, hands behind his head, the old glint in his eye. "The trick here is the gap between contract and publication. Making a science textbook is like an open-ended prison sentence: one to five years with good behavior. Aside from prying the manuscript out of the author, you've got design, illustrations, permissions, usually a DVD, a website, marketing campaign—"

"Fascinating," I interrupted, "but can we cut to the chase?"

"Here it comes." Tony pulled one foot up on the other knee. "Bruce canned me after I'd stocked his pond with enough fingerlings to keep Higher Ed in trout for several years. Those babies have been fattening up and hitting the pan ever since. Hence the continued rise in profits. However, with the pond full of fish, nobody's bothered much about small fry. So—yes, the Spring list looks plump and delicious, because Bruce is still publishing my books. But wait a year or two. You could fit all the new contracts he's signed into a goldfish bowl."

Lilah had been glaring at him throughout this speech with a cold fury that matched the weather. Now she turned to me. "You see why he's the monster?"

"Hey," Tony lifted his hands. "If you don't like the news, don't shoot the messenger."

"You call this news? Slandering my murdered husband in his own house?"

"Sorry, but reporting the facts isn't slander."

"Facts! Facts! You're all obsessed with facts. A bunch of junkies shooting up statistics." Lilah gave him a withering look. "I came here to talk to Cory about my nightmare, not you about fucking textbook publishing, which I've had enough of to last me the rest of my life."

She uncrossed her legs and slid her feet onto the floor. "Are we through? I'm tired of this, Cory. It's not getting us anywhere."

"Oh, Lilah, don't give up now! Not only are we getting somewhere, we're into the home stretch."

"Tally-ho!" Tony hoisted the cocoa pitcher. "Andiamo!"

Lilah sighed, grimaced, and tucked her feet up under her again. I didn't meet her eyes. True, our inquiry was sprinting toward the finish line; but I doubted she was going to like what nosed under the wire.

"You first had this dream on Labor Day weekend?" I asked. "How long was that after Paul died?"

"Bullseye," murmured Tony.

Lilah jutted her chin at him. "Three weeks."

"Hell of a short mourning period."

"What do you care? You were halfway around the world."

"I wasn't giving a party."

I intervened before Tony could reload and fire again. "Who was here the weekend Paul died? All the same people as now?"

Lilah nodded slowly. "Henry and Melinda were here Friday till Sunday—oh, and Gloria, and of course Edgar. Olive stopped in for drinks on Sunday afternoon, and so did Jeff, but I don't remember— Oh, yes I do. Olive must have come while I was asleep, because she woke me up when Paul fell off the deck. Then Jeff got in a fight with the police for breaking their barricade."

I looked at Tony. "But that doesn't mean Jeff couldn't have arrived earlier. We've established that one can hide a car nearby and sneak in the back way without being noticed. Right?"

He grinned. "What did I say about Mount Holyoke

girls?"

"How about Wayne Glynn, Lilah? Was he here?"

"No. That's right. He's the only one who wasn't."

"Unless he'd sneaked down for a secret fling with La Gloria," suggested Tony, "and she'd stowed him at her place."

"That's actually not so farfetched." Lilah grimaced at me. "Science publishing is a regular bunny hutch, as you might have noticed."

"You'd think the porn folks would pick up on it," Tony agreed. "Big Bill Ballantine Slings His Schlong—"

"Oh, shut up!" snapped Lilah. "You're no one to talk, Tony Cyr!"

"I'll match mine against Bill's any time. In fact, you can be our—"

"*Stop* it!"

"Lilah," I interposed, "don't you think there might be some connection between Paul's drowning and your dream?"

"Yes," she agreed immediately. "Didn't I tell you? That's why I wondered if the lamb shishkebabs set it off. I can still see Bruce standing by the grill jabbing skewers into the meat . . . I had to run inside to not get sick. It seemed so—oh, I don't know—"

"Ruthless," Tony contributed. "Typical."

"Will you cut it out?"

"Probably not." He sat back and stretched. "I can't help thinking it's relevant to Bruce getting himself killed that everybody who knew him thought he was a cold-hearted sadistic—"

"That's a lie!" Lilah scrambled angrily off her bed. "Get out of here, Tony Cyr! You *are* a monster! Bruce didn't get himself killed—somebody murdered him. And as far as I can see, the most likely person is *you*."

He looked so startled and disconcerted I almost felt sorry for him. After blinking a few times he stood and came over to face her. "Lilah, that's not funny."

"You're telling me!"

"It's ludicrous."

"Why? You hate him. You admitted it. All you've done all night is insult him. Why else did you come here?"

"Not to— Look. If I'd wanted— No, OK, I did *want* to, you're right. But if I were *going* to strangle Bruce, which I didn't, I sure as hell wouldn't have waited till now. What's to gain? My publishing career? He flushed that down the john along with the Press. Melinda? Fat chance, from her end or mine."

Lilah drew in breath as if to argue; paused, and exhaled one word: "Revenge."

"Not by killing him." Tony walked over to the window. "Jesus, Lilah, don't you get it? The bastard stomped my golden goose into fucking pâté! All the revenge I wanted was to watch him choke on it."

Nobody said anything for about ten seconds. Lilah combed the fringe on her shawl flat against her sleeve, as if struck by a sudden need for order amid chaos. Then she walked over and put her hand on Tony's shoulder.

"Do you believe me?" he demanded.

"Yes."

He looked searchingly into her face, his own expression faintly puzzled, as if he weren't sure what to make of this unexpected reversal. Lilah's hand didn't move from his shoulder.

For a long moment they gazed at each other. I'm not a believer in precognition, but I could see what was getting ready to happen as clearly as if I'd read the script.

I lowered my feet over the side of my bed and groped for my slippers.

Slowly Tony's hand went up to Lilah's cheek. His fingers brushed back her hair. Then his arms slid around her, and hers around him.

"Lilah," he murmured. "It's going to be all right."

She didn't speak, just nodded into his shoulder.

"Excuse me," I said.

They didn't hear. They were too engrossed in what appeared to me to be an extremely belated revelation.

I moved closer and spoke louder. "Hold it!"

Both of them turned as if I were the waitress and they weren't ready to order yet.

"In case you forgot," I said, "this is not a movie. It's a murder." I paused for impact. "And in the motive sweepstakes, you two have just pulled into a commanding lead."

"Cory, that's nuts." Though Lilah's brow had puckered, her voice was shining. "I didn't kill Bruce, and neither did Tony."

"She knows that," Tony assured her. "Don't you, Ms. Thorne?"

Impossible to doubt those two radiant faces; and unthinkable to take their word for it. Not without evidence. Not with so much at stake. I was glad—like Melinda—that I wasn't a cop.

"Yes," I admitted. "But I'm not the one you have to convince. Do yourselves a favor, OK? If we can't pin this thing on X before morning, keep the PDA down till the cops leave."

"PDA?" said Tony.

"That's not what this is, Cory! This is two very good friends who never, never should have lost touch with each other." Lilah squeezed Tony's arm.

"What's PDA?" Tony insisted.

"Public display of affection," she told him. "Frowned on by housemothers at women's colleges."

His mouth twitched as if to squelch a grin.

Then he looked back at me. "You know we didn't? Does that mean you know who did?"

"I've got a fairly good idea—"

"Cory! *Who?*"

"—but to make sure, we're going to have to set a trap."

"Tell me!" commanded Lilah. "Who killed Bruce? And *why?*"

"We?" countered Tony. "You're giving the front runners a piece of the action?"

"Well, of course!" said Lilah. "He was my husband, damn it, and he was strangled in my living room. If you don't want revenge for that, I do!"

"Oh, what the heck," said Tony with a fond glance at her. "Sure. Why not?"

"So, Cory!" directed Lilah. "Tell us everything!"

CHAPTER SEVENTEEN

When the Inquisition reconvened at seven-thirty, Tony and Lilah and I were ready . . . sort of.

We must have wasted ten minutes arguing before we'd even gotten to the trap. They both hated my theory. That was no surprise; so did I. Regarding motive, though, I couldn't see any way out. Look at the events since August through the prism of Lilah's dream, and how many possibilities were there?

Regarding X's identity I was less positive. On the one hand, *why* obviously depended on *who*, so if I'd got the motive right I should have the perpetrator. On the other hand, no direct evidence connected my suspect with Bruce's murder—or Paul, or the snakes, or the broken mirror. Still, since the trap we were setting involved using me as bait, I did wish Lilah wouldn't keep interrupting with reasons why I must be wrong. Proof first, verdict later.

"Hey there, Henry!" Tony's voice was hearty. "And Olive! You're looking wide awake for such a wee hour. Don't be shy. Step right up! Pick an end of the sofa, any end. And Edgar! Come in, come in."

"Ouch!" hissed Lilah. "That's my foot!"

"Sorry," I whispered back.

Her right ear and my left were pressed against the inner wall of the late Bruce Easton's clothes closet. I should have known, I reflected, that any shoe not tidily stowed on a shoe tree must have toes in it.

"How about if we shove these suits over?" whispered Lilah.

"Better not. The hangers might squeak, or we could trip on something, like for instance shoes."

"I used to call him a closet Imelda Marcos. Oh, Cory! I still don't see— I just can't believe Bruce would go along with—"

"Shh," I warned her. "Here come some more."

Tony welcomed Gloria and Jeff in the same clarion tone he'd used for the previous arrivals. We could hear better than I'd expected—a lucky break, since our next move would be cued by the conversation.

Olive, whom I pictured sitting on the sofa, asked Edgar if the snow had stopped. Edgar said he didn't know. Olive asked how that could be. Edgar said he'd come back here during a lull but it might not have lasted. Henry asked if Edgar had brought his dog. No, said Edgar. Bruce didn't allow Jingles in the house. The awkward silence that followed was broken by Edgar hailing Wayne Glynn. Evidently he felt he and Wayne had become buddies during their search for Lilah in the snow. Wayne, however, wanted Henry to know his only care was for introductory biology and that he realized fraternizing with the help was déclassé. I wondered if all this was as clear to them as it was to us, listening blindly through a wall.

"And Melinda! La pièce de résistance!"

Melinda I envisioned with a sleep-raddled scowl above a fresh velours sweatsuit, brushing Tony aside to go chat with her authors.

Her authors . . .

Lilah whispered something that sounded like "fat bitch."

"Let's get this show on the road, shall we?" said Tony.

"Where's Lilah?" Henry asked.

"And Cory?" Olive added.

"Lilah is resting. She's been badly upset by this whole business—"

"So are the rest of us, and we managed to show up!"

"Now, now, Melinda." That was Henry again. "As Bruce's wife, it stands to reason, what with finding the body, and then wandering through a blizzard—"

"I'm not saying she isn't unbalanced. I just don't see that as an excuse for shirking her responsibility. And even you must agree, Henry, that except for Tony, Lilah appears to have more responsibility—"

"Thank you, ladies and gentlemen, thank you," cut in our emcee. "To finish: Lilah is resting and Cory is with her. That's the bad news. The good news is that Lilah's memory is starting to come back. Cory's confident that, once her shock wears off, she can tell us what happened before we found her here with Bruce's body."

"Good news for us," remarked Jeff. "Maybe not for Lilah."

"What if she remembers she killed him?" asked Gloria. "Do you think her mind would just, like, *go*?"

"That would present an interesting legal dilemma," said Wayne Glynn. "If the defendant becomes insane as a result of the crime, does that constitute grounds for an insanity defense? Or does it mean the perpetrator must have been sane during the crime's commission, since to lose one's mind would appear to be the sanest possible reaction to killing one's spouse?"

"Can we cut the crap and get this done?" Jeff interrupted. "I want to go back to bed."

"You and me both," said Gloria.

I wished I could see Olive's face.

"OK, team," said Tony, "Let's put the ball in play. Who

has news? Jeff? You want to go first?"

Lilah tapped my knee. "Time for Phase Two."

I nodded. We extricated ourselves from Bruce's gallery of pin-stripes and emerged, disheveled, into light.

The three of us had agreed it was more urgent for Lilah and me to be in place on time than to listen. Our reasons differed: Tony figured he could handle this phase without us. I figured I already knew who'd strangled Bruce, so why bother? Lilah still hoped to hear something that would shatter my theory, but she understood we needed her to set up the tape deck and camcorder.

So she locked her bedroom door, while I crossed the hall to do my hair.

The curling iron was Lilah's idea, and a good one it was. Our contrasts in hair were subtle: streaky vs. solid auburn, wavy vs. straight. Theoretically X should be too preoccupied to notice until too late; plus I'd be hidden by a duvet. But why take chances? If X guessed that the redhead in the bed was an undercover journalist instead of a drug-dulled widow, my goose, like Tony's, would be pâté.

Plug cord into wall socket, flip switch, and wait for the red dot to turn black. You'd think a nation that could make microchips could invent a cordless curling iron. Or had it? Larry would know. I'd have to ask him when he got home from Seattle.

Assuming I lived that long . . .

I was gazing in the mirror, trying not to wonder if I'd ever see that loyal, brave face again, when something behind me shifted.

My heart ricocheted from my stomach to my throat. I pivoted, *en garde*.

No one there.

Then what—?

I faced the mirror again; reached again for the curling iron. On the wall my shadow moved with me.

As I should have known. Relax, Cory! Who's going to come in here? It's Lilah X wants to snuff, not you.

She must be almost ready by now . . . and the conference in the living room nearing the point where Tony would adjourn it till the cops arrived.

Damn this plastic phallus with its stubborn red dot! Hell, my grandmother's old metal curling iron was faster than this, heated in a stove flame.

I scowled at the dot; glanced up again, and saw not one reflection looking back at me but two.

My heart yo-yoed back up and down my windpipe.

"Cory."

I cleared my throat. "Gloria."

"I need to talk to you."

Take a deep breath and let it out. Try to sound unsurprised. "Is the conference over?"

"Uh-uh." She shook her head. "I said I had to use the bathroom." Then her reflection disappeared. I turned around. She was closing the door behind us.

I shoved the curling iron behind my cosmetics case. Had Gloria noticed it? Maybe yes; more likely no. With any luck she was too intent on her own problems to care about my hair.

"So, what's up?"

A nervous, mirthless giggle. "I don't exactly— I mean— Oh, shit. This is harder than I thought."

She didn't look as agitated as she sounded. Her clothes were all in place and fastened, her hair combed, her mascara repaired. And me with my quilted robe barely covering Lilah's white satin one.

Gloria sat on the foot of the bed she'd occupied earlier. "This is just between you and me."

"How can I promise that?" I countered. "We're suspects in a murder investigation. There are laws—"

"I mean it," she interrupted. "This hasn't got anything to

do with who killed Bruce. More like who didn't."

"Then why keep it a secret?" I asked, although I was fairly sure of the answer. "Why not tell them in there?"

"Because it's over and done with!" Gloria said passionately. "It can't help anything if it comes out! I'm only even telling you so Lilah won't worry about it."

But Lilah isn't worrying about it, I thought. She's crouched in a closet full of recording equipment, and I'm standing here with straight hair listening to a non-confession.

"Gloria," I said, "I appreciate the delicacy of your position, but I don't have time right now to beat around the bush. You're talking about that message written in soap on Bruce's bathroom mirror. Right?"

She gaped at me as if I were a Ouija board. Her mouth opened just far enough to let out a gasp.

I waited. Gloria whispered: "How did you know?"

"Because it doesn't fit. It's been sticking out of this mess like a piece from the wrong puzzle."

"But—what—"

"Nope. Sorry." I sauntered over to the bed. "Your turn to talk."

"Have you told anybody about this?"

"Not yet. And I won't, if nobody asks. Unless it's relevant to Bruce's murder."

"Cory, I swear to God I didn't kill him! On the Bible! Even if I wanted to I couldn't, and I didn't."

In spite of my assurance her forehead was glistening. I felt sorry for her, mired in high drama when her only wish was an apartment in Allston.

"You were trying to get him off your back about Jeff, was that it?"

A bitter nod. "I thought—I still think—Bruce put that snake's head in Jeff's food, made sure Jeff got it and then *blamed* it on Jeff to make him stay away from me."

"Why would Bruce do that?"

"Because he's such a rat! He always tried to run everybody's life. He never liked me in the first place because I was hired by Tony . . . plus I let him know from Day One that I don't take that crap from anybody. I mean, what the fuck business is it of his who I sleep with? Or who Jeff sleeps with, either? You know?"

"Sure."

"So when we were all hanging out after dinner I thought, OK, Bruce, you want snakes, I'll give you snakes! I was kind of drunk." She grimaced. "Now, I admit, it seems like an incredibly dumb idea."

I let that pass. "Did you and Jeff carry out this plan together?"

"No! Are you kidding?" Gloria's eyebrows went up. "Let him think I wanted him that bad? No way! He's stuck-up enough already."

"But you told him later? Or did he guess?"

She sighed glumly. "He went in there looking for aspirin and he saw that mirror and he just about flipped. He came stomping back into the bedroom—God, I thought he was going to kill me! Not that he *would*," she added hastily. "I don't think he's ever even hit me except for maybe a slap, you know, like if he's PO'd about something. He just yelled at me till I couldn't take any more, so I came in here."

And then you went back, I thought with a surge of exasperation. You'll risk your job to keep Bruce's nose out of your business; you'll brag about not taking crap from anybody; but you went back.

I moved toward the door. "Gloria, thanks. I appreciate your telling me this, and so will Lilah."

"But you won't tell anybody else, right?" She got to her feet. "I mean, if the cops knew, they might think it's important when it really isn't, and screw up their whole investigation, you know?"

"Don't worry."

I shut the door behind her. My aunt Louise used to tell me the best thing a woman can do for herself is become the secretary of some powerful executive. Where would I be now if I'd followed her advice instead of Rik Green's beckoning blue pencil?

Behind my cosmetics case the curling iron's dot had finally turned black. I lifted a strand of hair, twined it, and unfurled a perfect ringlet.

One down, a dozen to go.

That was no reason to feel sorry for Gloria, though. She'd made her own choices, same as I did. Amazingly (to me at least), most women preferred regular jobs to freelancing.

Curl number two was interrupted by a yawn. Delayed fear or plain exhaustion? Come on, Cory! Got to stay alert for the vigil ahead!

I rolled a third one, and a fourth. My joints cracked. My neck creaked. If this night ever ends, I vowed, I'm going to take a three-hour Jacuzzi and then sleep for a week.

I was unwrapping my sixth ringlet when a faint voice shouted from the bowels of the house: "Help! Fire! Fire!"

For three seconds I froze. Then I dropped the curling iron and yanked its plug.

Lilah: the real bait. Alone in her room while I primped and Tony tried to keep tabs on half a dozen murder suspects.

Before I could gather my scattered wits into a plan, the lights went out.

Automatically I checked the window. Ghostly lawn; stark black woods and sky. No floodlamps, no driveway lights, no reflections from bedroom windows.

My knee smacked painfully into the dresser. My brain was pumping as fast as my heart. X, like Gloria, must have sneaked out of the conference. Goddam Tony! Stupid, stupid, stupid of me to trust a near-stranger on a matter of life and death.

Or else had set the fire before the conference started, so the smoke would break it up.

Thinking of smoke, I smelled it. Not the wood fireplace kind but heavy and rancid . . . like a lawnmower starting. Like—gasoline.

By now I was groping in the drawer of my bedside table for a flashlight, matches, a candle. Nada. Niente. Damn! I'd have to feel my way to Lilah's room. Weapons . . . Would X be armed? Surely not, to have choked Bruce with a tie . . . but then that was part of the plan, wasn't it? Like hiding the tie in Bruce's stash box, where the cops couldn't miss it.

I dared not take the time to search for a suitable large heavy defensive object. Just get to Lilah—fast.

The hall was a chaos of smoke and noise. "Coats!" I heard Olive's shrill commanding cry in the foyer. "And boots! Everyone put on coats and boots!"

Lilah's door stood open. I called her name.

"Cory!"

Groping, my hand hit a shoulder. "Lilah! Are you OK?"

"Fine. But, Cory, we've got to put out the fire." She pulled me toward the foyer. "I've got my jewelry. Now, if I can just remember where Bruce keeps the extinguishers—"

With every step the smoke thickened. "It's too far along," I said. "From the smell, whoever set it was thorough."

We rounded the corner. A pocket-sized flashlight beam raked a hubbub of coats being yanked from hangers, handed out, and wriggled into. Olive and Gloria seemed to be in charge, judging from the tone and location of their voices.

"Tony?" I called.

"He's downstairs," answered Edgar's baritone. "Rescuing Professor Howrigan."

"What happened?"

"How did it start?" Lilah asked at the same time.

"Don't know." Edgar thrust a coat at me. Flat curls of fur: Persian lamb. I passed it to Lilah. "The prof went down to use the gents', and next thing we know he's yelling fire. Tony told the gals to get everybody dressed and me to shovel the doors clear. You got your car keys, Ms. Thorne? I figure that's where we'll bivouac till I can blow a path to the road."

"Tony's downstairs in the fire?" Lilah was aghast.

"No sweat. He knows this place inside out." Edgar tossed me an armful of damp tweed. "Gloria, where the— OK, never mind, here it is. Catch you folks later."

"Cory, I've got to go—"

"No." I grabbed Lilah's arm. "This is your house— you've got to get your guests out safely. Remember fire drills at school?"

"What about you?"

"Back in two minutes."

The flashlight I'd carried through the snow still lay on the kitchen counter where I'd left it. Now boots. I paused in the foyer long enough to make sure Lilah was wearing hers, and dashed back up the hall for mine. They'd be wet, but a lot better than bedroom slippers for fire-fighting in snowdrifts.

First, however, I needed to get out of this double bathrobe into jeans and a sweater.

A grim morning it promised to be, huddling in our cars until the plows cleared the roads. I'd better bring blankets. And my wallet, and keys . . .

I was pulling on my last dry wool sock when the door latch clicked.

The room went dead quiet.

Then a soft rustling sound: Slippers on tile floor? Whoever had shut the door was inside, and inching closer.

"Who's there?"

No answer.

"Look, this is no time for jokes. Who is it?"

Silence. My invisible visitor had stopped somewhere on the far side of Gloria's bed. I thought of the flashlight ten feet away on my dresser. Should I risk it?

No. I couldn't be sure where my adversary was; and if I couldn't see X, at least X couldn't see me, either.

That inner admission—that the person stalking me around my room was Bruce Easton's murderer—set my whole body trembling. In vain I commanded my nervous system to hold the line. This was too gruesome, being trapped in a burning house by someone I'd chatted with, dined with, decked a Christmas tree with . . .

I gritted my teeth to forestall any more attempts to compel a human response from my self-appointed nemesis. To make a sound would give away my position. Hold still, Cory, and think.

OK. I need a weapon. What? My bathrobe sash? Forget it. Nothing I can't force myself to use. Some kind of club, then. The bedside lamp? Too big and unwieldy. A shoe? Too flimsy. But what else is there?

Light flashed in my eyes. I recoiled. Another flash. X had a penlight and was shooting me as deliberately as a fashion photographer. Pinpointing where I was; while I, startled and blinded, stood exposed, unarmed, unable even to be sure whom I was confronting.

"Dammit, who is it?" I cried in spite of myself. "What do you want?"

This time I got an answer, a hoarse whisper: "You know."

Chills danced up my spine. I made myself breathe in and out before I spoke again. "How would I know? *What* would I know?"

No reply. Another muffled footstep told me X had reached the foot of Gloria's bed.

I was trapped in a cul-de-sac. Within seconds I had to make my move. But . . . fight or flee? Unless the shadow closing in on me was Edgar—in which case I was doomed—my decision could mean my life. If Jeff, best to dodge and delay. Olive or Gloria, mow her down. Henry, Wayne, or Melinda, fifty-fifty.

"You're giving me too much credit," I said, thinking frantically. "Whatever I might *suspect*, it's pure speculation."

Silence.

"Right now you're safe. Nobody's got any evidence against you. But if you attack me, whether you succeed or fail you're finished. There are too many people around here who know too much. In fact one of them could walk in any minute."

"No," said the hoarse whisper.

"You can't imagine they'll leave us alone in a burning house just because the lights—"

I didn't finish because X was jingling a fistful of keys. Bruce's keys. The bunch he'd grabbed hours ago on the ridiculously thin pretext of checking the padlocked basement for Lilah.

"No one will walk in," said Henry Howrigan, "because I locked the door."

He dropped the keys back into his pocket. "I knew as soon as Tony said Lilah's memory was coming back that the two of you were up to something. Flushing me out. So! Here I am."

I thought I could discern his faint silhouette against the room's white wall. If I could scramble across the bed before he rushed me . . .

Light glared in my eyes.

"You won't get away," said Henry. "Look what happened to Bruce. He thought he was too smart and too strong for me, but he was mistaken."

I blinked hard, trying to recover my sight. *Stall him, Cory.*

I said, "What good does it do you to kill me if you die of

smoke inhalation two minutes later?"

"I won't." He sounded unnervingly certain. "This wing is too far from the fire. I opened the door to the crawl space so enough smoke would get through to scare you and Lilah, but only the main house is burning. For the moment," he added.

"Where's Tony?"

"When I last saw him he was trying to douse the blaze. And calling my name. Appreciate it. Damn good fellow, Tony. Most likely realized by now I'm not there. And one fire extinguisher won't do the job. I used all the gasoline Bruce kept in the hall for the mowers—three or four liters."

His voice was moving toward the gap between the beds. "And what was Bruce doing the last time you saw him?" I inquired with desperate irony.

"Choking to death," said Henry. "Don't make a joke of it. It wasn't funny." Apparently he'd stopped at the foot of Gloria's bed. "Broke my heart, in fact. Believe it or not as you prefer, but nobody in this world loved Bruce Easton more than me."

"Then why . . .?"

"You know."

I knew enough to hazard a guess. "He was blackmailing you about Paul?"

"Naturally you spotted that right off," said Henry, "because you wrote about it in *Phases*. If you think I'm an expert on the subject, though, you're wrong. Learned quite a bit from your article."

At first I didn't follow. This was the Henry Howrigan I'd interviewed, all right: not stammering and timid but confident. Only something had gotten twisted in the reincarnation. He sounded proud—as if strangling the man who'd held his nose to the grindstone counted among his most successful experiments.

Then I realized it wasn't our interview he was talking

about. It was my feature story on child abuse.

I gulped. And said what Lilah refused to believe: "You killed Paul's snake to warn him to keep his mouth shut?"

"Exactly." Henry seemed relieved that I understood. "I didn't mean to hurt him. Even to touch him. I swear on my mother's grave, never in my life— But you understand. It was just that—oh, god!—he looked so much like Bruce."

My throat was dry. It's one thing to write a magazine piece about it. Or to add up the facts and reach a conclusion that may get your friend off the hook. It's another matter entirely to listen to a fellow houseguest, a tenured Harvard professor, someone across whose mahogany desk you've sat with a notebook and tape recorder, confess to raping a crippled child.

"And I didn't hurt him, did I?—not really, because he couldn't feel anything. But I had to be sure he wouldn't tell. If Bruce ever—well, if anybody! I'd be ruined. Which I don't deserve, because I'm not that kind of—one of those, who do that. But Olive, you see, wouldn't understand. She would refuse to marry someone who, even accidentally, even just once— Contrary to family values, she'd say. Not at all the thing for the new head of Chute Labs."

"How—" I could barely get words out. "How did Bruce fit in?"

Henry's voice tightened. "His own fault. I told him that when—before I—oh, well. Endless damned wining, dining, cajolery, seduction— Till he's got you. Then turn the screws. Change my book to nonmajors. Bring down the level. With that Glynn fellow. Travesty! But he promised— Bruce, that is—he gave me to understand, if I'd agree, he'd do anything. I said, You know what I want. But he must have thought, Lilah. Which I could never—" He stopped, sighed. "I went in the bedroom, expecting—hoping— And there she was instead, asleep, stark naked. Poor creature. Full of wine and Valium so she'd never know. Made me sick. Walked out on the deck to clear my head; and there's Paul in his chair. Thought I was dreaming. So fine, so incredibly perfect . . . Felt like a volcano erupting inside me. Hardly knew what happened. Then woke up. Nightmare! What to do? Bruce would never forgive me. Hold it over my head forever. So I went and got the snake and cut it in two. Just like you wrote. Showed Paul the pieces: Keep quiet or you too! Threw 'em in the pond. Didn't imagine he would— God in heaven!" His voice shook. "Rather have jumped in myself than that."

In my head jostled images that would no doubt fill my nightmares as long as I lived to have them. *Why didn't you, then?* Tormented by a lust he refused to face—and now Bruce's blood on his hands along with Paul's— *Dammit, Henry, how can you go on living?*

There was a soft thunk. Henry was long past such philosophical questions. As a garter snake or a paralyzed child clings to life, so does a killer. Henry had dropped his flashlight on the bed because he wanted both hands free for his third victim.

Though my brain balked, my body reacted. I threw myself on the bed and groped frantically for the flashlight.

He jumped on top of me before I found it. I tried to twist out from under and couldn't. A suffocating weight on my back, pressing my face into the blankets . . . My elbow jabbed upward as hard as I could, again and again, and finally freed one shoulder. As my head came up, a taut cord scraped across the back of my neck and caught on my ear.

"You're crazy!" Even now I couldn't believe that a man I knew wanted to strangle me. "Henry! Stop!"

I was hauling at the cord with all my strength, trying to get it away from my head and if possible away from him. Henry responded by jamming his knee into my back. I yelped and wriggled, but I couldn't dislodge him. The pain in my back was excruciating. I grabbed an arm that was flattening my nose and chomped into it.

Henry let out a startled scream. His grip slackened just long enough for me to roll both of us over and off the bed.

I'd hoped to land on top, but we hit the floor side by side. At least the odds were even. If only I could see! Were we close enough for me to slide under the bed? I was flailing blindly, aiming my knee where his groin should be, too entangled in bathrobes to hit. He hooked his leg over both of mine at the same time I caught his wrist. No cord in this hand. God, let him have dropped it! He was trying to scissor himself on top of me. I kicked hard and hit his shin. Trying to free his wrist, he slammed his elbow into my jaw. I heaved myself upward and pushed his arm down like a pump handle. He screamed. I clambered over his shoulder and twisted his arm behind his back. He thrashed, but I had him pinned.

He was grunting. I was panting, then coughing from the smoke I'd inhaled. I settled into the small of his back like a saddle and grabbed his other wrist. For the first time I noticed how icy the tile floor was under my bare knees. Both my bathrobes were hiked up around my waist.

Now what?

"Let go," he croaked.

I gave his arm a jerk that was meant to hurt. Now that I wasn't fighting for my life, I was so angry I could have killed him. What kind of supreme egomaniac are you, Henry Howrigan, to think you can murder everyone who threatens your master plan? What kind of psychopathic monster covers his tracks by torching a house full of his friends?

"Cory, you don't—"

"Shut up!" I cut him off. "Not one word till we've got witnesses!"

On cue the door rattled. A hoarse voice called my name. I called back and discovered that my throat hurt. As I pondered the irony of escaping strangulation only to suffocate, there was a series of clicks that had to be Tony Cyr and his credit card.

Then a beam the size of a spotlight lit up Henry and me and the smoke around us like the witch scene from *Macbeth: Fire burn and cauldron bubble!*

I looked down at my arms, double-sleeved, gripping the bony white wrists that had extinguished Bruce Easton's last spark; and I hoped somebody would get me out of here before I vomited on Henry's polyester turtleneck.

CHAPTER EIGHTEEN

We watched the house burn down from the first bend in the driveway. That is, Olive and I did, huddled under blankets in Bruce's Ferrari. I couldn't help remembering Henry's car getting stuck in this same spot eight hours ago when Olive and Jeff struck out for Boston. Although we didn't discuss it, I knew Olive must wish—as I did—that they'd succeeded.

The rest of our party, led by Tony, formed a combination bucket brigade and snowball artillery which gave the fire a run for its money. Lilah's aim, I was pleased to notice, hadn't suffered a bit from her years of domesticity and drugs. The Red Sox should be so lucky.

The roof collapsed shortly after sunrise. The firefighters backed off then, mopping their faces, thumping each other on the back in consolation. Nobody had really believed they could save the house; but the attempt had been a common cause when one was sorely needed. As they sagged against their cars, Olive and I opened our doors in tacit unison and crunched through the snow to offer sympathy and more hot cocoa.

Edgar, evidently less exhausted than his comrades, produced a camcorder. Lilah put her hand over the lens and made him lock it in the Ferrari's trunk. I silently applauded. Who here would ever want to relive this wretched morning?—streaks of azure and gold gleaming through charred rubble, steaming snow, and plumy black helices of smoke?

I was glad to see Gloria slip her arm around Olive. Rich, thin, and tan Mrs. Chute remained, but love had abandoned her. In her weary eyes I'd watched pain flare like the flames consuming the house, as she digested the tale her erstwhile fiancé had told me when he thought I'd never pass it on. Her questions sounded mechanical, except for the last one: *What will happen to him?*

That I preferred not even to think about. *Talk to Tony*, I advised her. He'd broken into my room full of apologies: tried to stop Henry from leaving the meeting, told him and Gloria to hold it or pee in their pants, but they'd dashed out toward opposite bathrooms. Anyhow, what harm could Henry do downstairs? Nada, if you forgot the damn fuse box.

Lilah, red-eyed and breathless, had joined us while Tony was tying Henry's wrists with the cord that had nearly strangled me. Hostess to the end, she soaked guest towels for all four of us to hold over our noses as she and I followed the men down the hall. I'd put on coat and boots over my bathrobes and socks and carried my suitcase, feeling more than ever as though I were back in college except for the bona fide inferno roaring behind the kitchen door.

After that, prisoner and warden had disappeared amid the general confusion. Tony popped up again flourishing buckets of melted snow; but where he'd stowed Henry I had no idea.

I made one attempt to help the firefighters and discovered that my knees had melted. Lilah assured me this was a normal post-stress reaction, and walked me down to the car where she'd already settled Olive.

"You don't think— Tony wouldn't let him get away, Cory, would he?"

"How far could he get in bedroom slippers?" I countered.

"I still can't believe it. Henry! It's too—" She waved her mittened hand in a gesture of speechlessness. "What made you first suspect it was him?"

"I kept remembering that comment of Tony's in the kitchen. That what we should be looking for in a houseful of frustrated ambitions and loose screws was somebody acting too normal."

Lilah shook her head. "But he *was* normal! All those months, years, working on his book— Even when Bruce teased him, or Melinda yelled at him, he never acted like he minded." She sighed. "He should have minded, is that what you're saying?"

I squelched an image of ruthless children jabbing a chained dog with sticks to make it snap. "Something like that."

"Still, who could ever imagine Henry would cut the head off a snake and put it in a puff pastry? Where did that *come from*? It's so *grotesque!* And then I keep thinking—oh, gawd, you know?—of him doing that to threaten Bruce, so he wouldn't stop him ditching the book for Olive and the Labs?—and Bruce just totally missing it."

"He didn't miss it, though. He got it right away." We were nearly to the Ferrari. "His mistake was not believing that Henry meant it."

"The rest of it I pretty much understand. Or at least I can follow what happened." Lilah faced me. "Bruce gave me Valium so I wouldn't get sucked into their showdown. He'd seen the message on our smashed mirror, which he assumed was also from Henry. That made him furious, because when were these nasty tricks going to stop? So he went to remind Henry they had a deal, and Henry flipped out and killed him."

I was on the verge of correcting this extremely generous interpretation when I saw Olive's stony face through the windshield. Enough. Let one of them, anyhow, keep her illusions. By my conservative accounting, Bruce Easton's hubris had already cost Lilah her home, her belongings, her stepson, and very nearly her sanity. If she chose to overlook his using her body as a carrot and his son's suicide as a stick—let her. Or at least let her therapist set her straight, not me.

Lilah was reflexively brushing snow off the hood of Bruce's car. "You know, I just can't picture Henry as this seething sexual cauldron. Can you? I mean, he seems so neuter." Her mittened hand lingered over a sloped headlight. "Is he—what? A pederast?"

"I don't think he was anything particular until too many pressures pushed him off a cliff," I said. "He seems to have been exhausted by the textbook, afraid he'd never satisfy Communicore, desperate to grab his chance to cut loose and hook up with Olive, and at the same time violently ambivalent about Bruce, his idol-cum-slave driver."

"Like those prisoners of war who get crushes on their guards." Under Lilah's mitten a patch of crimson appeared. "But to do what he did to Paul because of his weird thing for Bruce— Oh, *gawd!* That's the part I can't take. Especially," her mouth quivered, "knowing I was right there."

"You were out cold," I reminded her. "Listen, I'm freezing. Go put out your fire. I need to get some real clothes on, and Olive looks like she needs company."

That was only half true. What Olive looked like she needed was amnesia, or, failing that, a one-way ticket to her son's home in Short Hills.

However, I'd noticed two odd things about Henry's Cadillac, parked down the driveway, from which I wanted to distract both Lilah and Olive. From the tailpipe every few seconds issued a white wisp. Not a plume of exhaust like the Ferrari's; just a stray feather. And its windows were fogged.

How far away could Henry get in bedroom slippers? Out of reach of the cops, cameras, and lawyers who soon would surround the rest of us. Out of his albatross textbook contract and his personal nightmare . . . with the collusion of his ex-editor, that damn good fellow Tony Cyr.

Monday's *Boston Globe* headline showed what money, clout, and good manners can accomplish: *Biologist Kills Publisher, Self.* An argument erupted over a scientific issue, ran the account, during which the eminent professor accidentally strangled his distinguished friend and colleague. Unhinged by remorse, he plugged up the tailpipe of his car and asphyxiated himself. Not a word about cocaine, blackmail, old school ties, snakes, or crippled sons. Off-white lies: Bruce would have been pleased.

My *Phases* article, two weeks later, wasn't as sanitized. Lilah and I agreed before she took off that our fellow participants didn't need our protection, what with Chute Labs, Harvard University, and Communicore behind them. I recently got a card from her congratulating me on that and thanking me for everything else. The picture shows a sunny Mediterranean beach fringed with palm trees. Edgar is dealing with the insurance company, she reports, while she adjusts to widowhood in Corfu. Since leaving Oxbridge she hasn't touched a drug stronger than champagne. Jeff Abels, of all people, wired her a bottle of Taittinger to celebrate Olive's naming him to head Chute Labs, where Gloria now works as Mrs. Chute's personal secretary. After Melinda shot herself in the foot by trying to strong-arm the Board into publishing the aborted Howrigan/Glynn biology text, Bill Ballantine set his cap at Tony Cyr for Communicore Higher Ed's next president.

"But you know Tony," she finished. "He says he'd rather make his own messes than clean up someone else's. Olive and Jeff want him to start a publishing company at the Labs, which I hope he will, because otherwise he and Edgar have a lunatic plan to rebuild the guest wing and studio and turn the rest into a sculpture garden starring GUESS WHO!

He's threatening to fly over. Wish you were here!"

When I noticed what song I was humming, I had to laugh. No, this wasn't the femme fatale–suburban housewife who'd wept on my shoulder that she just couldn't take any more. That was Mrs. Bruce Easton. This was my role model, senior sister, mentor, Amazon—my friend, Lilah.

About the Author

CJ Verburg is a writer and editor in science and international literature, as well as a playwright and director. Launched into a publishing career by the late great editor Howard Boyer, who inspired and enjoyed this book, she also worked in theatre with the late great artist and writer Edward Gorey, subject of her print and e-book ***Edward Gorey On Stage: Playwright, Director, Designer, Performer: a Multimedia Memoir***.

Also from CJ Verburg and Boom-Books:
Croaked: an Edgar Rowdey Cape Cod Mystery
(see the next page for a sample)

Also from Boom-Books

By Charisse Howard
Dark Horseman:
Mystery, Adventure, and Romance in Regency Virginia

and the alphabetical *Regency Rakes & Rebels* novellas
Lady Annabelle's Abduction
Lady Barbara & the Buccaneer
The Countess & the Corsair

Croaked: an Edgar Rowdey Cape Cod Mystery
by CJ Verburg

"Everything I want in a mystery: wonderful kooky characters, a plot that keeps you turning pages, terrific dialog, humor, great local color, ...oh yes, and murders, too. . . . I enjoyed every minute of it. Highly recommended!" -- SW, Amazon

from **Chapter One**

If Lydia Vivaldi hadn't tried to read the Cape Cod Times Help Wanted ads while driving, she wouldn't have wound up on the side of 6A with a flat tire. Her yellow Morris Minor wouldn't have caught the eye of Alistair Pope, passing in his vintage Mercedes. Lydia wouldn't have joined Alistair at Leo's Back End for lunch; Leo wouldn't have hired her to replace his assistant cook, Sue, who had just stormed out in tears after Leo diluted her split-pea soup; and the murder rate in Quansett, Massachusetts, might have stayed at zero.

"Taste it!" Leo clunked down two cups. "On the house. Now tell me that's not perfect exactly how it is."

Lydia tasted. She was feeling dizzy—whether from not sleeping, skipping breakfast, or falling down a rabbit hole into Wonderland, she couldn't tell. Her mind groped for facts she could cling to. *Cape Cod is a sixty-mile peninsula which juts into the Atlantic Ocean south of Boston like a bent arm. The fingers are Provincetown, the elbow is Chatham, the armpit is Bourne. Quansett, on the biceps, dates to the late 1600s.*

That patchwork wall behind Leo must be the Back End's menu: squares of colored paper hand-printed with today's specials ("SPESHULS"). And this must be the Splat P Soop. Its problem (in Lydia's opinion) wasn't thickness but flavor.

If you didn't mind losing the vegetarians, as Leo clearly didn't, why not throw in a ham hock?

"I ask you! Any thicker you'd have to eat it with a fork."

She fished unobtrusively, found only a few meaty shreds. If stinginess was what kept Leo so skinny, it hadn't affected his customers. Of the twenty or so people in this two-room cafe, only the kid behind the cash register could be called thin. The mountainous aproned woman slinging burgers in the kitchen outweighed even Alistair.

Winters are milder than in Boston, thanks to the Gulf Stream bearing sea-warmth up from Florida and bouncing off the Cape toward Portugal. Springs are shorter, autumns longer. Golf is commonly played till Thanksgiving.

Her fingernails had gotten the worst of her battle with the flat tire. Yesterday's sparkly green polish was half chipped off. Green, like the streaks in her hair. Like her eyes, on the off chance anyone ever noticed.

Lydia set down her spoon and removed her sunglasses.

. . . Across the room, Edgar Rowdey skimmed the Cape Cod Times obituaries. Not (as a reviewer had once speculated) because he made his living from death. Yes, his miniature black-and-white books did follow one odd character after another through a dismal set of perils to a grotesque end. Edgar Rowdey's interest, however, was not in death per se. What fascinated him was people's reactions to death.

(For more, see your favorite bookstore or Boom-books)

Boom-Books.com

Printed in the USA
CPSIA information can be obtained
at www.ICGtesting.com
LVHW041949191124
797081LV00001B/58